Wish You Were Here

Wish You Were Here

RITA MAE BROWN

& SNEAKY PIE BROWN

ILLUSTRATIONS BY WENDY WRAY

BANTAM BOOKS   NEW YORK · TORONTO · LONDON · SYDNEY · AUCKLAND

WISH YOU WERE HERE

A BANTAM BOOK / DECEMBER 1990

LIBRARY OF CONGRESS CATALOGING-IN-PUBLICATION DATA

Brown, Rita Mae.
Wish you were here / Rita Mae Brown & Sneaky Pie Brown.
p. cm.
ISBN 0-553-05881-9
I. Title.
PS3552.R698W57 1990
813'.54—dc20   90-1071
                                                        CIP

PUBLISHED SIMULTANEOUSLY IN THE UNITED STATES AND CANADA

Bantam Books are published by Bantam Books, a division of Bantam Doubleday Dell Publishing Group, Inc. Its trademark, consisting of the words "Bantam Books" and the portrayal of a rooster, is Registered in U.S. Patent and Trademark Office and in other countries. Marca Registrada. Bantam Books, 666 Fifth Avenue, New York, New York 10103.

PRINTED IN THE UNITED STATES OF AMERICA
BVG   0 9 8 7 6 5 4 3 2 1

Dedicated to the memory of
Sally Mead
Director of the Charlottesville-Albemarle
Society for the Prevention of Cruelty to Animals

Acknowledgments

Gordon Reistrup helped me type and proofread, and Carolyn Lee Dow brought me lots of catnip. I couldn't have written this book without them.

Cast of Characters

Mary Minor Haristeen (Harry), the young postmistress of Crozet, whose curiosity almost kills the cat and herself

Mrs. Murphy, Harry's gray tiger cat, who bears an uncanny resemblance to authoress Sneaky Pie and who is wonderfully intelligent!

Tee Tucker, Harry's Welsh corgi, Mrs. Murphy's friend and confidant; a buoyant soul

Pharamond Haristeen (Fair), veterinarian, being divorced by Harry and confused by life

Boom Boom Craycroft, a high-society knockout who carries a secret torch

Kelly Craycroft, Boom Boom's husband

Mrs. George Hogendobber (Miranda), a widow who thumps her own Bible!

Bob Berryman, misunderstood by his wife, Linda

Ozzie, Berryman's Australian shepherd

Market Shiflett, owner of Shiflett's Market, next to the post office

Pewter, Market's fat gray cat, who, when need be, can be pulled away from the food bowl

Susan Tucker, Harry's best friend, who doesn't take life too seriously until her neighbors get murdered

Ned Tucker, a lawyer and Susan's husband

Jim Sanburne, mayor of Crozet

Big Marilyn Sanburne (Mim), queen of Crozet and an awful snob

Little Marilyn Sanburne, daughter of Mim, and not as dumb as she appears

Josiah Dewitt, a witty antiques dealer sought out by Big Marilyn and her cronies

Maude Bly Modena, a smart transplanted Yankee

Rick Shaw, Albemarle sheriff

Cynthia Cooper, police officer

Hayden McIntire, town doctor

Rob Collier, mail driver

Paddy, Mrs. Murphy's ex-husband, a saucy tom

Author's Note

Mother is in the stable mucking out stalls, a chore she richly deserves. I've got the typewriter all to myself, so I can tell you the truth. I would have kept silent, but that fat toad Pewter pushed her way onto the cover of *Starting from Scratch*. She took full credit for writing the book. Granted, Pewter's ego is in a gaseous state, ever-expanding, but that act of feline self-advertisement was more than I could bear.

Let me set the record straight. I am seven years old and for the duration of my life I have assisted Mother in writing her books. I never minded that she failed to mention the extent of my contribution. Humans are like that, and since they're such frail creatures (can you call fingernails claws?), I let it go. Humans are one thing. Cats are another, and Pewter, one year my junior, is not the literary lion she is pretending to be.

You don't have to believe me. Let me prove it to you. I am starting a kitty crime series. Pewter has nothing to do with it. I will, however, make her a minor character to keep peace in the house. This is my own work, every word.

I refuse to divulge whether this novel is a *roman à clef*. I will say only that I bear a strong resemblance to Mrs. Murphy.

Yours truly,

SNEAKY PIE

Mary Minor Haristeen, Harry to her friends, trotted along the railroad track. Following at her heels were Mrs. Murphy, her wise and willful tiger cat, and Tee Tucker, her Welsh corgi. Had you asked the cat and the dog they would have told you that Harry belonged to them, not vice versa, but there was no doubt that Harry belonged to the little town of Crozet, Virginia. At thirty-three she was the youngest postmistress Crozet had ever had, but then no one else really wanted the job.

Crozet nestles in the haunches of the Blue Ridge Mountains. The town proper consists of Railroad Avenue, which parallels the Chesapeake & Ohio Railroad track, and a street intersecting it called the Whitehall Road. Ten miles to the east reposes the rich and powerful small city of Charlottesville, which, like a golden fungus, is spreading east, west, north, and south. Harry liked Charlottesville just fine. It was the developers she didn't much like, and she prayed nightly they'd continue to think of Crozet and its three thousand inhabitants as a dinky little whistle stop on the route west and ignore it.

A gray clapboard building with white trim, next to the rail depot, housed the post office. Next to that was a tiny grocery store and a butcher shop run by "Market" Shiflett. Everyone appreciated this convenience because you could pick up your milk, mail, and gossip in one central location.

Harry unlocked the door and stepped inside just as the huge

railroad clock chimed seven beats for 7:00 A.M. Mrs. Murphy scooted
under her feet and Tucker entered at a more leisurely pace.

An empty mail bin invited Mrs. Murphy. She hopped in. Tucker
complained that she couldn't jump in.

"Tucker, hush. Mrs. Murphy will be out in a minute—won't you?"
Harry leaned over the bin.

Mrs. Murphy stared right back up at her and said, "*Fat chance. Let
Tucker bitch. She stole my catnip sockie this morning.*"

All Harry heard was a meow.

The corgi heard every word. "*You're a real shit, Mrs. Murphy. You've
got a million of those socks.*"

Mrs. Murphy put her paws on the edge of the bin and peeped
over. "*So what. I didn't say you could play with any of them.*"

"Stop that, Tucker." Harry thought the dog was growling for no
reason at all.

A horn beeped outside. Rob Collier, driving the huge mail truck,
was delivering the morning mail. He'd return at four that afternoon
for pickup.

"You're early," Harry called to him.

"Figured I'd cut you a break." Rob smiled. "Because in exactly
one hour Mrs. Hogendobber will be standing outside this door
huffing and puffing for her mail." He dumped two big duffel bags
on the front step and went back to the truck. Harry carried them
inside.

"Hey, I'd have done that for you."

"I know," Harry said. "I need the exercise."

Tucker appeared in the doorway.

"Hello, Tucker," Rob greeted the dog. Tucker wagged her tail.
"Well, neither rain nor sleet nor snow, et cetera." Rob slid behind the
wheel.

"It's seventy-nine degrees at seven, Rob. I wouldn't worry about
the sleet if I were you."

He smiled and drove off.

Harry opened the first bag. Mrs. Hogendobber's mail was on the
top, neatly bound with a thick rubber band. Rob, if he had the time,

put Mrs. Hogendobber's mail in a pile down at the main post office in Charlottesville. Harry slipped the handful of mail into the mail slot. She then began sorting through the rest of the stuff: bills, enough mail-order catalogues to provide clothing for every man, woman, and child in the United States, and of course personal letters and postcards.

Courtney Shiflett, Market's fourteen-year-old daughter, received a postcard from Sally McIntire, away at camp. Kelly Craycroft, the handsome, rich paving contractor, was the recipient of a shiny postcard from Paris. It was a photo of a beautiful angel with wings. Harry flipped it over. It was Oscar Wilde's tombstone in the Père Lachaise cemetery. On the back was the message "Wish you were here." No signature. The handwriting was computer script, like signatures on letters from your congressperson. Harry sighed and slipped it into Kelly's box. It must be heaven to be in Paris.

Snowcapped Alps majestically covered a postcard addressed to Harry from her lifelong friend Lindsay Astrove.

Dear Harry—

Arrived in Zurich. No gnomes in sight. Good flight. Very tired. Will write some more later.

Best,

LINDSAY

It must be heaven to be in Zurich.

Bob Berryman, the largest stock trailer dealer in the South, got a registered letter from the IRS. Harry gingerly put it in his box.

Harry's best friend, Susan Tucker, received a large package from James River Traders, probably those discounted cotton sweaters she'd ordered. Susan, prudent, waited for the sales. Susan was the "mother" of Tee Tucker, named Tee because Susan gave her to Harry on the seventh tee at the Farmington Country Club. Mrs. Murphy, two years the dog's senior, was not amused, but she came to accept it.

A Gary Larsen postcard attracted Harry's attention. Harry turned it over. It was addressed to Fair Haristeen, her soon-to-be-ex-husband, but not soon enough. "Hang in there, buddy" was the message from Stafford Sanburne. Harry jammed the postcard in Fair's box.

Crozet was still small enough that people felt compelled to take sides during a divorce. Perhaps even New York City was that small. At any rate, Harry reeled from fury to sorrow on a daily basis as she watched former friends choose sides, and most were choosing Fair.

After all, she had left him, thereby outraging other women in Albemarle County stuck in a miserable marriage but lacking the guts to go. That was a lot of women.

"Thank God they didn't have children," clucked many tongues behind Harry's back and to her face. Harry agreed with them. With children the goddamned divorce would take a year. Without, the limbo lasted only six months and she was two down.

By the time the clock struck eight the two duffel bags were folded over, the boxes filled, the old pine plank floor swept clean.

Mrs. George Hogendobber, an evangelical Protestant, picked up her mail punctually at 8:00 A.M. each morning except Sunday, when she was evangeling and the post office was closed. She fretted a great deal over evolution. She was determined to prove that humans were not descended from apes but, rather, created in God's own image.

Mrs. Murphy fervently hoped that Mrs. Hogendobber would prove her case, because linking man and ape was an insult to the ape. Of course, the good woman would die of shock to discover that God was a cat and therefore humans were off the board entirely.

That large Christian frame was lurching itself up the stairs. She pushed open the door with her characteristic vigor.

"Morning, Harry."

"Morning, Mrs. Hogendobber. Did you have a good weekend?"

"Apart from a splendid service at the Holy Light Church, no." She yanked out her mail. "Josiah DeWitt stopped by as I came home and gave me his sales pitch to part with Mother's Louis XVI bed, canopies and all. And on the Sabbath. The man is a servant of Mammon."

"Yes—but he knows good stuff when he sees it." Harry flattered her.

"H-m-m, Louis this and Louis that. Too many Louis's over there in France. Came to a bad end, too, every one of them. I don't think the French have produced anyone of note since Napoleon."

"What about Claudius Crozet?"

This stopped Mrs. Hogendobber for a moment. "Believe you're right. Created one of the engineering wonders of the nineteenth century. I stand corrected. But that's the only one since Napoleon."

The town of Crozet was named for this same Claudius Crozet, born on December 31, 1789. Trained as an engineer, he fought with the French in Russia and was captured on the hideous retreat from Moscow. So charmed was his Russian captor that he promptly removed Claudius to his huge estate and set him up with books and engineering tools. Claudius performed services for his captor until Frenchmen were allowed to return home. They say the Russian, a prince of the blood, rewarded the young captain with jewels, gold, and silver.

Joining Napoleon's second run at power proved dangerous, and Crozet immigrated to America. If he had a fortune, he carefully concealed it and lived off his salary. His greatest feat was cutting four railroad tunnels through the Blue Ridge Mountains, a task begun in 1850 and completed eight years later.

The first tunnel was west of Crozet: the Greenwood tunnel, 536 feet, and sealed after 1944, when a new tunnel was completed. Over the eastern portal of the Greenwood tunnel, carved in stone, is the legend: C. CROZET, CHIEF ENGINEER; E. T. D. MYERS, RESIDENT ENGINEER; JOHN KELLY, CONTRACTOR. A.D. 1852.

The second tunnel, Brooksville, 864 feet, was also sealed after 1944. This was a treacherous tunnel because the rock proved soft and unreliable.

The third tunnel was the Little Rock, 100 feet long and still in use by the C & O.

The fourth was the Blue Ridge, a long 4,723 feet.

Unused tracks ran to the sealed tunnels. They built things to last in the nineteenth century, for none of the rails had ever warped.

Crozet was reputed to have hidden his fortune in one of the tunnels. This story was taken seriously enough by the C & O Railroad that they carefully inspected the discontinued tunnels before sealing them after World War II. No treasure was ever found.

Mrs. Hogendobber left immediately after being corrected. She passed Ned Tucker, Susan's husband, on his way in. They exchanged pleasantries. Tee Tucker, barking merrily, rushed out to greet Ned. Mrs. Murphy climbed out of the mail bin and jumped onto the counter. She liked Ned. Everyone did.

He winked at Harry. "Well, have you been born again?"

"No, and I wasn't born yesterday either." She laughed.

"Mrs. H. was unusually terse this morning." He grabbed a huge handful of mail, most of it for the law office of Sanburne, Tucker, and Anderson.

"Count your blessings," Harry said.

"I do, every day." Ned smiled. Escaping a tirade of salvation on this hot July morning was just one blessing and Ned was a happy enough man to know there'd be many more. He stooped to rub Tucker's ears.

"You can rub mine, too," Mrs. Murphy pleaded.

"He likes me better than you." Tucker relished being the center of attention.

"Don't you love the sounds they make?" Ned kept scratching. "Sometimes I think they're almost human."

"Can you believe that?" Mrs. Murphy licked her front paws. Being human, the very thought! Humans lacked claws, fur, and their senses were dismal. Why, she could hear a doodlebug burrow in the sand. Furthermore, she understood everything humans said in their guttural way. They rarely understood her or other animals, much less one another. To get a reaction out of even Harry, who she confessed she did love, she had to resort to extravagant behavior.

"Yeah, I don't know what I'd do without my kids. Speaking of which, how're yours?"

Ned's eyes darted for a moment. "Harry, I'm beginning to think that sending Brookie to private school was a mistake. She's twelve going on twenty, and a perfect little snob too. Susan wants her to return to St. Elizabeth's in the fall but I say we yank her out of there and pack her back to public middle school with her brother. There she has to learn how to get along with all different kinds of people. Her grades fell and that's when Susan decided she was going to St. Elizabeth's. We went through public school, we learned, and we turned out all right."

"It's a tough call, Ned. They weren't selling drugs in the bathroom when you were in school."

"They were by the time we got to Crozet High. You had the good sense to ignore it."

"No, I didn't have the money to buy the stuff. Had I been one of those rich little subdivision kids—like today—who's to say?" Harry shrugged.

Ned sighed. "I'd hate to be a child now."

"Me too."

Bob Berryman interrupted. "Hey!" Ozzie, his hyper Australian shepherd, tagged at his heels.

"Hey, Berryman." Harry and Ned both called back to him out of politeness. Berryman's personality hovered on simmer and often flamed up to boil.

Mrs. Murphy and Tucker said hello to Ozzie.

"Hotter than the hinges of hell." Berryman sauntered over to his box and withdrew the mail, including the registered letter slip. "Shit, Harry, gimme a pen." She handed him a leaky ballpoint. He signed the slip and glared at the IRS notice. "The world is going to hell in a handbasket and the goddamned IRS controls the nation! I'd kill every one of those sons of bitches given half the chance!"

Ned walked out of the post office waving goodbye.

Berryman gulped some air, forced a smile, and calmed himself by petting Mrs. Murphy, who liked him although most humans found him brusque. "Well, I've got worms to turn and eggs to lay." He pushed off.

Bob's booted feet clomped on the first step as he closed the front door. As she didn't hear a second footfall, Harry glanced up from her stamp pads.

Walking toward Bob was Kelly Craycroft. His chestnut hair, gleaming in the light, looked like burnished bronze. Kelly, an affable man, wasn't smiling.

Wagging his tail, Ozzie stood next to Bob. Bob still didn't move. Kelly arrived at the bottom step. He waited a moment, said something to Bob which Harry couldn't hear, and then moved up to the second step, whereupon Bob pushed him down the steps.

Furious, his face darkening, Kelly scrambled to his feet. "You asshole!"

Harry heard that loud and clear.

Bob, without replying, sauntered down the steps, but Kelly, not a man to be trifled with, grabbed Bob's shoulder.

"You listen to me and you listen good!" Kelly shouted.

Harry wanted to move out from behind the counter. Good manners got the better of her. It would be too obvious. Instead she strained every fiber to hear what was being said. Tucker and Mrs. Murphy, hardly worried about how they'd look to others, bumped into each other as they ran to the door.

This time Bob raised his voice. "Take your hand off my shoulder."

Kelly squeezed harder and Bob balled up his fist, hitting him in the stomach.

Kelly doubled over but caught his breath. Staying low, he lunged, grabbing Bob's legs and throwing him to the pavement.

Ozzie, moving like a streak, sank his teeth into Kelly's left leg. Kelly hollered and let go of Bob, who jumped up.

"No" was all Bob had to say to Ozzie, and the dog immediately obeyed. Kelly stayed on the ground. He pulled up his pants leg. Ozzie's bite had broken the skin. A trickle of blood ran into his sock.

Bob said something; his voice was low. The color ran out of Kelly's face.

Bob walked over to his truck, got in, started the motor, and pulled out as Kelly staggered to his feet.

Jolted by the sight of blood, Harry shelved any concern about manners. She opened the door, hurrying over to Kelly.

"Better put some ice on that. Come on, I've got some in the refrigerator."

Kelly, still dazed, didn't reply immediately.

"Kelly?"

"Oh—yeah."

Harry led him into the post office. She dumped the ice out of the tray onto a paper towel.

Kelly was reading his postcard when she handed him the ice. He sat down on the bench, rolled up his pants leg, and winced when the cold first touched his leg. He stuck his mail in his back pocket.

"Want me to call Doc?" Harry offered.

"No." Kelly half smiled. "Pretty embarrassing, huh?"

"No more embarrassing than my divorce."

That made Kelly laugh. He relaxed a bit. "Hey, Mary Minor Haristeen, there is no such thing as a good divorce. Even if both parties start out with the best of intentions, when the lawyers get into it, the whole process turns to shit."

"God, I hope not."

"Trust me. It gets worse before it gets better." Kelly removed the ice. The bleeding had stopped.

"Keep it on a little longer," Harry advised. "It will prevent swelling."

Kelly replaced the makeshift ice pack. "It's none of my business, but you should have ditched Fair Haristeen years ago. You kept hanging in there trying to make it work. All you did was waste time. You cast your pearls before swine."

Harry wasn't quite ready to hear her husband referred to as swine, but Kelly was right: She should have gotten out earlier. "We all learn at our own rates of speed."

He nodded. "True enough. It took me this long to realize that Bob Berryman, ex–football hero of Crozet High, is a damned wimp. I mean, pushing me down the steps, for chrissake. Because of a bill. Accusing me of overcharging him for a driveway. I've been in business for myself for twelve years now and no one's accused me of overcharging."

"It could have been worse." Harry smiled.

"Oh, yeah?" Kelly glanced up quizzically.

"Could have been Josiah DeWitt."

"You got that right." Kelly rolled down his pants leg. He tossed the paper towel in the trash, said, "Harry, hang in there," and left the post office.

She watched him move more slowly than usual and then she returned to her tasks.

Harry was re-inking her stamp pads and cleaning the clogged ink out of the letters on the rubber stamps. She'd gotten to the point where she had maroon ink on her forehead as well as all over her fingers when Big Marilyn Sanburne, "Mim," marched in. Marilyn belonged to that steel-jawed set of women who were honorary men. She was called Big Marilyn or Mim to distinguish her from her daughter, Little Marilyn. At fifty-four she retained a cold beauty that turned heads. Burdened with immense hours of leisure, she stuck her finger in every civic pie, and her undeniable energy sent other volunteers to the bar or into fits.

"Mrs. Haristeen"—Mim observed the mess—"have you committed a murder?"

"No—just thinking about it." Harry slyly smiled.

"First on my list is the State Planning Commission. They'll never put a western bypass through this country. I'll fight to my last breath! I'd like to hire an F-14 and bomb them over there in Richmond."

"You'll have plenty of volunteers to help you, me included." Harry wiped, but the ink was stubborn.

Mim enjoyed the opportunity to lord it over someone, anyone. Jim Sanburne, her husband, had started out life on a dirt farm, and fought and scratched his way to about sixty million dollars. Despite Jim's wealth, Mim knew she had married beneath her and she was a woman who needed external proof of her social status. She needed her name in the Social Register. Jim thought it foolish. Her marriage was a constant trial. It was to Jim, too. He ran his empire, ran Crozet because he was mayor, but he couldn't run Mim.

"Well, have you reconsidered your divorce?" Mim sounded like a teacher.

"No." Harry blushed from anger.

"Fair's no better or worse than any other man. Put a paper bag over their heads and they're all the same. It's the bank account that's important. A woman alone has trouble, you know."

Harry wanted to say, "Yes, with snobs like you," but she shut up.

"Do you have gloves?"

"Why?"

"To help me carry in Little Marilyn's wedding invitations. I don't want to befoul them. Tiffany stationery, dear."

"Wait a minute, here." Harry rooted around.

"You put them next to the bin," Tucker informed her.

"I'll take you to the bathroom in a minute, Tucker," Harry told the dog.

"I'll knock them on the floor. See if she gets it." Mrs. Murphy nimbly trotted the length of the counter, carefully sidestepping the ink and stamps, and with one gorgeous leap landed on the shelf, where she pushed off the gloves.

"The cat knocked your gloves off the shelf."

Harry turned as the gloves hit the floor. "So she has. She must know what we're saying." Harry smiled, then followed Big Marilyn out to her copen-blue Volvo.

"Sometimes I wonder why I put up with her," Mrs. Murphy complained.

"Don't start. You'd be lost without Harry."

"She is good-hearted, I will admit, but Lord, she's slow."

"They all are," Tucker agreed.

Harry and Mim returned carrying two cardboard boxes filled with pale cream invitations.

"Well, Harry, you will know who is invited and who isn't before anyone else."

"I usually do."

"You, of course, are invited, despite your current, uh, problem. Little Marilyn adores you."

Little Marilyn did no such thing but no one dared not invite

Harry, because it would be so rude. She really did know every guest list in town. Because she knew everything and everybody, it was shrewd to keep on Harry's good side. Big Marilyn considered her a "resource person."

"Everything is divided up by zip code and tied." Mim tapped the counter. "And don't pick them up without your gloves on, Harry. You're never going to get that ink off your fingers."

"Promise."

"I'll leave it to you, then."

No sooner had she relieved Harry of her presence than Josiah DeWitt appeared, tipping his hat and chatting outside to Mim for a moment. He wore white pants and a white shirt and a snappy boater on his head, the very image of summer. He pushed open the door, touched the brim of his hat, and smiled broadly at the postmistress.

"I have affixed yet another date with the wellborn Mrs. Sanburne. Tea at the club." His eyes twinkled. "I don't mind that she gossips. I mind that she does it so badly."

"Josiah—" Harry never knew what he would say next. She slapped his hand as he reached into one of the wedding invitation boxes. "Government property now."

"That government governs best which governs least, and this one has its tentacles into every aspect of life, every aspect. Terrifying. Why, they even want to tell us what to do in bed." He grinned. "Ah, but I forgot you wear a halo on that subject now that you're separated. Of course, you wouldn't want to be accused of adultery in your divorce proceeding, so I shall assume yours is virtue by necessity."

"And lack of opportunity."

"Don't despair, Harry, don't despair. Anyway, you got a great nickname out of ten years of marriage . . . although Mary suits you now, because of the halo."

"You're awful sometimes."

"Rely on it." Josiah flipped through his mail and moaned, "Ned has given me the compliment of an invoice. Lawyers get a cut of everything, don't they?"

"Kelly Craycroft calls you Moldy Money." Harry liked Josiah because she could devil him. Some people you could and others you couldn't. "Don't you want to know why he calls you Moldy Money?"

"I already know. He says I've got the first dollar I ever made and it's moldering in my wallet. I prefer to think that capital, that offspring of business, is respected by myself and squandered by others, Kelly Craycroft in particular. I mean, how many paving contractors do you know who drive a Ferrari Mondial? And here, of all places." He shook his head.

Harry had to agree that owning a Ferrari, much less driving one, was on the tacky side. That's what people did in big cities to impress strangers. "He's got the money—I guess he can spend it the way he chooses."

"There's no such thing as a poor paving contractor, so perhaps you're right. Still"—his voice lowered—"so hopelessly flashy. At least Jim Sanburne drives a pickup." He absentmindedly slapped his mail on his thigh. "You will tell me, of course, who is and who isn't invited to Child Marilyn's wedding. I especially want to know if Stafford is invited."

"We all want to know that."

"What's your bet?"

"That he isn't."

"A safe bet. They were so close as children, too. Really devoted, that brother and sister. A pity. Well, I'm off. See you tomorrow."

Through the glass door Harry watched Susan Tucker and Josiah engage in animated conversation. So animated that when finished, Susan leaped up the three stairs in a single bound and flung open the door.

"Well! Josiah just told me you've got Little Marilyn's wedding invitations."

"I haven't looked."

"But you will and no time like the present." Susan opened the door by the counter and came around behind it.

"You can't touch that." Harry removed her gloves as Tucker joyfully jumped on Susan, who hugged and kissed her. Mrs. Murphy watched from her shelf. Tucker was laying it on pretty thick.

"Wonderful doggie. Beautiful doggie. Gimme a kiss." Susan saw Harry's hands. "Well, you can't touch the envelopes either, so for the next fifteen minutes I'll do your job."

"Do it in the back room, Susan. If anyone sees you we're both in trouble. Stafford will be in the one-double-oh zip codes and I think he's in one-double-oh two three, west of Central Park."

Susan called over her shoulder on her way to the back room: "If you can't live on the East Side of Manhattan, stay home."

"The West Side's really nice now."

"It's not here. Can you believe it?" Susan hollered from the back room.

"Sure, I believe it. What'd you expect?"

Susan came out and put the box under the counter. "Her own son. She's got to forgive him sometime."

"Forgiveness isn't a part of Big Marilyn Sanburne's vocabulary, especially when it impinges on her exalted social standing."

"This isn't the 1940's. Blacks and whites do marry now and the miscegenation laws are off the books."

"How many mixed marriages do you know in Crozet?"

"None, but there are a few in Albemarle County. I mean, this is so silly. Stafford's been married for six years now and Brenda is a stunning woman. A good one, too, I think."

"Are you going to have lunch with me? You're the only one left who will."

"It just seems that way because you're oversensitive right now. Come on, you'd better get out of here before someone else zooms through the door. You know how crazy Mondays are."

"Okay, I'm ready. My relief pitcher just pulled in." Harry smiled. It was nice having old Dr. Larry Johnson to cover the post office from 12:00 to 1:00 so she could take a lunch hour. It was also handy when she had errands to run during business hours. All she had to do was give him a call.

Dr. Johnson held the door for Harry, Susan, and the animals.

"Thank you, Dr. Johnson. How are you today?" Harry appreciated his gentlemanly gesture.

"I'm doing just fine, thank you."

"Good afternoon, Doctor," Susan said as Mrs. Murphy and Tucker greeted him with a chorus of purrs and yips.

"Hi, Susan. Good afternoon, Mrs. Murphy. And to you, too, Tee Tucker." Dr. Johnson reached down to pet Harry's buddies. "Where are you ladies headed?"

"We're just trotting up to Crozet Pizza for subs. Thanks for holding down the fort."

"My pleasure, as always. Have a good lunch," the retired doctor called after them.

Harry, Susan, Mrs. Murphy, and Tucker strolled down the shimmering sidewalk. The heat felt like a thick, moist wall. They waved at Market and Courtney Shiflett, working in the grocery store. Pewter, Market's chubby gray cat, indulged in a flagrant display of her private parts right there in the front window. On seeing Mrs. Murphy and Tucker, she said hello. They called back to her and walked on.

"I can't believe she's let herself go to pot like that," Mrs. Murphy whispered to Tucker. "All those meat tidbits Market feeds her. Girl has no restraint."

"Doesn't get much exercise either. Not like you."

Mrs. Murphy accepted the compliment. She had kept her figure just in case the right tom came along. Everyone, including Tucker, thought she was still in love with her first husband, Paddy, but Mrs. Murphy was certain she was over him. Over in capital letters. Paddy wore a tuxedo, oozed charm, and resented any accusation of usefulness. Worse, he ran off with a silver Maine coon cat and then had the nerve to come back thinking Mrs. Murphy would be glad to see him after the escapade. Not only was she not glad, she nearly scratched his eye out. Paddy sported a scar over his left eye from the fight.

Harry and Susan ordered huge subs at Crozet Pizza. They stayed inside to eat them, luxuriating in the air conditioning. Mrs. Murphy sat in a chair and Tucker rested under Harry's chair.

Harry bit into her sandwich and half the filling shot out the other end. "Damn."

"That's the purpose of a submarine sandwich. To make us look foolish." Susan giggled.

Maude Bly Modena came in at that moment. She started to walk over to takeout, then saw Harry and Susan. She ambled over for a polite exchange. "Use a knife and fork. What'd you do to your hands?"

"I was cleaning stamps."

"I, for one, don't care if my first class is blurred. Better than having you look like Lady Macbeth."

"I'll keep it in mind," Harry replied.

"I'd stay and chew the fat, ladies, but I've got to get back to the shop."

Maude Bly Modena had moved to Crozet from New York five years ago. She opened a packing store—cartons, plastic peanuts, papers, the works—and the store was a smash. An old railroad lorry sat in the front yard and she would put floral displays and the daily store discounts on the lorry. She knew how to attract customers and she herself was attractive, in her late thirties. At Christmastime there were lines to get into her store. She was a sharp businesswoman and friendly, to boot, which was a necessity in these parts. In time the residents forgave her that unfortunate accent.

Maude waved goodbye as she passed the picture window. Harry and Susan waved in return.

"I keep thinking Maude will find Mr. Right. She's so attractive."

"Mr. Wrong's more like it."

"Sour grapes."

"Am I like that, Susan? I hope not. I mean, I could rattle off the names of bitter divorced women and we'd be here all afternoon. I don't want to join that club."

Susan patted Harry's hand. "You're too sensitive, as I've said before. You'll cycle through all kinds of emotions. For lack of a better term, sour grapes is one of them. I'm sorry if I hurt your feelings."

Harry squirmed in her seat. "I feel as if there's no coating on my nerve endings." She settled in her chair. "You're right about Maude.

She's got a lot going for her. There ought to be someone out there for her. Someone who would appreciate her—and her business success too."

Susan's eyes danced. "Maybe she's got a lover."

"No way. You can't burp in your kitchen but what everyone knows it. No way." Harry shook her head.

"I wonder." Susan poured herself more Tab. "Remember Terrance Newton? We all thought we knew Terrance."

Harry thought about that. "Well, we were teenagers. I mean, if we had been adults, maybe we'd have picked up on something. The vibes."

"An insurance executive we all know goes home, shoots his wife and himself. My recollection is the adults were shocked. No one picked up on anything. If you can keep up your facade, people accept that. Very few people look beneath the surface."

Harry sighed. "Maybe everyone's too busy."

"Or too self-centered." Susan drummed the table with her fingers. "What I'm getting at is that maybe we don't know one another as well as we think we do. It's a small-town illusion—thinking we know each other."

Harry quietly played with her sub. "You know me. I think I know you."

"That's different. We're best friends." Susan polished off her sandwich and grabbed her brownie. "Imagine being Stafford Sanburne and not being invited to your sister's wedding."

"That was a leap."

"Like I said, we're best friends. I don't have to think in sequence around you." Susan laughed.

"Stafford sent Fair a postcard. 'Hang in there, buddy.' Come to think of it, that's what Kelly said to me. Hey, you missed it. Kelly Craycroft and Bob Berryman had a fight, fists and all."

"You wait until now to tell me!"

"So much else has been going on, it slipped my mind. Kelly said it was about a paving bill. Bob thinks he overcharged him."

"Bob Berryman may not be Mr. Charm but that doesn't sound like him, to fight over a bill."

"Hey, like I said, maybe we don't really know one another."

Harry picked tomatoes out of her sandwich. They were the culprits; she was sure the meat, cheese, and pickles would stay inside without those slimy tomatoes. She slapped the bread back together as Mrs. Murphy reached across the plate to hook a piece of roast beef. "Mrs. Murphy, that will do." Harry used her commanding mother voice. It would work at the Pentagon. Mrs. Murphy withdrew her paw.

"Maybe we should rejoice that Little Marilyn's made a match at last," Susan said.

"You don't think that Little Marilyn bagged Fitz-Gilbert Hamilton by herself, do you?"

Susan considered this. "She's got her mother's beauty."

"And is cold as a wedge."

"No, she isn't. She's quiet and shy."

"Susan, you've liked her since we were kids and I never could stand Little Marilyn. She's such a momma's baby."

"You drove your mother wild."

"I did not."

"Oh, yeah, how about the time you put your lace underpants over her license plate and she drove around the whole day not knowing why everyone was honking at her and laughing."

"That." Harry remembered. She missed her mother terribly. Grace Minor had died unexpectedly of a heart attack four years earlier, and Cliff, her husband, followed within the year. He couldn't make a go of it without Grace and he admitted as much on his deathbed. They were not rich people by any means but they left Harry a lovely clapboard house two miles west of town at the foot of Little Yellow Mountain and they also left a small trust fund, which paid for taxes on the house and pin money. A house without a mortgage is a wonderful inheritance, and Harry and Fair were happy to move from their rented house on Myrtle Street. Of course, when Harry asked Fair to leave, he complained bitterly that he had always hated living in her parents' house.

"Fitz-Gilbert Hamilton is ugly as sin, but he's never going to need food stamps and he's a Richmond lawyer of much repute—at least that's what Ned says."

"Too much fuss over this marriage. You marry in haste and repent in leisure."

"Don't be sour." Susan's eyes shot upward.

"The happiest day of my life was when I married Pharamond Haristeen and the next happiest day of my life was when I threw him out. He's full of shit and he's not going to get any sympathy from me. God, Susan, he's running all over town, the picture of the wounded male. He has dinner every night with a different couple. I heard that Mim Sanburne offered her maid to do his laundry for him. I can't believe it."

Susan sighed. "He seems to relish being a victim."

"Well, I sure don't." Harry practically spat. "The only thing worse than being a veterinarian's wife is being a doctor's wife."

"That's not why you want to divorce him."

"No, I guess not. I don't want to talk about this."

"You started it."

"Did I?" Harry seemed surprised. "I didn't mean to. . . . I'd like to forget the whole thing. We were talking about Little Marilyn Sanburne."

"We were. Little Marilyn will be deeply hurt if Stafford doesn't show up, and Mim will die if he does—her event-of-the-year marriage marred by the arrival of her black daughter-in-law. Life would be much simpler if Mim would overcome her plantation mentality." Susan drummed the table again.

"Yeah, but then she'd have to join the human race. I mean, she's emotionally impotent and wants to extend her affliction universally. If she changed her thinking she might have to feel something, you know? She might have to admit that she was wrong and that she's wounded her children, wounded and scarred them."

Susan sat silent for a moment, viewing the remnants of the once-huge sub. "Yeah—here, Tucker."

"*Hey, hey, what about me?*" Mrs. Murphy yelled.

"Oh, here, you big baby." Harry shoved over her plate. She was full.

Mrs. Murphy ate what was left except for the tomatoes. As a kitten, she once ate a tomato and vowed never again.

Harry strolled back to the post office, and the rest of the day ran on course. Market dropped by some knucklebones. Courtney picked up the mail while her dad talked.

After work Harry walked back home. She liked the two-mile walk in the mornings and afternoons. Good exercise for her and the cat and the dog. Once home, she washed her old Superman-blue truck, then weeded her garden. She cleaned out the refrigerator after that and before she knew it, it was time to go to bed.

She read a bit, Mrs. Murphy curled up by her side with Tucker snoring at the end of the bed. She turned out her light, as did the other residents of Crozet ensconced behind their high hedges, blinds, and shutters.

It was the end of another day, peaceful and perfect in its way. Had Harry known what tomorrow would bring, she might have savored the day even more.

2

Mrs. Murphy performed a somersault while chasing a grasshopper. She never could resist wigglies, as she called them. Tucker, uninterested in bugs, cast a keen eye for squirrels foolish enough to scamper down Railroad Avenue. The old tank watch, her father's, on Harry's wrist read 6:30 A.M. and the heat rose off the tracks. It was a real July Virginia day, the kind that compelled weathermen and weatherwomen on television to blare that it would be hot, humid, and hazy with no relief in sight. They then counseled the viewer to drink plenty of liquids. Cut to a commercial for, surprise, a soft drink.

Harry reflected on her childhood. At thirty-three she wasn't that old but then again she wasn't that young. She thought the times had become more ruthlessly commercial. Even funeral directors advertised. Their next gimmick would be a Miss Dead America contest to see who could do the best work on the departed. Something had happened to America within Harry's life span, something she couldn't quite put her finger on, but something she could feel, sharply. There was no contest between God and the golden calf. Money was God, these days. Little pieces of green paper with dead people's pictures on them were worshipped. People no longer killed for love. They killed for money.

How odd to be alive in a time of spiritual famine. She watched the cat and dog playing tag and wondered how her kind had ever drifted so far away from animal existence, that sheer delight in the moment.

Harry did not consider herself a philosophical woman, but lately she had turned her mind to deeper thoughts, not just to the purpose of her own life but to the purpose of human life in general. She wouldn't even tell Susan what zigzagged through her head these days, because it was so disturbing and sad. Sometimes she thought she was mourning her lost youth and that was at the bottom of this. Maybe the upheaval of the divorce forced her inward. Or maybe it really was the times, the cheapness and crass consumerism of American life.

Mrs. George Hogendobber, at least, had values over and above her bank account, but Mrs. Hogendobber vainly clung to a belief system that had lost its power. Right-wing Christianity could compel those frightened and narrow-minded souls who needed absolute answers but it couldn't capture those who needed a vision of the future here on earth. Heaven was all very fine but you had to die to get there. Harry wasn't afraid to die but she wouldn't refuse to live either. She wondered what it must have been like to live when Christianity was new, vital, and exciting—before it had been corrupted by collusion with the state. That meant she would have had to have lived before the second century A.D., and as enticing as the idea might be, she wasn't sure she could exist without her truck. Did this mean she'd sell her soul for wheels? She knew she wouldn't sell her soul for a buck, but machines, money, and madness were tied together somehow and Harry knew she wasn't wise enough to untangle the Gordian knot of modern life.

She became postmistress in order to hide from that modern life. Majoring in art history at Smith College on a scholarship had left her splendidly unprepared for the future, so she came home upon graduation and worked as an exercise rider in a big stable. When old George Hogendobber died, she applied for the post office job and won it. Odd, that Mrs. Hogendobber had had a good marriage and that Harry was engaged in hand-to-hand combat with the opposite sex. She wondered if Mrs. Hogendobber knew something she didn't or if George had simply surrendered all hope of individuality and that was why the marriage had worked. Harry had no regrets about her job, small though it might seem to others, but she did have regrets about her marriage.

"Mom's pensive this morning." Mrs. Murphy brushed up against Tucker. "Divorce stuff, I guess. Humans sure make it hard on themselves."

Tucker flicked her ears forward and then back. "Yeah, they seem to worry a lot."

"I'll say. They worry about things that are years away and may never happen."

"I think it's because they can't smell. Miss a lot of information."

Mrs. Murphy nodded in agreement and then added, "Walking on two legs. Screws up their backs and then it affects their minds. I'm sure that's the source of it."

"I never thought of that." Tucker saw the mail driver. "Hey, I'll race you to Rob."

Tucker cheated and tore out before Mrs. Murphy could reply. Furious, Mrs. Murphy shot off her powerful hindquarters and stayed low over the ground.

"Girls, girls, you come back here."

The girls believed in selective hearing and Tucker made it to the mail truck before Mrs. Murphy, but the little tiger jumped into the vehicle.

"I won!"

"You did not," Tucker argued.

"Hello, Mrs. Murphy. Hello, Tucker." Rob was pleased at the greeting he'd received.

Harry, panting, caught up with the cat and the dog. "Hi, Rob. What you got for me this morning?"

"The usual. Two bags." He rattled around in the truck. "Here's a package from Turnbull and Asser that Josiah DeWitt has to sign and pay for." Rob pointed out the sum on the front.

Harry whistled. "One hundred and one dollars duty. Must be a mess of shirts in there. Josiah has to have the best."

"I was reading somewhere, don't remember where, that the

mark-up in the antiques business can be four hundred percent. Guess he can afford those shirts."

"Try to get him to pay for anything else." Harry smiled.

Boom Boom Craycroft, Kelly's pampered wife, drove east, heading toward Charlottesville. Boom Boom owned a new BMW convertible with the license plate BOOMBMW. She waved and Harry and Rob waved back.

Rob gazed after her. Boom Boom was a pretty woman, dark and sultry. He came back to earth. "Today I'll carry the bags in, miss. You can save women's liberation for tomorrow."

Harry smiled. "Okay, Rob, butch it up. I love a man with muscles."

He laughed and hauled both bags over his shoulders as Harry unlocked the door.

After Rob left, Harry sorted the mail in a half hour. Tuesdays were light. She settled herself in the back room and made a cup of good coffee. Tucker and Mrs. Murphy played with the folded duffel bag and by the time Harry emerged from the back room, Mrs. George Hogendobber was standing at the front door and the duffel was moving suspiciously. Harry didn't have the time to pull Mrs. Murphy out. She unlocked the front door and as Mrs. Hogendobber came in, Mrs. Murphy shot out of the bag like a steel ball in a pinball machine.

"*Catch me if you can!*" she called to Tucker.

The corgi ran around in circles as Mrs. Murphy jumped on a shelf, then to the counter, ran the length of the counter at top speed, hit the wall with all four feet and shoved off the wall with a half turn, ran the length of the counter, and did the same maneuver in the opposite direction. She then flew off the counter, ran between Mrs. Hogendobber's legs, Tucker in hot pursuit, jumped back on the counter, and then sat still as a statue as she laughed at Tucker.

Mrs. Hogendobber gasped, "That cat's mental!"

Harry, astonished at the display of feline acrobatics, swallowed and replied, "Just one of her fits—you know how they are."

"I don't like cats myself." Mrs. H. drew herself up to her full height, which was considerable. She had the girth to match. "Too independent."

Yes, many people say that, Harry thought to herself, and all of them are fascists. This was a cherished assumption she would neither divulge nor purge.

"I forgot to tell you to watch Diane Bish Sunday night on cable. Such an accomplished organist. Why they even show her feet, and last Sunday she wore silver slippers."

"I don't have cable."

"Oh, well, move into town. You shouldn't be out there at Yellow Mountain alone, anyway." Mrs. Hogendobber whispered, "I hear Mim dumped off the wedding invitations yesterday."

"Two boxes full."

"Did she invite Stafford?" This sounded innocent.

"I don't know."

"Oh." Mrs. Hogendobber couldn't hide her disappointment.

Josiah came in. "Hello, ladies." He focused on Mrs. Hogendobber. "I want that bed." He frowned a mock frown.

Mrs. Hogendobber was not endowed with much humor. "I'm not prepared to sell."

Fair came in, followed by Susan. Greetings were exchanged. Harry was tense. Mrs. Hogendobber seized the opportunity to slip away from the determined Josiah. Across the street Hayden McIntire, the town physician, parked his car.

Josiah observed him and sighed, "Ah, my child-ridden neighbor." Hayden had fathered many children.

Fair quietly opened his box and pulled out the mail. He wanted to slip away, and Harry, not using the best judgment, called him back.

"Wait a minute."

"I've got a call. Cut tendon." His hand was on the doorknob.

"Dammit, Fair. Where's my check?" Harry blurted out from frustration.

They had signed a settlement agreement whereby Fair was to pay $1,000 a month to Harry until the divorce, when their joint assets would be equally divided. While not a wealthy couple, the two had worked hard during their marriage and the division of spoils would most certainly benefit Harry, who earned far less than Fair. Fortunately, Fair considered the house rightfully Harry's and so that was not contested.

She felt he was jerking her around with the money. Typical Fair. If she didn't do it, it didn't get done. All he could concentrate on was his equine practice.

For Fair's part, he thought Harry was being her usual nagging self. She'd get the goddamned check when he got around to it.

Fair blushed. "Oh, that, well, I'll get it off today."

"Why not write it now?"

"I've got a call, Harry!"

"You're ten days late, Fair. Do I have to call Ned Tucker? I mean, all that does is cost me lawyer's fees and escalate hostilities."

"Hey," he yelled, "calling me out in front of Susan and Josiah is hostile enough!" He slammed the door.

Josiah, transfixed by the domestic drama, could barely wipe the smile off his face. Having avoided the pitfalls of marriage, he thoroughly enjoyed the show couples put on. Josiah never could understand why men and women wanted to marry. Sex he could understand, but marriage? To him it was the ball and chain.

Susan, not transfixed, was deeply sorry about the outburst, because she knew that Josiah would tell Mim and by sunset it would be all over town. The divorce was difficult enough without public displays. She also guessed that Fair, good passive-aggressive personality that he was, was playing "starve the wife." Husbands and their lawyers loved that game . . . and quite often it worked. The soon-to-be-ex wife would become dragged down by the subtle battering and give up. Emotionally the drain was too much for the women, and they would kiss off what they had earned in the marriage. This was made all the more difficult because men took housework and women's labor for granted. No dollar value was attached to it. When the wife withdrew that labor, men usually didn't perceive its value; instead they felt something had been done to them. The woman was a bitch.

After the sting wore off, Susan knew Fair would immediately set about to find another woman to love, and the by-product of this love would mean that the new wife would do the food shopping, juggle the social calendar, and keep the books. All for love.

Did Susan do this for Ned? In the beginning of the marriage, yes. After five years and two kids she had felt she was losing her mind. She balked. Ned was ripshot mad. Then they got to talking, really talking. She was fortunate. So was he. They found common ground. They learned to do with less so they could hire help. Susan took a part-time job to bring in some money and get out of the house. But Susan and Ned were meant for each other, and Harry and Fair were not. Sex brought them together and left them together for a while, but they weren't really connected emotionally and they certainly weren't connected intellectually. They were two reasonably good people who needed to free themselves to do what came next, and sadly, they weren't going to free themselves without anger, recrimination, and dragging their friends into it.

Susan's thoughts were abruptly short-circuited.

A siren echoed in the background, growing louder until the Crozet Rescue Squad ambulance flashed down the road, effectively ending the Harry versus Fair reverberation. They all ran out in front of the post office.

Harry, without thinking, touched Josiah's arm. "Not old Dr. Johnson." He had been her childhood physician and was becoming stooped and frail.

"He'll live to be one hundred. Don't worry." Josiah patted her hand.

The ambulance turned south on the Whitehall Road, also known as Route 240.

Big Marilyn Sanburne's Volvo sped to Shiflett's Market. She stopped and slammed the door of her car.

She thumped over to the group. "I damn near got run off the road by the Rescue Squad. They probably scare to death as many people as they save."

"Amen," Josiah agreed. He started to leave.

Harry called him back. "Josiah, you've got to sign and pay for a Turnbull and Asser package."

"It came." He beamed and then the glow went into remission. "How much?"

"One hundred and one dollars," Harry answered.

Josiah bore the blow. "Well, some things one cannot postpone from motives of economy. Consider the people I am compelled to meet."

"Di and Fergie," Harry solemnly intoned.

In fact, Josiah was in the vicinity of the Royals whilst in London buying up George III furniture before taking a hovercraft across the channel to acquire more of his beloved Louis XV.

Mim wheeled on Josiah, her constant escort whenever she could dump husband Jim. "Still dining out on that story."

"My dear Mim, I merely do business with royalty. You know them as friends." An allusion to the obscure Romanian countess much touted by Big Marilyn, who, when she was eighteen, paraded the European beauty about Crozet.

In the late fifties, Mim had looted Europe for Fabergé boxes and George III furnishings, her favorite period. Jim Sanburne didn't know what he was getting into when he married Mim—but then, who does? In Paris, Mim encountered a friend of the countess who told her the woman was a bakery assistant from Prague, albeit a beautiful one. Whoever she was, she was smart enough to outwit Mim, and Mrs. Sanburne did not take kindly to a reminder, nor did she appreciate the fact that the countess seduced Jim—but then, he was an easy lay. She made him pay for that indiscretion.

Pewter thundered out of the market as a customer opened the door. She was so fat that when she ran, her stomach wobbled from side to side.

Susan giggled. "Someone ought to put that cat on a diet." She diverted the topic of conversation but didn't mind Mim's moment of discomfort.

Pewter stood on her hind legs and scratched the post office door. "*Let me in.*"

Harry opened the door for her as the humans kept talking outside. Pewter burst into the P.O., filled with importance. Even Mrs. Murphy paid attention to her.

"*Guess what?*" The gray whiskers swept forward and Pewter leaped onto the counter—not easy for her, but she was so excited she made it in one try.

Tucker craned her head upward. "*I wish you'd come down here and tell your tale.*"

Pewter brushed aside the corgi's request. "*Market got a call from Diana Farrell, of the Rescue Squad. You know Market does duty on weekends sometimes and they're friends.*"

"*Get to the point, Pewter.*" Mrs. Murphy swished her tail.

"*If that's your attitude, I'm leaving. You can find out from someone else.*"

"*Don't go,*" Tucker pleaded.

"*I am. I am most certainly going. I know when I'm not wanted.*" Pewter was in a real huff. She puffed her tail, and as Harry opened the door to come in she ran out.

"*You're so rude,*" Tucker complained.

"*She's a windbag.*" Mrs. Murphy did not feel like apologizing.

Josiah was paying out money and grumbling.

"*She may be chatty,*" Tucker said, "*but if she ran over here in this blistering heat, it had to be something big.*"

Mrs. Murphy knew Tucker was right, but she said nothing and curled up on the counter instead. Tucker, out of sorts, whined for Harry to open the door beside the counter. Harry did and Tucker lay down on her big pillow under the counter.

An hour passed with people coming and going. Maude Bly Modena opened her copy of *Vogue* and she and Harry read their horoscopes.

Maude declared that there were only twelve horoscope readings. Whatever the horoscope was for your sign, it would be moved to the next sign tomorrow. So if you were a Scorpio, your reading would move to Sagittarius the following day, and Libra's reading would then be yours. It took twelve days to complete the cycle. When Harry giggled with disbelief, Maude said people don't remember their horoscopes from one day to the next. They'd never remember twelve days' worth.

Maude said that instead of remembering an entire reading, remember the phrase "Opposite sex interested and shows it." That phrase will move through each sign in succession.

By the time Maude finished, Harry was laughing so hard she didn't care if Maude's theory was true or not. The important thing was that it was fun and Harry needed to know she could still have fun. Divorce was not the end of the world.

Harry's projection for August was "Revise routine. Rebuild for future. Important dates: 7th, 14th, and 29th." Important for what, this stellar prophecy declined to reveal. Harry swore she'd test Maude's theory after Maude left. She clipped the horoscope but within fifteen minutes it had gotten mixed up with postal patron notices.

Little Marilyn Sanburne came in and cooed about her wedding, sort of. With Little Marilyn a coo came from the more obscure regions of her throat. Harry pretended to be interested but personally felt Little Marilyn was making a huge mistake. She couldn't even get along with herself, much less anyone else.

A full hour passed before Market Shiflett pushed through the door.

"Harry, I would have come over sooner but it's been bedlam—sheer bedlam." He wiped his brow.

"Are you all right?" Harry noticed he looked peaked. "Can I get you something?"

He waved no, and then leaned up against the counter to steady himself. "Diana Farrell called me. Kelly Craycroft—at least they think it's Kelly Craycroft—was found dead about ten this morning."

Tucker jumped up. "See, Mrs. Murphy? I told you she knew something big."

Mrs. Murphy realized her mistake but couldn't do a damn thing about it now.

"My God, how?" Harry was stunned. She thought maybe a heart attack. Kelly was at that dangerous age for a man.

"Don't rightly know. The body's all tore up. Found him in one of the big cement grinders. He's not even in one piece. Diana said that if he was shot in the head or any other part of the body, they'd never know. Sheriff's Department has impounded the mixer. Guess they'll search for some lead in there. You know, Kelly was always climbing to the top of that mixer to show it to people."

"Murder—you're talking about murder." Harry's eyes widened.

"Well, hell, Harry, a big strong man like Kelly don't just fall into a cement mixer. Someone pushed him in."

"Maybe it isn't him. Maybe it's some drunk or—"

"It's him. Ferrari parked right there. Didn't show up at the office. Since his car was there, everyone figured he was on the grounds somewhere. They didn't really know until one of the men started up the grinder and it sounded funny."

Harry shuddered at the thought of what that poor fellow saw when he looked into the mixer.

"He wasn't a saint but who is? He couldn't have made anyone mad enough to kill him."

"Made someone mad enough." Market exhaled. He didn't like the news, but there was something special about being the messenger of such tidings and Market was not a man immune to those few moments of privileged status. "Thought you ought to know."

As he turned to leave, Harry called out, "Your mail."

"Oh, yeah." Market fished out the mail in his box and left.

Harry sat down on the stool behind the counter. She needed to order her mind. Then she went to the phone and rang up Appalachia Equine. Fair was out, so she left a message for him to call her pronto. Then she dialed Susan.

"Doodle, doodle, doodle." Susan answered the phone. She'd grown tired of "Hello."

"Susan!"

Susan knew from the sound of Harry's voice that something was amiss. "What's wrong?"

"Kelly Craycroft's body was found in a cement mixer. Market just told me, and he said it was murder."

"Murder?!"

3

Rick Shaw, Albemarle County sheriff, hitched up the broad Sam Browne belt. His gun felt even heavier in this stinking heat and it didn't help that he'd put on a pound or two in the last eighteen months. Before he became sheriff he had been more active but now he spent too much time behind his desk. His appetite did not diminish, however, and he began to think that the red tape he had to wade through actually increased his appetite through frustration. The sheriff who preceded him died fat as a tick. This was not a happy thought.

This was not a happy case. Rick had grown accustomed to the vileness of men. He'd seen shoot-outs, drunken knife fights, and corpses of people who had been bludgeoned to death. The traffic accidents weren't much better but at least they weren't premeditated. Albemarle County suffered about two murders a year, usually domestic. This was different, and he sensed it the minute he stepped out of the car.

Officer Cynthia Cooper had arrived on the scene first. A tall young woman with sense as well as experience, she had cordoned off the area. The fingerprint team was on the way but Rick didn't hope for much there. The staff at Craycroft Concrete stood in the sun, too hot to be standing around like that but they were dazed.

Someone was screaming somewhere, and according to Officer Cooper, Kelly's wife was at home, sedated. He regretted that and would have to have a word with Hayden McIntire, the doctor. Sedating should be done after the questioning, not before.

A BMW screeched through the entrance. Kelly Craycroft's wife vaulted from her seat and raced for the mixer.

"Boom Boom!" Rick hollered at her.

Boom Boom soared over the cordoning and roughly pushed her way past Diana Farrell of the Rescue Squad. Clai Cordle, another nurse and squad member, couldn't stop her either.

Cynthia Cooper made a flying tackle but it was a second too late and Boom Boom was climbing up the ladder to the opening of the mixer.

"He's my husband! You can't keep me from my husband!"

"You don't want to see that, girl." Rick moved his bulk as quickly as he could.

Cynthia scurried up the ladder and grabbed Boom Boom's ankle but not before the raven-haired woman lifted her head over the side of the mixer. Immobile for a second, she fell back into Cynthia Cooper's arms in a dead faint, nearly knocking the young police-woman off the ladder.

Rick reached up and held Cynthia around the waist as Diana ran over to help. They got Boom Boom to the ground.

Diana broke open the amyl nitrite.

Cynthia snatched it from her hand. "All she's got are these few moments before this hits her again. Let her have them."

Rick cleared his throat. He hated this. He also hated that Boom Boom might throw up when she came to and he fervently hoped she wouldn't. Blood and guts were one thing. Vomit was another.

Boom Boom moaned. She opened her eyes. Rick held his breath. She sat up and swallowed. He exhaled. She wasn't going to throw up. She wasn't even going to cry.

"He looks like something in the Cuisinart." Boom Boom's voice sounded flat.

"Don't think about it," Officer Cooper advised.

"I'll remember the sight for the rest of my natural life." Boom

Boom struggled to her feet. She swayed a bit and Rick steadied her. "I'm all right. Just . . . give me a minute."

"Why don't we go over to the office. The air conditioning will help."

Officer Cooper and Boom Boom walked over to the small office and Rick motioned to Diana and Clai to get the body pieces out of the mixer. "Don't let Boom Boom see the bag."

"Keep her inside," Diana requested.

"Do what I can but she's a wild one. Been that way since she was a kid." Rick took off his hat and entered the office.

Marie Williams, Craycroft Concrete's secretary, sobbed. At the sight of Boom Boom she emitted a wail.

Boom Boom stared at her in disgust. "Pull yourself together, Marie."

"I loved him. I just loved him. He was the best man in the world to work for. He'd bring me roses on Secretary's Day. He'd give me time off when Timmy was sick. Didn't dock my pay." A fresh outburst followed this.

Boom Boom hit the chair with a thump. Behind her a huge poster of a sitting duck slurping a drink, bullet holes in the wall behind him, gave the room a festive air. If Marie kept this up she'd throw her in the mixer. Boom Boom loathed displays of emotion. Circumstances did not alter her opinion on this.

"Mrs. Williams, why don't you come into Mr. Craycroft's office with me. Maybe you can explain his daily routine. We can't touch anything until the prints men come in."

"I understand." Marie shuffled off with Officer Cooper, shutting the door behind her.

"You don't really know if that's my husband in there." Boom Boom's voice didn't sound normal.

"No."

She leaned back in the chair. "It is, though."

"How do you know?" Rick's voice was gentle but probing.

"I feel it. Besides, his car is parked here and Kelly was never far from that car. Loved it more than anything, even me, his wife."

"Do you have any idea how this could have happened?"

"Apart from someone pushing him into the mixer, no." Her eyes glittered.

"Enemies?"

"Pharamond Haristeen—well, that's old. They aren't enemies anymore."

Rick knew the story of Fair making a pass at Boom Boom at last year's Hunt Club ball. Much liquor had been consumed but not enough for people to forget the overture. He'd need to question Fair. Emotions, like land mines, could explode when you least expected them to . . . years after an event. It wouldn't be impossible for Fair to be a murderer, only improbable. "What about business troubles?"

Boom Boom smiled a wan smile. "Kelly had the Midas touch."

Rick smiled back at her. "All of central Virginia knows that." He paused. "Perhaps he got into a disagreement over a bill or a paving bid. People get crazy about money. Anything, anything at all that comes to mind."

"Nothing."

Rick placed his hand on her shoulder. "I'll have Officer Cooper drive you home."

"I can drive."

"No, you can't. For once you'll do as I say."

Boom Boom didn't argue. She felt shakier than she wanted to admit. In fact, she'd never felt so terrible in her life. She loved Kelly, in her vague fashion, and he loved her in return.

Rick glanced up to see how the body removal was progressing. It wasn't easy. Even Clai Cordle, stomach of iron, was green around the gills.

Rick opened the door, blocking Boom Boom's view. "Clai, Diana, hold up a minute, will you? Officer Cooper's going to run Boom Boom home."

"Okay." Diana suspended her labors.

"Officer Cooper."

"Yo," Cynthia called out, then opened the door.

"Carry Boom Boom home, will you?"

"Sure."

"Find anything in there?"

Marie followed behind Officer Cooper. "Everything's filed and cross-filed, first alphabetically and then under subject matter. I did it myself."

As Boom Boom and Officer Cooper left, Rick went into the small, clean office with Marie.

"He believed in 'a place for everything and everything in its place,' " Marie whimpered.

Rick scanned the top of Kelly's desk. A silver-framed portrait of Boom Boom was on the right-hand corner. A Lamy pen, very bulky, was placed on a neat diagonal over Xeroxed papers.

Rick leaned over, careful not to touch anything, and read the top sheet.

> My Whig principles have been strengthened by the Mexican War. It broke out just as I was preparing to depart for Europe; my trunks were actually ready; that and the Oregon question, made me unpack them. Now my son is in it. Some pecuniary interest is at stake, the political horizon is clouded and I am forced to wait until all this ends. Since I have had my surfeit of war, I am for peace; but at this time I am still more so. Peace, peace rises at the top of all my thoughts and the feeling makes me twice a Whig. As soon as things are settled I cross the Atlantic. I might do it now, of course, but I do not wish to go for only a few months and my stay might now be curtailed by events.
>
> > Very respectfully, Y'r most obed't.
> > C. CROZET

"I don't recall Kelly being interested in history."

Marie shrugged. "Me neither, but he'd get these whims, you know."

Rick put his thumb under the heavy belt again, taking some of the weight off his shoulder and waist. "Crozet was an engineer. Maybe he wrote about paving or something. Built all our turnpikes, you know. Route 240, too, if I remember Miss Grindle's teachings in fourth grade."

"What a witch." Marie had had Miss Grindle too.

"Never had any disciplinary problems at Crozet Elementary when Miss Grindle was there."

"From the War Between the States until the Korean War." Marie half giggled, then caught herself. "How can I laugh at a time like this?"

"Need to. Your emotions will be a roller coaster for a while."

Tears welled up in Marie's eyes. "You'll catch him, won't you? Whoever did this?"

"I'm gonna try, Marie. I'm gonna try."

4

"Are you sure you want to do this?" Susan peered into Harry's face.

"You know I have to."

Not paying her condolences to Boom Boom would have been a breach of manners so flagrant it would be held against Harry forever. Not actively held against her, mind, just remembered, a black mark against her name in the book. Even if she had more good marks than bad, and she hoped that she did, it didn't pay to play social percentages in Crozet.

It wasn't just facing the jolt of a shocking death that caught Harry; it was having to face the entire social spectrum. Since asking Fair to leave, Harry had kept pretty much to herself. Of course, Fair would be at the Craycrofts'. Even if his big truck was not parked in the driveway she knew he'd be there. He was well brought up. He understood his function at a time like this.

The gathered Crozet residents would not only be able to judge how Boom Boom held up during the hideous crisis, but they'd also be able to judge the temperature of the divorce, a crisis of a different sort. Behaving bravely was tremendously important in Crozet. Stiff upper lip.

Harry often thought if she wanted a stiff upper lip she'd grow a moustache.

"*Are you going to leave me here?*" Tee Tucker asked.

"*Yeah, what about me?*" Mrs. Murphy wanted to know.

Harry looked down at her friends. "Susan, either we take the kids or you'll have to run me back home."

"I'll run you home. Really isn't proper to take the animals to the Craycrofts', I guess."

"You're right." Harry shooed Mrs. Murphy and Tucker out the post office door and locked it behind her.

Pewter, lounging in the front window of Market's store, yawned and then preened when she saw Mrs. Murphy. Pewter's countenance radiated satisfaction, importance, and power, however momentary.

Mrs. Murphy seethed. "*A fat gray Buddha, that's what she thinks she is.*"

Tucker said, "*You like her despite herself.*"

Mrs. Murphy and Tucker glanced at each other during the ride home.

Tucker rolled her eyes. "*Humans are crazy. Humans and ants—kill their own kind.*"

"*I've had a few thoughts along those lines myself,*" Mrs. Murphy replied.

"*You have not. Stop being cynical. It isn't sophisticated. You'll never be sophisticated, Mrs. Murphy. You came from Sally Mead's SPCA.*"

"*You can shut up any time now, Tucker. Don't take your bad mood out on me just because we have to go home.*"

Once in the house, Mrs. Murphy hopped on a chair to watch Susan and Harry drive off.

"*You know what I found out at Pewter's?*" Tucker asked.

"*No.*"

"*That it smelled like an amphibian over behind the cement mixer.*"

"*How would she know? She wasn't there.*"

"*Ozzie was,*" Tucker matter-of-factly replied.

"*When did you find this out?*" the cat demanded.

"*When I went to the bathroom. I thought I'd go over and chat with Pewter to try and smooth over your damage.*" Tucker enjoyed chiding Mrs. Murphy. "*Anyway, when Bob Berryman stopped by the store, Ozzie told me everything. Said it smelled like a big turtle.*"

"*That makes no sense.*" Mrs. Murphy paced on the back of the chair. "*And just what was Ozzie doing over there, anyway?*"

"*Didn't say. You know, Murph, a tortoise scent is very strong.*"

Not to people. The tiger thought.

"*Ozzie said Sheriff Rick Shaw and the others walked over the scent many times. Didn't wrinkle their noses. How they can miss that smell I'll never know. It's dark and nutty. I'd like to go over there and have a sniff myself.*" Tucker began trotting up and down the living room rug.

"*It probably has nothing to do with this ... mess.*" Mrs. Murphy thought a minute. "*But on the other hand ...*"

"*Want to go?*" Tucker wagged her tail.

"*Let's go tonight when Harry's asleep.*" Mrs. Murphy was excited. "*If there's a trace, we'll pick it up. We can't leave now. Harry's upset. If she comes back from the Craycrofts' and finds us gone it will make her even more upset.*"

"*You're right,*" the dog concurred. "*Let's wait until she's asleep.*"

Cars lined the long driveway into the imposing Craycroft residence.

Josiah and Ned parked people's cars for them. Susan and Harry pulled up.

Josiah opened Harry's door. "Hello, Harry. Terrible, terrible," was all the normally garrulous fellow could say.

When Harry walked into the house she found enough food to feed the Sandanistas, and was glad she'd brought flowers for the table. She was not glad to see Fair but damned if she'd show it.

Boom Boom sat in a huge damask wing chair by the fireplace. Drained and drawn, she was still beautiful, made more so, perhaps, by her distress.

Harry and Boom Boom, two years apart in school, were never close but they got along—until last year's Hunt Club ball. Harry put it out of her mind. She had heard the gossip that Boom Boom wanted to catch Fair, and the reverse. Were men rabbits? Did you snare them? Harry never could figure out the imagery many women used in discussing the opposite sex. She didn't treat her men friends any differently than her women friends and Susan swore that was the source of her marital difficulties. Harry would rather be a divorcée than a liar and that settled that.

Boom Boom raised her eyes from Big Marilyn Sanburne, who was sitting next to her, dispensing shallow compassion. Her eyelids flickered for a split second and then she composed herself and held out her hand to Fair, who had just walked up to her.

"I'm so sorry, Boom Boom. I . . . I don't know what to say." Fair stumbled verbally.

"You never liked him anyway." Boom Boom astonished the room, which was filled with most of Crozet.

Fair, befuddled, squeezed her hand, then released it. "I did like him. We had our differences but I did like him."

Boom Boom accepted this and said, "It was correct of you to come. Thank you." Not kind, not good, but correct.

Harry received better treatment. After extending her sympathy she went over to the bar for a ginger ale and to get away from Fair. What rotten timing that they had arrived so close together. The heat and the smoldering emotion made her mouth dry. Little Marilyn Sanburne poured a drink for her.

"Thanks, Marilyn."

"This is too awful for words."

Harry, ungenerously, thought that it might be too awful for a number of reasons, one being that Little Marilyn's impending wedding was eclipsed, temporarily at least, by this event. Little Marilyn, not having been in the limelight, just might learn to like it. Her marriage was the one occasion when her mother wouldn't be the star, or so she thought.

"Yes, it is."

"Mother's wretched." Little Marilyn sipped a stiff shot of Johnny Walker Black.

Mim's impeccable profile betrayed no outward sign of wretchedness, Harry thought to herself. "I'm sorry," she said to Little Marilyn.

Jim Sanburne blew into the living room. Mim joined him as he walked over to Boom Boom, whispered in her ear, and patted her hand.

Difficult as it was, he toned down his volume level. When finished with Boom Boom he hauled his huge frame around the room. Working a room, second nature to Jim, never came easily to his wife. Mim expected the rabble to pay court to her. It galled her that her husband sought out commoners. Commoners do vote, though, and Jim liked getting reelected. Being mayor was like a toy to him, a relaxation from the toils of expanding his considerable wealth. Since God rewarded Mim and Jim with money, it seemed to her that lower life forms should realize the Sanburnes were superior and vote accordingly.

Perhaps it was to Marilyn's credit that she grasped the fact that Crozet did not practice equality . . . but then, what community did? For Mim, money and social position meant power. That was all that mattered. Jim, absurdly, wanted people to like him, people who were not listed in the Social Register, people who didn't even know what it was, God forbid.

A tight smile split her face. An outsider like Maude Bly Modena would mistake that for concern for Kelly Craycroft's family. An insider knew Mim's major portion of sympathy was reserved for herself, for the trial of being married to a super-rich vulgarian.

Harry didn't know what possessed her. Maybe it was the suppressed suffering in the Craycroft house, or the sight of Mim grimly doing her duty. Wouldn't everyone be better off if they bellowed fury at God and tore their hair? This containment oddly frightened her. At any rate she stared Little Marilyn right in those deep blue eyes and said, "Marilyn, does Stafford know you're getting married?"

Little Marilyn, thrown, stuttered, "No."

"We aren't close, Marilyn. But if I never do anything else for you in your life let me do this one thing: Ask your brother to your wedding. You love him and he loves you." Harry put down her ginger ale and left.

Little Marilyn Sanburne, face burning, said nothing, then quickly sought out her mother and father.

*

Bob Berryman's hand rested on the doorknob of Maude's shop. She had turned the lights out. No one could see them, or so they thought.

"Does she suspect?" Maude whispered.

"No," Berryman told her to reassure her. "No one suspects anything."

He quietly slipped out the back door, keeping to the deep shadows. He had parked his truck blocks away.

Pewter, out for a midnight stroll, observed his exit. She made a mental note of it and of the fact that Maude waited a few moments before going upstairs to her apartment over the shop. The lights clicked on, giving Pewter a tantalizing view of the bats darting in and out of the high trees near Maude's window.

That night Mrs. Murphy and Tucker tried to distract Harry from her low mood. One of their favorite tricks was the Plains Indian game. Mrs. Murphy would lie on her back, reach around Tucker, and hang on like an Indian under a pony. Tucker would yell, "Yi, yi, yi," as though she were scared, then try to dump her passenger. Harry laughed when they did this. Tonight she just smiled.

The dog and cat followed her to bed and when they were sure she was sound asleep they bolted out the back door, which contained an animal door that opened into a dog run. Mrs. Murphy knew how to throw the latch, though, and the two of them loped across the meadows, fresh-smelling with new-mown hay.

There wasn't a car on the road.

About half a mile from the concrete plant Mrs. Murphy spied glittering eyes in the brush. "Coon up ahead."

"Think he'll fight?" Tucker stopped for a minute.

"If we have to make a detour, we might not get back by morning."

Tucker called out, "We won't chase you. We're on our way to the concrete plant."

"The hell you won't," the raccoon snarled.

"Honest, *we* won't." Mrs. Murphy sounded more convincing than Tucker.

"*Maybe you will and maybe you won't. Give me a head start. I might believe you then.*" With that the wily animal disappeared into the bushes.

"Let's go," Mrs. Murphy said.

"*And let's hope he keeps his promise. I'm not up for a fight with one of those guys tonight.*"

The raccoon kept his word, didn't jump out at them, and they arrived at the plant within fifteen minutes.

The dew held what scent there was on the ground. Much had evaporated. Gasoline fumes and rock dust pervaded. Human smells were everywhere, as was the scent of wet concrete and stale blood. Tucker, nose to the ground, kept at it. Mrs. Murphy checked out the office building. She couldn't get in. No windows were open; there were no holes in the foundation. She grumbled.

A tang exploded in Tucker's nostrils. "*Here!*"

Mrs. Murphy raced over and put her nose to the ground. "*Where's it go?*"

"*It doesn't.*" Tucker couldn't fathom this. "*It's just a whiff, like a little dot. No line. Like something spilled.*"

"*It does smell like a turtle.*" The cat scratched behind her ears.

"*Kinda.*"

"*I've never smelled anything quite like it—have you?*"

"*Never.*"

5

Even Mrs. George Hogendobber's impassioned monologue on the evils of this world failed to rouse Mrs. Murphy and Tucker. Before Mrs. Hogendobber had both feet through the front door she had declared that Adam fell from grace over the apple, then man broke the covenant with God, a flood cleansed us by killing everyone but Noah and family, Moses couldn't prevent his flock from worshipping the golden calf, and Jezebel was on every street corner, to say nothing of record covers. These pronouncements were not necessarily in historical order but there was a clear thread woven throughout: We are by nature sinful and unclean. This, naturally, led to Kelly Craycroft's death. Mrs. H. sidestepped revealing exactly how Hebrew history as set down in the Old Testament culminated in the extinction of a paving contractor.

Harry figured if Mrs. Hogendobber could live with her logical lacunae, so could she.

Tossing her junk mail in the wastebasket, Mrs. Hogendobber spoke exhaustingly of Holofernes and Judith. Before reaching their gruesome biblical conclusion she paused, a rarity in itself, walked over to the counter, and glanced over. "Where are the animals?"

"Out cold. Lazy things," Harry answered. "In fact, they were so sluggish this morning that I drove them to work."

"You spoil those creatures, Harry, and you need a new truck."

"Guilty as charged."

Josiah entered as Harry uttered the word *guilty*.

"I knew it was you all along." He pointed at Harry. The soft pink of his Ralph Lauren polo shirt accented his tan.

"You shouldn't joke about a thing like that." Mrs. Hogendobber's nostrils flared.

"Oh, come now, Mrs. Hogendobber, I'm not joking about the Craycroft murder. You're oversensitive. We all are. It's been a terrible shock."

"Indeed it has. Indeed it has. Put not thy faith in worldly things, Mr. DeWitt."

Josiah beamed at her. "I'm afraid I do, ma'am. In a world of impermanence I take the best impermanence I can find."

A swirl of color rose on Mrs. Hogendobber's beautifully preserved cheeks. "You're witty and sought-after and too clever by half. People like you come to a bad end."

"Perhaps, but think of the fun I'll have getting there, and I really can't see that you're having any fun at all."

"I will not stand here and be insulted." Mrs. Hogendobber's color glowed crimson.

"Oh, come on, Mrs. H., you don't walk on water," Josiah coolly replied.

"Exactly! I can't swim." Her color deepened. She felt the insult keenly; she would never think of comparing herself to Jesus. She turned to Harry. "Good day, Harry." With forced dignity, Mrs. Hogendobber left the post office.

"Good day, Mrs. Hogendobber." Harry turned to the howling Josiah. "She has absolutely no sense of humor and you're too hard on her. She's quite upset. What seems a trifle to you is major to her."

"Oh, hell, Harry, she bores you every bit as much as she bores me. Truth?"

Harry wasn't looking for an argument. She was conversant with Mrs. Hogendobber's faults and the woman did bore her to tears, but Mrs. Hogendobber was fundamentally good. You couldn't say that about everybody.

"Josiah, her values are spiritual and yours aren't. She's overbearing and narrow-minded about religion but if I were sick and called her at three in the morning, she'd be there."

"Well"—his color was brighter now, too—"I hope you know I would come over too. You only have to ask. I value you highly, Harry."

"Thank you, Josiah." Harry wondered if he valued her at all.

"Did I tell you I am to be Mrs. Sanburne's walker for the funeral? It's not Newport but it's just as important."

Josiah often escorted Mim. They had their spats but Mim was not a woman to attend social gatherings without clinging to the arm of a male escort, and Jim would be in Richmond on the day of Kelly's funeral. Josiah adored escorting Mim; unlike Jim, he placed great store on status, and like Mim he needed much external proof of that status. They'd jet to parties in New York, Palm Beach, wherever the rich congregated. Mim and Josiah thought nothing of a weekend in London or Vienna if the guest list was right. What bored Jim about his wife thrilled Josiah.

"I dread the funeral." Harry did, too.

"Harry, try Ajax."

"What?"

Josiah pointed to her hands, still discolored from cleaning the stamps two days ago.

Harry held her hands up. She'd forgotten about it. Yesterday seemed years away. "Oh."

"If Ajax fails, try sulfuric acid."

"Then I won't have any hands at all."

"I'm teasing you."

"I know, but I have a sense of humor."

"Darn good one too."

The late afternoon sun slanted across the crepe myrtle behind the post office. Mrs. Murphy stopped to admire the deep-pink blossoms glowing in the hazy light. Harry locked the door as Pewter stuck her nose out from behind Market's store. Courtney could be heard calling her from inside.

"*Where are you going?*" the large cat wanted to know.

"Maude's," came Tucker's jaunty reply.

Pewter, dying to confide in someone, even a dog, that she had seen Bob Berryman sneak out of Maude's shop, switched her tail. Mrs. Murphy was such a bitch. Why give her the advantage of hot news, or at least warm news? She decided to drop a hint like a leaf of fragrant catnip. "*Maude's not telling all she knows.*"

Mrs. Murphy's head snapped around. "*What do you mean?*"

"*Oh . . . nothing.*" Pewter's delicious moment of torment was cut short by the appearance of Courtney Shiflett.

"There you are. You come inside." She scooped up the cat and took her back into the air-conditioned store.

Harry waved at Courtney and continued on her way to Maude Bly Modena's. She thought about going in the back door but decided to go through the front. That would give her the opportunity to see if anything new was in the window. Beautiful baskets spilling flowers covered the lorry in the front yard. Colorful cartons full of seed packets were in the window. Maude advertised that packing need not be boring and anything that would hold or wrap a present was her domain. She carried a good stock of greeting cards too.

Upon seeing Harry through the window, Maude waved her inside. Mrs. Murphy and Tucker trotted into the store.

"Harry, what can I do for you?"

"Well, I was cutting up the newspaper to send Lindsay a clipping about Kelly's death and then I decided to send her a CARE package."

"Where is she?"

"Heading toward Italy. I've got an address for her."

Mrs. Murphy nestled into a basket filled with crinkly paper. Tucker stuck her nose into the basket. Crinkly sounds pleased the cat, but Tucker thought, *Give me a good bone, any day.* She nudged Mrs. Murphy.

"*Tucker, this is my basket.*"

"*I know. What do you think Pewter meant?*"

"*A bid for attention. She wanted me to beg her for news. And I'm glad that I didn't.*"

As the two animals were discussing the finer points of Pewter's personality, Harry and Maude had embarked on serious girl talk about divorce, a subject known to Maude, who endured one before moving to Crozet.

"It's a roller coaster." Maude sighed.

"Well, this would be a lot easier if I didn't have to see him all the time and if he'd take a little responsibility for what happened."

"Don't expect the crisis to change him, Harry. You may be changing. I think I can say that you are, even though we haven't known each other since B.C. But your growth isn't his growth. Anyway, my experience with men is that they'll do anything to avoid emotional growth, avoid looking deep inside. That's what mistresses, booze, and Porsches are all about." Maude removed her bright red-rimmed glasses and smiled.

"Hey, I don't know. This is all new to me." Harry sat down, suddenly tired.

"Divorce is a process of detachment, most especially detachment from his ability to affect you."

"He sure as hell can affect me when he doesn't send the check."

Maude's eyes rolled. "Playing that game, is he? Probably trying to weaken you or scare you so you'll accept less come judgment day. My ex tried it, too. I suppose they all do or their lawyers talk them into it and then when they have a moment to reflect on what a cheap shot it is—if they do—they can wring their hands and say, 'It wasn't my idea. My lawyer made me do it.' You hang tough, kiddo."

"Yeah." Harry would, too. "Not to change the subject, but are you still jogging along the C and O Railroad track? In this heat?"

"Sure. I try and go out at sunrise. It really is beastly hot. I passed Jim this morning."

"Jogging?" Harry was incredulous.

"No, I passed him as I ran back into town. He was out with the sheriff. Horrible as Kelly's death was, I do think Jim is getting some kind of thrill out of it."

"I doubt this town has had much excitement since Crozet dug the tunnels."

"Huh?" Maude's eyes brightened.

"When Claudius Crozet finished the last tunnel through the Blue Ridge. Well, actually, the town was named for him after that. Just a figure of speech. You have to realize that those of us who went to grade school here learned about Claudius Crozet."

"Oh. That and Jefferson, Madison, and Monroe, I guess. Virginia's glories seem to be in the past, as opposed to the present."

"I guess so. Well, let me take this big Jiffy bag and some colored paper and get out of your hair and get Mrs. Murphy out of your best basket."

"I love a good chat. How about some tea?"

"No thanks."

"Little Marilyn was in today, all atwitter. She needed tiny baskets for her mother's yacht party." Maude burst out laughing and so did Harry.

Big Marilyn's yacht was a pontoon boat that floated on the ten-acre lake behind the Sanburne mansion. She adored cruising around the lake and she especially liked terrorizing her neighbors on the other side. Between her pontoon boat and her bridge night with the girls, Mim kept herself emotionally afloat, forgive the pun.

She'd also gone quite wild when she redecorated the house for the umpteenth time and made over the bar so that it resembled a ship. There were little portholes behind the bar. Life preservers and colorful pennants graced the walls, as well as oars, life vests, and very large saltwater fish. Mim never caught a catfish, much less a sailfish, but she commissioned her decorators to find her imposing fish. Indeed they did. The first time Mrs. Murphy beheld the stuffed trophies she swooned. The idea of a fish that big was too good to be true.

Mim also had DRYDOCK painted over the bar. The big golden letters shone with dock lights she had cleverly installed. Throw a few fish-nets around, a bell, and a buoy, and the bar was complete. Well, it was really complete when Mim inaugurated it with a slosh of martinis for her bridge girls, the only other three women in Albemarle County she remotely considered her social equals. She'd even had matchbooks and little napkins made up with DRYDOCK printed on them, and she was hugely pleased when the girls noticed them as they smacked their martini glasses onto the polished bar.

Mim enjoyed more success in getting the girls to the bar than she did in getting them to her pontoon boat, which also had gold letters painted along the side: Mim's Vim. With the big wedding coming up, Mim knew she had the bargaining card to get her bridge buddies on the boat, where she could at last impress them with her abilities as captain. It wasn't satisfying to do something unless people saw you do it. If the bridge girls wanted good seats at the wedding, they would board Mim's Vim. Mim could barely wait.

Little Marilyn could happily wait, but being the dutiful drudge that she was, she appeared in Maude's shop to buy baskets as favors, baskets that would be filled with nautical party favors for the girls.

"Have you ever seen Mim piloting her yacht?" Harry howled.

"That captain's cap, it's too much." Maude was doubled over just thinking about it.

"Yeah, it's the only time she removes her tiara."

"Tiara?"

Harry giggled. "Sure, the Queen of Crozet."

"You are wicked." Maude wiped her eyes, tearing from laughter.

"If you'd grown up with these nitwits, you'd be wicked too. Oh, well, as my mother used to say, 'Better the devil you know than the devil you don't.' Since I know Mim, I know what to expect."

Maude's voice dropped. "I wonder. I wonder now if any of us know what to expect?"

6

The coroner's report lay opened on Rick Shaw's desk. The peculiarity in Kelly's body was a series of scars on the arteries into his heart. These indicated tiny heart attacks. Kelly, fit and forty, wasn't too young for heart attacks, but these would have been so small he might not have noticed when they occurred.

Rick reread the page. The skull, pulverized, yielded little. If there had been a bullet wound there'd be no trace of it. When the men combed through the mixer no bullets were found.

Much of the stomach was intact. Apart from a Big Mac, that yielded nothing.

There was a trace of cyanide in the hair samples. Well, that was what killed him but why would the killer mutilate the body? Finding the means of death only provoked more questions.

Rick smacked together the folder. This was not an accidental death but he didn't want to report it as a murder—not yet. His gut feeling was that whoever killed Kelly was smart—smart and extremely cool-headed.

Cynthia Cooper knocked.

"Come in."

"What do you think?"

"I'm playing my cards close to my chest for a bit." Rick slapped the report. He reached for a cigarette but stopped. Quitting was hell. "You got anything?"

"Everybody checks out. Marie Williams was right where she said she was on Monday night, and so was Boom Boom, if we can believe her servants. Boom Boom said she thought her husband was out of town on business and she was waiting for him to call. Maybe, maybe not. But was she alone? Fair Haristeen said he was operating late that evening, solo. Everyone else seems to have some kind of alibi."

"Funeral's tomorrow."

"The coroner was mighty quick about it."

"Powerful man. If the family wants the body buried by tomorrow, he'll get those tissue samples in a hurry. You don't rile the Craycrofts."

"Somebody did."

7

Boom Boom held together throughout the service at Saint Paul's Episcopal Church at the crossroads called Ivy. An exquisite veil covered her equally exquisite features.

Harry, Susan, and Ned discreetly sat in a middle pew. Fair sat on the other side of the church, in the middle. Josiah and Mim, both elegantly dressed in black, sat near the pulpit. Bob Berryman and his wife, Linda, were also in a middle pew. Old Larry Johnson, acting as an usher, spared Maude Bly Modena a social gaffe by keeping her from marching down the center aisle, which she was fixing to do. He firmly grabbed her by the elbow and guided her toward a rearward pew. Maude, a Crozet resident for five years, didn't merit a forward pew, but Maude was a Yankee and often missed such subtleties. Market and Courtney Shiflett were in back, as were Clai Cordle and Diana Farrell of the Rescue Squad.

The church was covered in flowers, signifying the hope of rebirth through Christ. Those who could, also gave donations to the Heart Fund. Rick had to tell Boom Boom about the tiny scars on the arteries and she chose to believe her husband had suffered a heart attack while inspecting equipment and fallen in. How the mixer could have been turned on was of no interest to her, not today anyway. She could absorb only so much. What she would do when she could really absorb events was anybody's guess. Better to bleed from the throat than to cross Boom Boom Craycroft.

8

Life must go on.

Josiah showed up at the post office with a gentleman from Atlanta who'd flown up to buy a pristine Louis XV bombé cabinet. Josiah liked to bring his customers down to the post office and then over to Shiflett's Market. Market smiled and Harry smiled. Customers exclaimed over the cat and dog in the post office and then Josiah would drive them back to his house, extolling the delights of small-town life, where everyone was a character. Why anyone would believe that human emotions were less complex in a small town than in a big city escaped Harry but urban dwellers seemed to buy it. This Atlanta fellow had "sucker" emblazoned across his forehead.

Rob came back at eleven. He'd forgotten a bag in the back of the mail truck and if she wouldn't tell, neither would he.

Harry sat down to sort the mail and read the postcards. Courtney Shiflett received one from one of her camp buddies who signed her name with a smiling face instead of a dot over the "i" in "Lisa." Lindsay Astrove was at Lake Geneva. The postcard, again brief, said that Switzerland, crammed with Americans, would be much nicer without them.

The mail was thin on postcards today.

Mim Sanburne marched in. Mrs. Murphy, playing with a rubber band on the counter, stopped. When Harry saw the look on Mim's face she stopped sorting the mail.

"Harry, I have a bone to pick with you and I didn't think that the funeral was the place to do it. You have no business whatsoever telling Little Marilyn whom to invite to her wedding. No business at all!"

Mim must have thought that Harry would bow down and say "Yes, Mistress." This didn't happen.

Harry steeled herself. "Under the First Amendment, I can say anything to anybody. I had something I wanted to say to your daughter and I did."

"You've upset her!"

"No, I've upset you. If she's upset she can come in here and tell me herself."

Suprised that Harry wasn't subservient, Big Marilyn switched gears. "I happen to know that you read postcards. That's a violation, you know, and if it continues I shall tell the postmaster at the head office on Seminole Trail. Have I made myself clear?"

"Quite." Harry compressed her lips.

Mim glided out, satisfied that she'd stung Harry. The satisfaction wouldn't last long, because the specter of her son would come back to haunt her. If Harry was brazen enough to speak to Little Marilyn, plenty of others were speaking about it too.

Harry turned the duffel bag upside down. One lone postcard slipped out. Defiantly she read it: "Wish you were here," written in computer script. She flipped it over and beheld a gorgeous photograph, misty and evocative, of the angel in an Asheville, North Carolina, cemetery. She turned it over and read the fine print. This was the angel that inspired Thomas Wolfe when he wrote *Look Homeward, Angel*.

She slipped it in Maude Bly Modena's box and didn't give it a second thought.

9

A pensive Pharamond Haristeen drove his truck back from Charlottesville. Seeing Boom Boom had rattled him. He couldn't decide if she was truly sorry that Kelly was dead. The zing had fled that marriage years ago.

No armor existed against her beauty. No armor existed against her icy blasts, either. Why wouldn't a woman like Boom Boom be sensible like Harry? Why couldn't a woman like Harry be electrifying like Boom Boom?

As far as Fair was concerned, Harry was sensible until it came to the divorce. She threw him out. Why should he pay support until the settlement was final?

It came as a profound shock to Fair when Harry handed him his hat. His vanity suffered more than his heart but Fair seized the opportunity to appear the injured party. The elderly widowed women in Crozet were only too happy to side with him, as were single women in general. He moped about and the flood of dinner invitations immediately followed. For the first time in his life, Fair was the center of attention. He rather liked it.

Deep in his heart he knew his marriage wasn't working. If he cared to look inward he would discover he was fifty percent responsible for the failure. Fair had no intention of looking inward, a quality that doomed his marriage and would undoubtedly doom future relationships as well.

Fair operated on the principle "If it ain't broke, don't fix it," but emotional relationships weren't machines. Emotional relationships didn't lend themselves to scientific analysis, a fact troubling to his scientifically trained mind. Women didn't lend themselves to scientific analysis.

Women were too damned much trouble, and Fair determined to live alone for the rest of his days. The fact that he was a healthy thirty-four did not deter him in this decision.

He passed Rob Collier on 240 heading east. They waved to each other.

If the sight of Boom Boom at her husband's funeral wasn't enough to unnerve Fair, Rick Shaw had zeroed in on him at the clinic, asking questions. Was he under suspicion? Just because two friends occasionally have a strained relationship doesn't mean that one will kill the other. He said that to Rick, and the sheriff replied with "People have killed over less." If that was so, then the world was totally insane. Even if it wasn't, it felt like it today.

Fair pulled up behind the post office. Little Tee Tucker stood on her hind legs, nose to the glass, when she heard his truck. He walked over to Market Shiflett's store for a Coca-Cola first. The blistering heat parched his throat, and castrating colts added to the discomfort somehow.

"Hello, Fair." Courtney's fresh face beamed.

"How are you?"

"I'm fine. What about you?"

"Hot. How about a Co-Cola?"

She reached into the old red bin, the kind of soft-drink refrigerator used at the time of World War II, and brought out a cold bottle. "Here, unless you want a bigger one."

"I'll take that and I'll buy a six-pack, too, because I am forever drinking Harry's sodas. Where's your dad?"

"The sheriff came by and Dad went off with him."

Fair smirked. "A new broom sweeps the place clean."

"Sir?" Courtney didn't understand.

"New sheriff, new anything. When someone takes over a job they

have an excess of enthusiasm. This is Rick's first murder case since
he was elected sheriff, so he's just busting his ... I mean, he's
anxious to find the killer."

"Well, I hope he does."

"Me too. Say, is it true that you have a crush on Dan Tucker?"
Fair's eyes crinkled. How he remembered this age.

Courtney replied quite seriously, "I wouldn't have Dan Tucker if
he was the last man on earth."

"Is that so? He must be just awful." Fair picked up his Cokes and
left. Pewter scooted out of the market with him.

Tucker ran around in circles when Fair stepped into the post
office with Pewter on his heels. Maude Bly Modena rummaged
around in her box, while Harry was in the back.

"Hi, Maudie."

"Hi, Fair." Maude thought Fair a divine-looking man. Most women
did.

"Harry!"

"What?" The voice filtered out from the back door.

"I brought you some Cokes."

"Three hundred thirty-three"—the door opened—"because that's
what you owe me." Harry appreciated his gesture more than she
showed.

Fair shoved the six-pack across the counter.

Pewter hollered, *"Mrs. Murphy, where are you?"*

Tucker walked over and touched noses with Pewter, who liked
dogs very much.

"I'm counting rubber bands. What do you want?" Mrs. Murphy replied.

Harry grabbed the Cokes off the counter. "Mrs. Murphy, what
have you done?"

"I haven't done anything," the cat protested.

Harry appealed to Fair. "You're a veterinarian. You explain this."
She pointed to the rubber bands tossed about the floor.

Maude leaned over the counter. "Isn't that cute? They get into
everything. My mother once had a calico that played with toilet

paper. She'd grab the end of the roll and run through the house with it."

"*That's nothing.*" Pewter one-upped her: "*Cazenovia, the cat at Saint Paul's Church, eats communion wafers.*"

"Pewter wants on the counter." Fair thought the meow meant that. He lifted her onto the counter, where she rolled on her back and also rolled her eyes.

The humans thought this was adorable and fussed over her. Mrs. Murphy, boiling with disgust, jumped onto the counter and spat in Pewter's face.

"Jealousy's the same in any language." Fair laughed and continued to pet Pewter, who had no intention of relinquishing center stage.

Tucker moaned on the floor. "*I can't see anything down here.*"

Mrs. Murphy walked to the edge of the counter. "*What are you good for, Tee Tucker, with those short stubby legs?*"

"*I can dig up anything, even a badger.*" Tucker smiled.

"*We don't have any badgers.*" Pewter now rolled from side to side and purred so loudly the deaf could appreciate her vocal abilities. The humans were further enchanted.

"*Don't push your luck, Pewter,*" Tucker warned. "*Just because you've got the big head over knowing what happened before we did doesn't mean you can come in here and make fun of me.*"

"This is the most affectionate cat I've ever seen." Maude tickled Pewter's chin.

"*She's also the fattest cat you've ever seen,*" Mrs. Murphy growled.

"Don't be ugly," Harry warned the tiger.

"*Don't be ugly.*" Pewter mocked the human voice.

Mrs. Murphy paced the counter. A mail bin on casters rested seven feet from the counter top. She gathered herself and arched off the counter, smack into the middle of the mail bin, sending it rolling across the floor.

Maude squealed with delight and Fair clapped his hands together like a boy.

"She does that all the time. Watch." Harry trotted up behind the now-slowing cart and pushed Mrs. Murphy around the back of the

post office. She made choo-choo sounds when she did it. Mrs.
Murphy popped her head over the side, eyes big as eight balls, tail
swishing.

"*Now this is fun!*" the cat declared.

Pewter, still being petted by Maude, was soured by Mrs. Murphy's
audacious behavior. She put her head on the counter and closed her
eyes. Mrs. Murphy might be bold as brass but at least Pewter behaved like a lady.

Maude leafed through her mail as she rubbed Pewter's ears. "I
hate that!"

"Another bill? Or how about those appeals for money in envelopes that look like old Western Union telegrams? I really hate that."
Harry continued to push Mrs. Murphy around.

"No." Maude shoved the postcard over to Fair, who read it and
shrugged his shoulders. "What I hate is people who send postcards
or letters and don't sign their names. For instance, I must know
fourteen Carols and when I get a letter from one of them, if the
return address isn't on the outside I haven't a clue. Not a clue. Every
Carol I know has two-point-two children, drives a station wagon,
and sends out Christmas cards with pictures of the family. The
message usually reads 'Season's Greetings' in computer script, and
little holly berries are entwined around the message. What's bizarre
is that their families all look the same. Maybe there's one Carol
married to fourteen men." She laughed.

Harry laughed with her and pretended to look at the postcard for
the first time while she rocked Mrs. Murphy back and forth in the
mail bin and the cat flopped on her back to play with her tail. Mrs.
Murphy was putting on quite a show, doing what she accused
Pewter of doing: wanting to be the center of attention.

Harry said, "Maybe they were in a hurry."

"Who do you know going to North Carolina?" Fair asked the
logical question.

"Does anyone *want* to go to North Carolina?" Maude's voice
dropped on "want."

"No," Harry said.

"Oh, North Carolina's all right." Fair finished his Coke. "It's just that they've got one foot in the nineteenth century and one in the twenty-first and nothing in between."

"You do have to give them credit for the way they've attracted clean industry." Maude thought about it. "The state of Virginia had that chance. You blew it about ten years ago, you know?"

"We know." Fair and Harry spoke in unison.

"I was reading about Claudius Crozet's struggle with the state of Virginia to finance railroads. He foresaw this at the end of the 1820's, before anything was happening with rail travel. He said Virginians should commit everything they had to this new form of travel. Instead they batted his ideas down and rewarded him with a pay cut. Naturally, he left, and you know what else? The state didn't do a thing about it until 1850! By that time New York State, which had thrown its weight behind railroads, had become the commercial center of the East Coast. If you think where Virginia is placed on the East Coast, we're the state that should have become the powerful one."

"I never knew that." Harry liked history.

"If there're any progressive projects, whether commercial or intellectual, you can depend on Virginia's legislature to vote 'em down." Maude shook her head. "It's as if the legislature doesn't want to take any chances at all. Vanilla pudding."

"Yeah, that's true." Fair agreed with her. "But on the other hand, we don't have the problems of those places that are progressive. Our crime rate is low except for Richmond. We've got full employment here in the county and we live a good life. We don't get rich quick but we keep what we've got. Maybe it isn't so bad. Anyway, you moved here, didn't you?"

Maude considered this. "Touché. But sometimes, Fair, it gets to me that this state is so backward. When North Carolina outsmarts us and enjoys the cornucopia, what can you think?"

"Where'd you learn about railroads?"

"Library. There's a book, a long monograph really, on Crozet's life. Not having the benefit of being educated in Crozet, I figured I'd better catch up, so to speak. Pity the railroad doesn't stop here anymore. Passenger service stopped in 1975."

"Occasionally it does. If you call up the president of the Chesapeake and Ohio Railroad and request a special stop—as a passenger and descendent of Claudius Crozet—they're supposed to stop for you right next to the post office here at the old depot."

"Has anyone tried it lately?" Maude was incredulous.

"Mim Sanburne last year. They stopped." Fair smiled.

"Think I'll try it," Maude said. "I'd better get back to my shop. Keep thy shop and thy shop keeps thee. 'Bye."

Pewter lolled on the counter as Harry put the Cokes in the small refrigerator in the back. Mrs. Murphy stayed in the mail bin hoping for another ride.

"Are these a peace offering?" Harry shut the refrigerator door.

"I don't know." And Fair didn't. He'd gotten in the habit, over the years, of picking up Cokes for Harry. "Look, Harry, can't we have a civil divorce?"

"Everything is civil until it gets down to money."

"You hired Ned Tucker first. Once lawyers get into it, everything turns to shit."

"In 1658 the Virginia legislature passed a law expelling all lawyers from the colony." Harry folded her arms across her chest.

"Only wise decision they ever made." Fair leaned against the counter.

"Well, they rescinded it in 1680." Harry breathed in. "Fair, divorce is a legal process. I had to hire a lawyer. Ned's an old friend."

"Hey, he was my friend too. Couldn't you have brought in a neutral party?"

"This is Crozet. There are no neutral parties."

"Well, I got a Richmond lawyer."

"You can afford Richmond prices."

"Don't start with money, goddammit." Fair sounded weary. "Divorce is the only human tragedy that reduces to money."

"It's not a tragedy. It's a process." Harry, at this point, would be bound to contradict or correct him. She half knew she was doing it but couldn't stop.

"It's ten years of my life, out the window."

"Not quite ten."

"Dammit, Harry, the point is, this isn't easy—and it wasn't my idea."

"Oh, don't pull the wounded dove with me. You were no happier in this marriage than I was!"

"But I thought everything was fine."

"As long as you got fed and fucked, you thought everything was fine!" Harry's voice sank lower. "Our house was a hotel to you. My God, if you ran the vacuum cleaner, angels would sing in the sky."

"We didn't have money for a maid," he growled.

"So it was me. Why is your time more valuable than my time? Jesus Christ, I even bought you your clothes, your jockey shorts." For some reason this was significant to Harry.

Fair, quiet for a moment to keep from losing his temper, said, "I make more money. If I had to be out on call, well, that's the way it had to be."

"You know, I don't even care anymore." Harry unfolded her arms and took a step toward him. "What I want to know is, were you, are you, sleeping with Boom Boom Craycroft?"

"No!" Fair looked wounded. "I told you before. I was drunk at the party. I—okay, I behaved as less than a gentleman . . . but that was a year ago."

"I know about that. I was there, remember? I'm asking about now, Fair."

He blinked, steadied his gaze. "No."

As the humans recriminated, Tucker, tired of being on the floor, out of the cat action, said, "Pewter, we went over to Kelly Craycroft's concrete plant."

Alert, Pewter sat up. "Why?"

"Wanted to sniff for ourselves."

"How can Mrs. Murphy smell anything? She's always got her nose up in the air."

"Shut up." Mrs. Murphy stuck her head over the mail bin.

"How uncouth." Pewter pulled back her whiskers.

"I was talking to Tucker, but you can shut up too. I'll kill two birds with one stone."

"Why were you telling me to shut up? I didn't do anything." Tucker was hurt.

"I'll tell you later," the tiger cat replied.

"It's no secret. Ozzie's probably blabbed it over three counties by now—ours, Orange, and Nelson. Maybe the whole state of Virginia knows, since Bob Berryman delivers those stock trailers everywhere and Ozzie goes with him," Tucker yipped.

"Nine states." Mrs. Murphy knew Tucker was going to tell.

"Tell me. What did Ozzie blab and why did you go to the concrete plant?" Pewter's pupils enlarged.

"Ozzie said there was a funny smell. And there was." Tucker liked this turnabout.

Pewter scoffed, "Of course, there was a funny smell, Tucker. A man was ground into hamburger meat and the day sweltered at ninety-seven degrees. Even humans can smell that."

"It wasn't that." Mrs. Murphy crawled out of the mail bin, disappointed that Harry had lost interest and was giving her full attention to Fair.

"Rescue Squad smells." Pewter was fishing.

"Smelled like a turtle."

"What?" The fat cat swept her whiskers forward.

Mrs. Murphy jumped up on the counter and sat next to Pewter. Since Tucker was going to yap she might as well be in the act. "It did. By the time we got there most of the scent was gone but there was this slight amphibian odor."

Pewter wrinkled her nose. "I did hear Ozzie say something about a turtle, but I didn't pay too much attention. There was so much going on." She sighed.

"Ever smell 'Best Fishes'?" Pewter's mind returned to food, her favorite topic. "Now that's a good smell. Mrs. Murphy, doesn't Harry have any treats left?"

"Yes."

"Think she'll give me one?"

"I'll give you one if you promise to tell us anything you hear about Kelly Craycroft. Anything at all. And I promise not to make fun of you."

"I promise." The fat chin wobbled solemnly.

Mrs. Murphy jumped off the counter and ran over to the desk. The lower drawer was open a crack. She squeezed her paw in it and hooked out a strip of dried beef jerky. She picked it up and gave it to Pewter, who devoured it instantly.

10

Bob Berryman laughed loudly during the movie *Field of Dreams*. He was alone. Apart from Bob, Harry and Susan didn't know anyone else in the theater. Charlottesville, jammed with new people, was becoming a new town to them. No longer could you drive into town and expect to see your friends. Not that the new people weren't nice—they were—but it was somewhat discomforting to be born and raised in a place and suddenly feel like a stranger.

The new residents flocked to the county in such numbers that they couldn't be absorbed quickly enough into the established clubs and routines. Naturally, the new people created their own clubs and routines. Formerly, the four great social centers—the hunt club, the country club, the black churches, and the university—provided stability to the community, like the four points of a square. Now young blacks drifted away from the churches, the country club had a six-year waiting list for membership, and the university was in the community but not of the community. As for the hunt club, most of the new people couldn't ride.

The road system couldn't handle the newcomers either. The state of Virginia was dickering about paving over much of the countryside with a bypass. The residents, old and new, were bitterly opposed to the destruction of their environment. The Highway Department people would be more comfortable in a room full of scorpions, because this was getting ugly. The obvious solution, of improving the central corridor road, Route 29, or even elevating a direct road over the existing route, did not occur to the powers-that-be in Richmond. They cried, "Expensive," while ignoring the outrageous sums they'd already squandered in hiring a research company to do their dirty work for them. They figured the populace would direct their wrath at the research company, and the Highway Department could hide behind the screen. The Republican party, quick to seize the opportunity to roast the reigning Democrats, turned the bypass into a political hot potato. The Highway Department remained obstinate. The Democrats, losing power, began to feel queasy. It was turning into an interesting drama, one in which political careers would be made and unmade.

Harry believed that whatever figure was published, you should double it. For some bizarre reason, government people could not hold the line on spending. She observed this in the post office. The regulations, created to help, just made things so much worse that she ran her post office as befitted the community, not as befitted some distant someone sitting on a fat ass in Washington, D.C. The same was true for the state government. They wouldn't travel the roads they'd build; they wouldn't have their hearts broken because beautiful farmland was destroyed and the watershed was endangered. They'd have a nice line on the map and talk to the governor about traffic flow. Every employee would justify his or her position by complicating the procedure as much as possible and then solving the complications.

Meanwhile the citizens of Albemarle County would be told to accept the rape of their land for the good of the counties south of them, counties that had contributed heavily to certain politicians' war chests. No one even considered the idea of letting people raise money themselves for improving the central corridor. Whatever the extra cost would be, compared to a bypass, Albemarle would pay for it. Self-government—why, the very thought was too revolutionary.

Harry, raised to believe the government was her friend, had learned by experience to believe it was her enemy. She softened her stance only with local officials whom she knew and to whom she could talk face-to-face.

One good thing about newcomers was, they were politically active. Good, Harry thought. They're going to need it.

She and Susan batted these ideas around at the Blue Ridge Brewery. Ice-cold beer on a sticky night tasted delicious.

"So?"

"So what, Susan?"

"You've been sitting here for ten minutes and you haven't said a thing."

"Oh. I'm sorry. Lost track of time, I guess."

"Apparently." Susan smiled. "Come on, what gives? Another bout with Fair?"

"You know, I can't decide who's the bigger asshole, him or me. What I do know is, we can't be in the same room together without an argument. Even if we start out on friendly terms . . . we end up accusing each other of . . ."

Susan waited. No completion of Harry's sentence was forthcoming. "Accusing each other of what?"

"I asked him if he'd slept with Boom Boom."

"What?" Susan's lower lip dropped.

"You heard me."

"And?"

"He said no. Oh, it went on from there. Every mistake I'd made since we dated got thrown in my face. God, I am so bored with him, with the situation"—she paused—"with myself. There's a whole world out there and right now all I can think of is this stupid divorce." Another pause. "And Kelly's murder."

"Fortunately the two are not connected." Susan took a long draft.

"I hope not."

"They aren't." Susan dismissed the thought. "You don't think they are either. He may not have been the husband you needed, but he's not a murderer."

"I know." Harry pushed the glass away. "But I don't know him anymore—and I don't trust him."

"Ever notice how friends love you for what you are? Lovers try to change you into what they want you to be." Susan drank the rest of Harry's beer.

Harry laughed. "Mom used to say, 'A woman marries a man hoping to change him and a man marries a woman hoping she'll never change.' "

"Your mother was a pistol." Susan remembered Grace's sharp wit. "But I think men try to change their partners, too, although in a different way. It's so confusing. I know less about human relationships the older I get. I thought it was supposed to be the other way around. I thought I was supposed to be getting wiser."

"Yeah. Now I'm full of distrust."

"Oh, Harry, men aren't so bad."

"No, no—I distrust myself. What was I doing married to Pharamond Haristeen? Am I that far away from myself?"

Back home, Mrs. Murphy prowled.

Tucker, in her wicker basket, lifted her head. *"Sit down."*

"Am I keeping you awake?"

"No," the dog grumbled. *"I can't sleep when Mommy's away. I've seen other people take their dogs to the movies. Muffin Barnes sticks her dog in her purse."* Muffin was a friend of Harry's.

"Muffin Barnes's dog is a chihuahua."

"Zat what he is?" Tucker, stiff-legged, got out of the basket. *"Wanna play?"*

"Ball?"

"No. How about tag? We can rip and tear while she isn't here. Actually, we should rip and tear. How dare she go away and leave us here. Let's make her pay."

"Yeah!" Mrs. Murphy's eyes lit up.

An hour later, when Harry flipped the lights on in the living room, she exclaimed, "Oh, my God!"

The ficus tree was tipped over, soil was thrown over the floor, and soiled kittyprints dotted the walls. Mrs. Murphy had danced in the moist dirt before hitting the walls with all four feet.

Harry, furious, searched for her darlings. Tucker hid under the bed in the back corner against the wall, and Mrs. Murphy lay flat on the top shelf of the pantry.

By the time Harry cleaned up the mess she was too tired to discipline them. To her credit, she understood that this was punishment for her leaving. She understood, but was loath to admit that the animals trained her far better than she trained them.

11

The prospect of the weekend lightened Harry's step as she walked along Railroad Avenue, shiny from last night's late thunderstorm, which had done nothing to lower the exalted temperature. Mrs. Murphy and Tucker, forgiven, scampered ahead.

The moment she caught sight of them, Pewter tore down the avenue to greet them.

"I didn't know she could move that fast." Harry whistled out loud.

When Pewter ran, the flab under her belly swayed from side to side. She started yelling half a block away from her friends. "I've been waiting outside the store for you!"

Panting, Pewter slid to a stop at Tucker's feet.

Harry, thinking that the animal had exhausted herself, stooped to pick her up. "Poor Fatty."

"Lemme go." Pewter wiggled free.

"What is it?" Mrs. Murphy rubbed against Harry's legs to make her feel better.

"Maude Bly Modena." The chartreuse eyes glittered. "Dead!"

"How?" Mrs. Murphy wanted details.

"Train ran over her."

"In her car, you mean?" Tucker was impatient waiting for Pewter to catch her breath as they continued walking toward the post office.

"No!" Pewter picked up the pace. "Worse than that."

"Pewter, I've never heard you so chatty." Harry beamed.

Pewter replied, "*If you'd pay attention you might learn something.*" She turned to Mrs. Murphy. "*They think they're so smart but they only pay attention to themselves. Humans only listen to humans and half the time they don't do that.*"

"*Yes.*" Mrs. Murphy wanted to say "*Get on with it,*" but she prudently bit her lip.

"*As I was saying, it was worse than that. She was tied to the track, I don't know where exactly, but when the six o'clock came through this morning, the engineer couldn't stop in time. Cut her into three pieces.*"

"*How'd you find out?*" Tucker blinked at the thought of the grisly sight.

"*Unfortunately, Courtney heard about it first. Market let her come in and open up for the farm trade, the five A.M. crew. The Rescue Squad roared by—Rick Shaw too. Officer Cooper, in the second squad car, ran in for coffee. That's how we found out. Courtney phoned Market and he came right down. There's some weirdo out there killing people.*"

"*Like a serial killer, you mean?*" Tucker was very concerned for Harry's safety.

"*It's bad enough that humans kill once.*" Pewter sucked in her breath. "*But every now and then they throw one who wants to kill over and over.*"

Mrs. Murphy murmured, "*I liked Maude.*"

"*I did too.*" Tucker hung her head. "*Why don't people kill their sick young like we do? Why do they let them live and cause damage?*"

"*Well, as I understand it, these psychos*"—Pewter had an opinion on everything—"*can appear mentally normal.*"

"*That's no excuse for the ones they know are nuts from the beginning.*" Mrs. Murphy couldn't cover her distress.

"*They think it's wrong to weed out litters.*" Tucker's claws clicked on the pavement.

"*Yeah, they let the sickies grow up and kill them instead.*" Pewter laughed a harsh laugh. "*No one better come after Courtney or Market. I'll scratch their eyes out.*"

Harry noticed the three animals were attentive to one another.

"*Whoever this is has something to cover up,*" Mrs. Murphy thought out loud.

"*Yes, they have to cover up that they're demented and they'll kill again, during a full moon, I bet,*" Pewter said.

"*No. I don't mean that.*" Mrs. Murphy's eyes became slits. Tucker had lived with Mrs. Murphy since she was a six-week-old puppy. She knew how the cat thought. "*This person is after something—or has something to hide. It might not be a thrill killer.*"

"*Don't you find it peculiar that he or she leaves the bodies about? Doesn't a killer try and bury the body?*" Pewter figured that's what vultures were for, but then, people were different.

"*That struck me about Kelly's body.*" Mrs. Murphy ignored a caterpillar, so intense was her concentration. "*The killer is displaying the bodies . . .*" Her voice drifted off because Market Shiflett emerged from his store and was waving at Harry.

"Harry, Harry!"

Harry heard the fear in his voice and ran down to the store. "What's the matter?"

"S'awful, just awful."

Harry put her arm around him. "Are you all right? Want me to call the Doc?" She meant Hayden McIntire.

Market nodded he was fine. "It's not me, Harry. It's another murder—Maude Bly Modena."

"What?!" Harry's color fled from her cheeks.

"I'm keeping my girl inside. There's a monster out there!"

"What happened, Market?" Harry, shocked, put her hand against the store window to steady herself.

"That poor woman was tied to the railroad tracks like in some silent movie. The fellow saw her—the brakeman, I guess, on the morning passenger train—but too late, too late. Oh, that poor woman." His lower lip trembled.

"Who else knows?" Harry's mind was moving at the speed of light.

"Why do you ask?" Market was surprised at the question.

"I'm not sure, Market, I . . . Woman's intuition."

"Do you know something?" His voice rose.

"No, I don't know a damn thing but I'm going to find out. This has to stop!"

"Well"—Market rubbed his chin—"Courtney knows, Rick Shaw and Officer Cooper, and Clai and Diana of the Rescue Squad, of course. Train people know, including the passengers. Train stopped. A lot of people know."

"Yes, yes." Her voice trailed off.

"What are you thinking?"

"That I wish so many people didn't know already. Controlling the information might have been a way to snag a clue."

"Yeah." The phone rang inside. "I've got to pick that up. Let's stick together, Harry."

"You bet."

Market opened the door and Pewter scooted in, calling her good-byes over her shoulder.

A miserable Harry unlocked the door to the post office, Mrs. Murphy and Tucker behind.

"Come on."

Mrs. Murphy looked at Tucker. *"You thinking what I'm thinking?"*

Tucker replied, *"Yes, but we don't know where."*

"Damn!" Mrs. Murphy fluffed her tail in fury and walked dramatically into the post office.

Tucker followed as Harry picked up the phone and started dialing. *"It could be miles and miles from here."*

"I know!" Mrs. Murphy crabbed. *"And we'll lose the scent—if it's there."*

"It held a little bit the other time. That day was stinky hot too."

Mrs. Murphy leaned up against the corgi. *"I hope so. Buddy-bud, we're going to have to use our powers to get to the bottom of this. Harry's smart but her nose is bad. Her ears aren't too good either. People can't move very fast. We've got to find out who's doing this so we can protect her."*

"I'll die before I let anyone hurt Harry!" Tucker barked loudly.

"Susan, there's been another murder."

"I'll be right there," Susan replied.

She started to dial Fair at the clinic but hung up the phone. It was a knee-jerk reaction to call him.

"Rick Shaw came by for Ned," Susan said as Harry unlocked the front door. It was 7:30 A.M.

"What's he want with Ned?"

"He wants him to organize a Citizen's Alert group. Harry, this is unbelievable. This is Crozet, Virginia, for Pete's sake, not New York City."

"Unbelievable or not, it's happening. Did Rick say anything about Maude?"

"What do you mean?"

"I mean, was she alive when she was run over?" Harry's entire body twitched at the thought and a wave of nausea engulfed her.

"I thought of that too. I asked him. He said they didn't know but they believed not. The coroner would know exactly when she died."

"If Rick said that, it means she was dead already. I mean, you'd have to be pretty stupid not to tell after a certain point. Did he say anything else?"

"Only that it happened out near the Greenwood tunnel, out on that first part of track."

Harry said, almost to herself, "What was she doing out that far?"

"God only knows." Susan sniffed. "What if this—this creature starts after our children?"

"That's not going to happen. I'm sure of it."

"How would you know?" A note of anger crept into Susan's voice.

"I'm sorry. I didn't mean to ignore your concern for the children, and you should keep the kids in at night. It's just that—well, I don't know. A feeling."

"There's a madman loose! Tell me what Kelly Craycroft and Maude Bly Modena had in common! Tell me that!"

"If we can figure that out, we might catch the killer." Command rang through Harry's voice. She was a born leader, although she never acknowledged it and even avoided groups.

Susan knew Harry had made up her mind. "You aren't trained in this sort of thing."

"Neither are you. Will you help me?"

"What do I have to do?"

"The police ask routine questions. That's fine, because they learn a lot. We need to ask different questions—not just 'Where were you on the night of . . . ?' but 'How did you feel about Kelly's Ferrari and how did you feel about Maude's big success with her store?' Emotions. Maybe emotions will get us closer to an answer."

"Count me in."

"I'll take Mrs. Hogendobber and Little Marilyn for starters. How about if you take Boom Boom and Mim. No, wait. Let me take Boom Boom. I have my reasons. You take Little Marilyn."

"Okay."

Rob sailed through the front door. He dropped the mail sacks like lead when Harry told him the news. He absolutely couldn't believe this was happening, but who could?

Tucker and Mrs. Murphy overheard Harry reveal the location of the murder.

"We can't get there by ourselves unless we're willing to be gone an entire day."

"Can't do that." Tucker pulled at her collar. The metal rabies tag tinkled.

"So, how are we going to get out there? We need Harry to take us in the truck."

"Half of Crozet will go out there. People have a morbid curiosity," Tucker observed.

"When she gets in that truck, no matter when, we'd better pitch a fit."

"Gotcha."

Mrs. Hogendobber was stopped by Market Shiflett as she ascended the post office steps. She emitted a piercing yell upon hearing the news.

Josiah, crossing the street, hesitated for a split second and then came over to see what was amiss.

"This is the work of the Devil!" Mrs. Hogendobber put her hand on the wall for support.

"It's shocking." Josiah tried to sound comforting but he never would like Mrs. Hogendobber. "Come on, Mrs. H., let me help you inside the post office." He swung open the door.

"When did you hear?" Mrs. Hogendobber's voice sounded even.

"On the radio this morning." Josiah fanned Mrs. H., now sitting by the stamp meter. "Would you like me to take you home?" Josiah offered.

"No, I came for my mail and I'm going to get it." Resolutely, Mrs. Hogendobber stood up and strode to her postal box.

Harry and Josiah followed her as Fair screeched up out front, killing the engine before turning off the key as his foot slipped off the clutch.

"You could have come right through the window," Mrs. Hogendobber admonished him.

Fair shut the door behind him. "I thought I'd give the taxpayers a break and not do that."

"This old building could use a rehab." Josiah turned the key in his box.

"Do you know about that sweet Maude Bly Modena? Murdered! In cold blood." Mrs. Hogendobber breathed heavily again.

"Now, now, don't get yourself overexcited," Josiah warned her.

"Quite right." Mrs. Hogendobber controlled herself. "So much evil in the land. Still, I never thought it would come home." She touched her eyebrow, trying to remember. "The last bad thing that happened here—apart from the drunken-driving accidents—why, that would be the robberies at the Farmington Country Club. Remember?"

"That was in 1978." Harry recalled the incident. "A gang of high-class thieves broke into the homes there and took the silver and the antiques."

"And left the silver plate." Mrs. Hogendobber didn't realize how funny that was and couldn't understand why, for a moment, Harry, Fair, and Josiah laughed.

"The theft wasn't funny, Mrs. H.," Harry explained. "But on top of being robbed, everyone would find out who had good stuff and who didn't. I mean, it added insult to injury."

Mrs. Hogendobber found no humor in it and made a harrumphf. "Well, this has been too much for one morning. I bid you adieu."

"Are you sure you don't want me to see you home?" Josiah offered again.

"No . . . thank you." And she was gone.

"Didn't they find that stuff stashed in a barn in Falling Water, West Virginia?" Fair asked.

"They did, and that was a stupid place to put it too." Josiah shut his mailbox.

"Why?" Harry asked.

"Putting exquisite pieces like that in a barn. Rodents could chew them or defecate on the furniture. The elements could expand and contract the woods. Just dumb. They knew good stuff from bad but they didn't know how to take care of it."

"Maybe they packed them up or crated them." Fair wasn't very knowledgeable about antiques.

"No, I remember the TV reports. They showed the inside of the barn." Josiah shook his head. "No matter, that's small beer compared to . . . this." He walked over to the counter where Fair was leaning. "What do you think?"

"I don't know."

"What about you, Harry?" Josiah's face registered concern.

"I think whoever did this was one of us. Someone we know and trust."

Josiah instinctively stepped back. "Why do you think that?"

"What's the killer doing? Flying in and out of Charlottesville to murder his victims? It has to be a local."

"Well, it doesn't have to be someone from Crozet." Josiah was offended at the idea.

"Why not? It's not so strange when you think about it." Fair ran his fingers through his thick hair. "Something goes wrong between friends or lovers; the hurt person blows. It can happen here. It has happened here."

Josiah slowly walked to the door and put his hand on the worn doorknob. "I don't like to think about it. Maybe it will stop now." He left and for good measure circled around the post office to Mrs. Hogendobber's house to make sure she arrived home safely.

"What can I do for you?" Harry, even-toned, asked Fair.

"Oh, nothing. I heard on the way to work and I thought I'd see if you were all right. You liked Maude."

Harry, touched, lowered her eyes. "Thanks, Fair. I did like Maude."

"We all did."

"That's it. That's what I need to find out. We all liked Maude. We mostly liked Kelly Craycroft. To the eye, everything looks normal. Underneath, something's horribly wrong."

"Find the motive and you find the killer," Fair said.

"Unless he or she finds you first."

12

Harry paused before knocking on Boom Boom Craycroft's dark-blue front door. She'd brought the cat and the dog along because when she left for her lunch break the animals carried on like dervishes. First the ficus tree, now this. Must be the heat. She glanced over her shoulder. Mrs. Murphy and Tucker, good as gold, sat in the front seat of the truck. The windows, wide open, gave them air but it was too hot to be in the truck. She turned around and opened the truck door.

"Now, you stay here."

The minute Harry disappeared through the front door of the Craycroft house, that order was forgotten.

Boom Boom's West Highland white shot around from behind the back of the house. "*Who's here? Who's here, and you'd better have a good reason to be here!*"

"*It's us, Reggie,*" Tucker said.

"*So it is.*" Reggie wagged his tail and touched noses with Tucker. He touched noses with Mrs. Murphy, too, even though she was a cat. Reggie had manners.

"*How are you?*"

"*As good as can be expected.*"

"*Bad, huh?*" Tucker was sympathetic.

"*She's just grim. Never smiles. I wish I could do something for her. I miss him too. He was a lot of fun, Kelly.*"

"Do you have any idea what happened? Did he take you places that humans didn't know about?" Mrs. Murphy asked.

"No. I'm supposed to be a house dog. I've seen the concrete plant a few times but that's it."

"Did he seem worried recently?"

"No, he was happy as a dog with a bone. Every time he made money he was happy and he made lots of it. Bones to them, I guess. He wasn't home much but when he was, he was happy."

Inside, Harry wasn't getting much from Boom Boom either.

"A nightmare." Boom Boom snapped open her platinum cigarette case. "And now Maude. Does anyone know if she has people?"

"No. Susan Tucker offered to put up the relatives but Rick Shaw told her that Maude had no siblings and her parents were dead."

"Who's going to claim the body?" Boom Boom, having undergone a funeral, was keenly aware of the technical responsibilities.

"I don't know but I'll be sure to mention that to Susan."

"I've gone over that last day a thousand times in my head, Harry. I've gone over the week before and the week before that and I can't think of a thing. Not a sign, not a hint, not anything. He kept me separate from the business but I had little interest in it anyway. Concrete and pouring foundations and roadbeds never was my idea of thrills." Boom Boom lit her dark Nat Sherman cigarette. "If he roughed a man up in business, I wouldn't know."

"Kelly might have crossed someone. He was very competitive." Harry picked up a crystal ashtray with a silver rim around it and felt its perfect proportions.

"He liked to win, I'll grant you that, but I don't think he was unfair. At least, he wasn't with me. Look, Harry, we've known each other since we were children. You know for the last few years Kelly and I were almost more like brother and sister than husband and wife, but he was a good friend to me. He was . . . good." Her voice got thick.

"I'm so sorry. I wish I could say or do something." Harry touched her hand.

"You've been kind to call on me. I never knew how many friends I had. He had. People have been wonderful—and I can be hard to be wonderful to . . . sometimes."

Harry thought to herself that someone was being anything but wonderful. Which one? Who? Why?

Boom Boom mused, "Kelly would have been amazed to see how many people did love him."

"Perhaps he knows. I'd like to think that."

"Yes, I'd like to think that too."

Harry put the ashtray back. She paused. "Have the cops gone over everything? His office?"

"Even his office here at home. The only thing on his desk the day he died was the day's mail."

"May I peek in the office? I don't want to be rude, but I think if there's anything that we can do to help Rick Shaw, we should. Perhaps if I poke around I'll find a clue. Even a blind pig finds an acorn sometimes."

"You've read too many mysteries sitting there in the post office." Boom Boom stood up and Harry did also.

"Spy thrillers this year."

"And for that you went to Smith College?" Boom Boom felt Harry should do more with her life, but who was she to judge? Boom Boom truly was the idle rich.

The walnut paneling glowed in the bright afternoon light. Neatly placed in the middle of an unblemished desk pad bound by red Moroccan leather was Kelly's mail.

"May I?" Harry didn't reach for the mail.

"Yes."

Harry picked it up and rifled through the letters, including the postcard, the beautiful postcard of Oscar Wilde's tombstone. She replaced the mail as she found it. At that moment she was more concerned with a certain evasiveness Boom Boom displayed toward her. She and Boom Boom got along well enough, but today there was something not right between them.

It wasn't until later, when she had left Boom Boom and was

rumbling past the tiny trailer park on Route 240, that she realized Maude had received a postcard of a beautiful tombstone as well. With the same inscription: "Wish you were here." My God, someone was telling them, I wish you were dead. It was a sick joke. She put her pedal to the metal.

"Hey, slow down," Mrs. Murphy said. "I don't like to drive fast."

Harry careened into Susan's manicured driveway, hit the brakes, and vaulted out of the truck. The cat and dog hit the turf too.

Susan stuck her head out the upstairs window. "You'll kill yourself driving that old truck like that."

"I found something."

Susan raced down the stairs and flung open the front door. Harry told Susan what she discovered, swore her to secrecy, and then they called Rick Shaw. He wasn't there, so Officer Cooper received the information.

Harry hung up the phone. "She didn't seem very excited about it."

"They shag so many leads. How's she to know if this is anything special?" Susan laced her sneakers. "Let's hope another one doesn't show up."

"Damn, I forgot to look."

"For what?"

"For the postmark on Kelly's card. Was it from Paris?"

"Let's go to Maude's shop and look at the postcard she received."

Maude's shop, closed, beckoned the passerby. The window boxes burst with pink and purple petunias. The sidewalk was swept clean.

Susan tried the door. "Locked."

Harry circled to the back and jimmied a window. The minute she got it open, Mrs. Murphy shot up on the windowsill and gracefully dropped into the shop. Harry followed and Susan handed Tucker to her and then followed herself.

The back room, an avalanche of packing materials, greeted them.

"I didn't know there were that many plastic peanuts in the world," Susan observed.

Harry made a beeline for Maude's rolltop desk in the front room.

"What if someone sees you there?"

"They can report me for breaking and entering." Harry snatched the mail, which was kept in boxes on the desk. "Found it!" She quickly flipped over the postcard. "Well, there goes that theory."

"What's it say?"

"Come here and read it. No one's going to arrest us."

Susan joined her. " 'Wish you were here.' " She then noticed the postmark. "Oh." It read Asheville, North Carolina.

Harry slid open the center drawer. A huge ledger book, pencils, erasers, and a ruler rattled. She reached for the ledger book. Sometimes accounting columns tell a story.

Footsteps on the sidewalk made her freeze. She closed the drawer.

"Let's get out of here," Susan whispered.

When Harry returned to the post office and relieved Dr. Johnson, she called Boom Boom and asked her to look at the postcard. It was marked PARIS, REPUBLIC OF FRANCE.

Baffled, Harry put down the receiver. Okay, the postmarks confused her. Still, she wasn't giving up. Those postcards were important. Whoever the killer was, he or she had a sense of humor, maybe even a sense of the absurd. Even the disposition of the corpses was macabre and trashy.

She racked her brain to think of who had a sharp sense of humor: everybody in Crozet except for Mrs. Hogendobber.

The shroud of mortality drew closer. Who could be next? Was she in danger? If only she could discover the link between Kelly and Maude, maybe she'd know that her friends would be safe. But if she discovered that link, she wouldn't be safe.

```
╔═══════════╗
║    13     ║
╚═══════════╝
```

Harry was taken aback by the number of people milling about the railroad track. Getting there wasn't easy. People had to drive out to 691 and then cut right on 690. Bob Berryman, Josiah, Market, and Dr. Hayden McIntire glumly stared at the tracks.

When Mrs. Murphy and Tucker sped into the brush, Harry barely noticed.

Harry joined the men. She cast her eyes downward and saw blood spattered everywhere. Flies buzzed on the ground, feasting on what hadn't soaked up. Even the creosote odor of the railroad ties didn't blot out the sweltering odor of blood.

Josiah grimaced. "I had no idea that it could be so bad."

"Considering how many pints of blood are in the human body—" Hayden spoke like a physician.

Berryman, sweating profusely, cut him off. "I don't want to know." He backed away to his four-wheel-drive Jeep. Ozzie howled inside, furious that he couldn't get out. Berryman roared out of there, tearing hunks of earth as he went.

"I didn't mean to upset him," Hayden apologized.

"Don't worry about it." Market pinched his nose. "Damn, are we ghouls or what?"

"Of course not!" Josiah snapped. "Maybe we'll find something the police didn't. How much faith do you have in Rick Shaw? When he reads, his lips move."

"He's not that bad," Harry protested.

"Well, he's not that good." Hayden stuck up for Josiah.

Harry swept her eyes along the tracks. The cat and dog rummaged in the high weeds and then burst onto the tracks about one hundred yards west of where she was standing. At least they're happy, she thought.

"We know one thing," Harry stated.

"What?" Market pinched his nose again.

"She walked here."

"How do you know that?" Josiah peered intently at her features.

"Because there's no sign that the grasses are beaten down. If she'd been dragged there'd be a path even though it rained. A human's body is literally dead weight." The smell was getting to Harry and she moved away from the track.

"She could have been carried." Josiah joined her.

"Have to be a strong man." Hayden moved off the track too. "Don't know if the killer is male or female, although men commit over ninety percent of the murders in this country, statistically."

Josiah replied, "Not exactly. The women are too smart to get caught."

Market, the last to leave even though the stench turned his stomach, doubted that. "Maude was a good five feet ten inches. The road's back a stretch. The strongest among us was Kelly. The next strongest is Fair. No one else could have carried her, other than Jim Sanburne, and he has a bum back."

"A four-wheel-drive could have come up here." Josiah watched the animals as they moved closer.

"Cooper said no tire tracks," Market volunteered.

"She walked? So what?" Josiah thrust his hands into his pockets.

"Where was Fair last night?" Hayden asked, none too innocently.

"Ask him," Harry shot back.

"She walked out here in the middle of the night?" Market was thinking out loud. "Why?"

"She liked her jogging and usually ran along the track," Harry told them.

"Damn good jogger to get all the way out to Greenwood," Market said.

"In the middle of the night?" Hayden rubbed his chin.

"Beat the heat," Josiah offered. "Hey, how about Berryman getting squeamish like that?"

"He wasn't squeamish in school," Market recalled. "Hell, I saw the trainer stick a needle in his knee once during a football game. Took a bad hit, you know. Twisted his knee a bit. Anyway, Kooter Ashcomb—"

"I remember him!" Harry smiled.

Kooter was an old man by the time Harry attended Crozet High.

"Yeah, well, Kooter stuck a hypodermic needle right in his knee and drew out the fluid. Played the rest of the game, too."

"We win?" Harry wondered.

"You bet." Market folded his arms across his chest. Market liked remembering playing fullback a lot more than he liked the present.

"Back to Maude." One line of perspiration rolled down the side of Harry's face. "Did she come out here alone? Did she come out here to meet someone? Did she come out here with someone?"

"I had no idea you were so logical, Harry," Josiah observed.

"Obvious questions and I'm sure Rick Shaw and company have asked them too." Harry wiped away the sweat.

"Wish we could find some tracks." Hayden, not being a hunting man, wouldn't even know how to look.

In the distance, the finger of a dark thundercloud hooked over the Blue Ridge.

"No tracks if you walk on the train bed." Harry felt bad. The reality of Maude's death, the blood, began to press on her head. She felt a throbbing at her temples.

"There's nothing here"—Josiah's voice dropped—"except that." He pointed up to the stained site.

"But there is! There is!" Tucker barked.

Mrs. Murphy and Tucker swarmed over the site of the murder. Harry mistook this for attraction to the blood.

"Get out of there!" she shouted.

"Don't be mad at them, Harry. They're only animals," Market chided her.

"There's something here! That same smell is here!" Tucker barked.

Harry ran up to the dog and collared her. "You come with me right now!"

Mrs. Murphy ran alongside Harry. *"Don't do that! Come back. Come back and sniff!"*

Harry couldn't go back and it was just as well, because if she'd gotten down on her hands and knees to catch the scent she would also have seen a few strands of Maude's blood-soaked hair missed by the Sheriff's Department. That would have done her in.

Tucker and Mrs. Murphy had thoroughly investigated the area around the murder location. Not until they examined the exact site did they catch the faint amphibian odor. No track, no line. But again it was in one place, although this time there was more of it than a dot. There were a few dots, fading fast.

But no one would listen to them and they rode home in disgrace with Harry, who thought the worst of her best friends.

Later that evening the thunderstorm lashed Crozet. Marilyn Sanburne was put out because the power failed and she had a soufflé in the oven. Jim, just back from his business trip, said the hell with it. They could eat sandwiches. He was also being driven wild by the telephone ringing. As the mayor of murder hamlet, as one reporter called it, Jim was expected to say something. He did. He told them to "fuck off," and Mim screamed, "I hate the 'f' word." She would have left to go visit one of her cronies, but the storm was too intense. Instead, she flounced into her room and slammed the door.

Bob Berryman drove around aimlessly. A huge tree ripped out by the high winds crashed across the road. He avoided hitting it. Shaken, he turned the truck around and drove some more. Ozzie sat next to him wondering what was going on.

14

Boom Boom Craycroft thought the worst of everybody. Much as she tried to keep her emotions to herself they kept spilling over, and since she wouldn't express her sorrow, what she expressed was anger. Right now she was furious with Susan Tucker and she took a sabbatical on manners.

"I don't give a good goddam what you think. And I don't care if whoever killed Maude killed Kelly. I want whoever killed Kelly and I'm going to get him."

Susan hung her head. To a passerby it would appear she was addressing her golf ball with her five iron, an unusual choice off the tee. "Boom Boom, calm yourself. You were the one who wanted to play golf. You said sitting home would drive you crazy."

Boom Boom, warming up, swung her wood and dug up a clump of Farmington Country Club turf. If the greensman had been there he would have suffered a coronary. Susan, wordlessly, replaced Boom Boom's divot, then hit a beauty off the tee.

"Been a woody and you'd be on the green," Boom Boom advised. "I don't know why I kept this golf date with you. You do the screwiest things on a golf course."

"I still beat you."

"Not today you won't." Boom Boom stuck the tee in the ground, put the ball on it, and without a practice swing, socked away. The ball rose with a pleasing loft and then veered left, only to disappear in the rough.

"Shit!" Boom Boom threw her club on the ground. Not satisfied, she stamped on it. "Shit! Fuck! Damn!"

Susan held her breath during the indiscriminate rampage, which concluded with Boom Boom turning her expensive leather golf bag upside down. Balls and gloves fell out of the open zippers. Exhausted from her fury, Boom Boom sat on the ground.

"Honey, it's the pits." Susan sat next to her and put her arm around her. "Would you like to go home?"

"No. I hate it there more than I hate it here." Boom Boom shook when she inhaled. "Let's play. I feel better when I'm moving. I'm sorry I yelled at you when you were giving me the third degree. I didn't mind Rick Shaw so much but those grotesque newspeople ought to be horsewhipped. I slammed the door in their faces. I just didn't want to hear it from you."

"I am really sorry. Harry and I think if those of us who know one another as friends snoop around we might find something. It's a horrendous strain and I haven't helped."

"You have. I got to scream and holler and throw my bag on the ground. I feel better for it." She nimbly got up, righted her bag.

Susan picked up the balls. "Here." She noticed the brand name. "When did you buy these?"

"Last week. Ought to be gold-plated, the expensive buggers. See my initials on them." She pointed to a red B.B.C. carefully incised into the gleaming white surface.

"How'd you do that?"

"I didn't. Josiah did. He's got tools for everything. He cracks me up, buying this gilded junk, making repairs on it, and then selling it to some parvenu for a bundle."

"He is funny, though." Susan reached her ball.

Boom Boom waited until Susan was midway into her backswing. "Josiah said Mim has a purse with a lock on it. Isn't that perfect?" She laughed.

Naturally Susan's shot was ruined. "Damn you."

The ball plunked into the water, sending up a plume.

That made Boom Boom temporarily happy. She found her ball,

walked around it as though it were a snake, and finally hit it out of the rough. Not a bad shot.

"If you do think of anything, you will tell me?"

"Yes." Boom Boom picked up her bag. She wouldn't use golf carts because that defeated the purpose of golf for her. On weekends she'd use one because the club forced her to, and she complained plenty about it. She even pointed out one fat board member at the Nineteenth Hole and declared if he'd get out of his golf cart and walk, he might stop resembling the Michelin tire boy.

Susan peered into the water. The Canada geese peered back at her as they glided by. She carried a ball retriever for this very purpose and with some finesse she liberated her ball from the depths.

"I ought to get one of those."

"Especially when you're paying what you're paying for golf balls." Susan folded the retriever back and placed it in her bag. She then dropped her ball.

"Why do you think this is the work of one person?" Boom Boom had quieted enough to return to Susan's earlier question.

"Two gruesome murders—spectacularly gruesome—and within the same week."

"That's superficial evidence. The second murderer could be a copycat. The details of Kelly's murder covered the front page of the paper, the evening news, and God knows what else. A person wouldn't have to be too clever to figure out that the time is right to settle a score, and goodbye Maude Bly Modena."

"I never thought of that."

"I thought of something else too."

"What?"

"Susan, what if the police aren't telling us everything? What if they're holding something back?"

"I never thought of that either." Susan shuddered.

15

Rick Shaw hunched over another coroner's report. Normally, the office sank into a stupor on weekends except for the drunk-driving jobs. Not this weekend. People were tense. He was tense, and the damned newspaper was keeping a reporter on his tail. The bird perched in the parking lot after he threw him out of the office.

There was no evidence of sexual abuse. The victim had been dead for two hours before the train ran over her, which the coroner also reported. However, there were no bullet wounds, no bruises on the neck, and no contusions of any sort. Again, there was a tiny trace of cyanide in the hair. Whoever was killing these people with cyanide knew a great deal about chemistry. He or she wasn't wasting the cyanide. The killer took the victim's body weight into account.

Rick shook his head and closed the report, then sidled over to Officer Cooper's desk, where he filched a cigarette from an open pack. Illicit pleasure soon to be replaced by guilt, but not until the cigarette was smoked.

A deep draw soothed him. He'd have to remember to buy a pack of Tic Tacs on the way home or his wife would smell his breath. He studied a map of the county on the wall. The positions of the two bodies were in the same general vicinity, a few miles apart. The killer was most likely a local but not necessarily a Crozet resident. Albemarle County covered 743 square miles and anyone could drive in and out of Crozet fairly easily. Of course, they knew one another out there. A stranger would be reported. No such report. Even a resident of Charlottesville or a friend from out of town would be noticed. No such notice.

The postmistress and Market Shiflett were poised at the hub of social activity. Officer Cooper had mentioned that the postmistress had an idea about postcards. People usually think what they do is relevant, and Mary Minor Haristeen was no exception. He checked out the postcards within an hour of Harry's call and the postmarks were from different locales.

Still, he decided to call Harry. After a few pleasantries he thanked her for being alert, said he'd examined the postcards and they seemed okay to him.

"Could I have them—temporarily?" Harry asked him.

He considered this. "Why?"

"I want to match them with the inks that I have in the office—just in case."

"All right, if you promise not to harm them."

"I won't."

"I'll have Officer Cooper drop them by."

After Rick Shaw's call, Harry called Rob, and he agreed to "borrow" the first postcard from France that he came across at the main post office. She swore she'd give it back to him by the next day.

Then she remembered she was supposed to interrogate Mrs. Hogendobber. She called Mrs. H., who was surprised to hear from her but agreed on a tea-time get-together.

16

Mrs. Hogendobber served a suspiciously green tea. Little chocolate cupcakes oozing a tired marshmallow center reposed on a plate of Royal Doulton china. Mrs. Hogendobber snapped one up, devouring it at a gobble.

She reminded Harry of a human version of Pewter. Stifling a giggle, Harry reached for a leaking cupcake so as not to appear ungrateful for the sumptuous repast—well, repast.

"I stopped drinking caffeine. Made me testy." Mrs. H.'s little finger curled when she held her cup. "I purged soft drinks, coffee, even orange pekoe teas from my household."

Obviously, she had not purged refined sugar.

"I wish I had your willpower," Harry said.

"Stick to it, my girl, stick to it!" Another chocolate delight disappeared between the pink-lipsticked lips.

Mrs. Hogendobber's neat clapboard house was located on St. George Avenue, which ran roughly parallel to Railroad Avenue. A sweeping front porch with a swing afforded the large lady a vantage point. A trellis along the sides of the porch, choking with pink tea roses, allowed her to see everything while not being seen. The Good Lord said nothing about spying, so Mrs. Hogendobber spied with a vengeance. She chose to think of it as being curious about her fellow man.

"I'm so glad you agreed to see me," Harry began.

"Why wouldn't I?"

"Uh, well, come to think of it, why not?" Harry smiled, reminding Mrs. H. of when Harry was a cute seven-year-old.

"I'm here to, oh, root around for clues to the murders. The telling detail, thoughts—you're so observant."

"You have to get up early in the morning to put one over on me." Mrs. H. lapped up the compliment, and truthfully, she didn't miss much. "My late husband, God rest his soul, used to say, 'Miranda, you were born with eyes in the back of your head.' I could anticipate his wants and he thought I had special powers. No special powers. I was a good wife. I paid attention. It's the little things that make a marriage, my dear. I hope you have reviewed your marriage and will reconsider your acts. I doubt there are any men out there better than Fair—only different. They're all trouble in their unique ways." She poured herself more tea and opened her mouth but no sound escaped. "Where was I?"

". . . trouble in their unique ways." Harry hardly thought of herself in those terms.

"If you'd kick off those sneakers and buy some nice smocks instead of those jeans, I think he'd come to his senses."

"Love usually involves losing your senses, not coming to them."

Mrs. H. pondered this. "Yes . . . yes."

Before she could launch on to another tangent, Harry inquired, "What did you think of Maude Bly Modena?"

"I thought she was a Catholic. Italian-looking, you know. The shop proved how shrewd she was. Now I never socialized with her. My social life is the Church, and well, as I said, I think Maude was Catholic." Mrs. Hogendobber cleared her throat on "Catholic." "I, like yourself, only knew her for five years. Not a great deal of time but enough to get a feel for a person, I guess. She seemed quite fond of Josiah."

"What did you feel then?"

The bosom heaved. She was dying to be allowed to wander into the subjective. "I felt that she was hiding something—always, always."

"Like what?"

"I wish I knew. She didn't cheat anyone at the shop. I never heard of her shortchanging or overcharging but there was something, oh, not quite right. She spoke very little of her background." Unlike Mrs. Hogendobber, who fairly galloped down Memory Lane, given half a chance to speak of her past.

"She didn't tell me much either. I assumed she was discreet. After all, she was a Yankee."

"Not one of us, my dear, not one of us. Her manners were adequate. She missed the refinements, of course—they all do. But then there's Mim, who is overrefined, if you ask me."

"I liked her. I even grew accustomed to the accent." Uneasiness crept into Harry's heart. She felt that poor Maude wasn't here to defend herself and she was sorry for asking about her.

"I couldn't understand much of what she said. I relied on tone of voice, hand gestures, that sort of thing. I bet she's from a Mafia family."

"Why?"

"Well, she was Catholic and Italian."

"It doesn't follow that she was from a Mafia family."

"No, but you can't prove otherwise."

Driving home, Harry started to laugh. It was all so horrible and horribly funny. Did a person have to die before you discovered the truth about her? As long as someone is alive the chance exists that whatever you have said about her will get back to her. Therefore, Harry and most of Crozet measured their words. You thought twice before you spoke, especially if you intended to say what you thought.

The other thing Harry learned from Mrs. Hogendobber was the time, occupants, and license plate number of every car that had rolled down St. George Avenue in the last twenty-four hours. The Citizens' Alert was Mrs. Hogendobber's opportunity to be rewarded for her natural nosiness.

17

Ned Tucker dreamed of sleeping late on Sunday mornings but the alarm clanged at 6:30 A.M. He opened his eyes, cut off the offending noise, and sat up. The digital clock blinked the time in a turquoise-blue color. It occurred to Ned that a generation of American children wouldn't know how to tell time with a conventional clock. Then again, they couldn't add and subtract either. Calculators performed that labor for them.

Harry said she hated digital clocks. They reminded her of little amputees. No hands. Ned smiled, thinking about Harry. Susan turned over and he smiled even more. His wife could sleep through an earthquake, a thunderstorm, you name it. He'd give her an extra forty-five minutes and feed the kids. The chores of fatherhood comforted him. What worried him was the example he set. He didn't want to be a slave to his job but he didn't want to be too lazy either. He didn't want to be too stern but he didn't want to be too lax. He didn't want to treat his son any differently from his daughter but he knew he did. It was so much easier to love a daughter—but then, that was what Susan said about their son.

A shower and a shave brightened Ned; a cup of coffee popped him in gear. He'd need to awaken Brookie and Dan in twenty minutes to get them up for church. He decided to take what precious quiet time he had and peruse the bills. Everything was more expensive than it should have been and his heart dropped each time he wrote a check. First he scanned his bank statement. A five hundred dollar withdrawal last Monday really woke him up. He made no such withdrawal last Monday and neither did Susan. Anything over two hundred dollars had to be discussed between them. He wanted to crumple the statement but neatly put it aside. Couldn't contact the bank until tomorrow anyway.

The telephone rang at seven o'clock. Ned picked it up. "Hello."

"Ned, you're up as early as I am so I hope I'm not being rude in calling." Josiah DeWitt, mellow-voiced, sounded serious.

"What can I do for you?" Ned wondered.

"You are, were, Maudie's lawyer, am I right?"

"Yes." Ned hadn't thought of Maude since he got up. Being reminded brought back the uneasiness, the nagging suspicions.

"Since she has no living relatives I'd like to claim the body"—he sighed—"or what's left of it, and give her a decent burial. It's not right that she be left to a potter's field."

As Josiah was tight as the bark on a tree, Ned was astonished. "I think we can work this out, Josiah," he said, then added, "But if you'll allow me, I'll take up a collection for the interment. We should all pull our weight on this."

"I'd be most grateful." Josiah did sound relieved. "Do you know of anyone who might have a plot, who could help us out there?"

"I'll ask Herbie Jones. He'll know." Herbie Jones was the minister at Crozet Lutheran Church.

"Do we even know what denomination Maude was?" Josiah asked.

"No, but Herb has always had a wide embrace. I don't think he'd mind if she were a Muslim. Would you like me to inquire about a service also?"

"Yes—I think we should. And one more thing, Ned: I'd like to run her store and buy it when that's feasible. I don't know what paperwork will be involved but Maudie built a good business. It was her love, you know. I'll keep it up in her honor, and for the profit too. She'll come back to haunt me if I don't make a profit."

"She left her estate to the M.S. Foundation, so we will need to negotiate with them."

"Really?" Josiah was consumed with interest but refrained from boring in.

"She had a brother who died from the disease."

"You know more about Maude than any of us." Josiah was envious.

"Not really. But I'll do what I can. It would be wonderful to keep the shop going and I can't see that the M.S. Foundation has the personnel or the desire to come out here to Crozet and sell packing materials. I'll do my best."

"Thank you."

"No, Josiah, thank you. I wish Maude could know what good friends she had." And he thought to himself that good friend or not, Josiah was quick to see a way to make more money.

18

A persistent owl hooted in the distance. Mrs. Murphy and Tucker padded in the moonlight toward Maude Bly Modena's store. Tucker, restless, jauntily moved along, her tail wagging. They'd be back long before Harry woke up, so Tucker treated herself to small sniffs and explorations along the way.

As they approached the building Mrs. Murphy stiffened. Tucker stopped in her tracks.

"There's someone in there," Mrs. Murphy whispered. "Let me jump up on the window box. Maybe I can see who it is. You come sit by the front door. If he runs out, you can trip him."

Tucker quickly hopped up the steps and lay flat against the door. The only sound was the click-click of her claws and the tinkle of her rabies tag.

Mrs. Murphy tiptoed the length of the window box. She pressed her face against the glass panes. She couldn't see clearly because whoever it was had crawled under the desk.

Mrs. Murphy carefully dropped onto the earth. "S-s-st, come on."

They circled to the back as Mrs. Murphy explained why she couldn't see.

"I can't smell anything with the windows and door closed but we can pick up the scent by the back door or by a window."

Tucker, nose to the ground, needed no encouragement. She hit the trail by the back door. "I got him."

Before Mrs. Murphy could put her nose down to identify the scent the back door opened. Tucker crouched down and tripped the man coming out as Mrs. Murphy, claws at the ready, leaped onto his back. He stifled a shout, dropping his letters, which scattered in the light evening breeze.

He thrashed around but couldn't reach Mrs. Murphy, who was far more agile than he. Tucker sank her fangs clean into his ankle.

He yowled. A few houses down, a light clicked on in an upstairs bedroom. The man gathered up the letters as Mrs. Murphy jumped off and scurried up a tree. Tucker scooted around the corner of the house and they both watched Bob Berryman run with a limp down the back alleyway. In a few moments they heard the truck start up and peel out onto St. George Avenue.

Mrs. Murphy backed down the tree. She liked climbing up much more than she liked coming down. Tucker waited at the base.

"Bob Berryman!" Tucker couldn't believe it.

"Let's go inside." Mrs. Murphy trotted to the back door, which Bob had left open in his haste to escape his attackers.

Tucker, head down, followed this trail. Berryman had entered through the back door. He passed through the storage room and went directly to and under the desk. He stopped at no other place. Tucker, intent on the scent, bumped her head into the back of the desk.

Mrs. Murphy, close behind her, laughed. "Look where you're going."

"Your eyes are better than mine," Tucker growled. "But my nose is golden, cat. Remember that."

"So, golden nose, what was he doing under the desk?" Mrs. Murphy snuggled in next to Tucker.

"His hands slid over the sides, the top, and the back." She followed the line.

Mrs. Murphy, pupils open to the maximum, stared. "A secret compartment."

"Yeah, but how'd he get it open?"

"I don't know, but he's a clumsy man. It can't be that hard." Mrs. Murphy stood on her hind legs and gently batted the sides of the desk.

A loud slam scared the bejesus out of both of them. They shot out from under the desk. Mrs. Murphy's tail looked like a bottlebrush. The hair on the back of Tucker's neck bristled. No other sound assailed their sensitive ears.

Mrs. Murphy, low to the ground, whiskers to the fore, slowly, one paw at a time, headed for the back room. Tucker, next to her, also crouched as low as she could, which was pretty low. When they reached the storage room they saw that the door was closed.

"Oh, no!" Tucker exclaimed. "Can you reach the doorknob?"

Mrs. Murphy stretched her full length. She could just get her paws on the old ceramic doorknob but she couldn't turn it the whole way. She exhausted herself trying.

Finally, Tucker said, "Give up. We're in for the night. Once people start moving about I'll set up a howl that will wake the dead."

"Harry will be frantic."

"I know but there's nothing we can do about it. We're already in her bad graces for our work at the railroad tracks. Boy, are we in for it now."

"No, she won't be mad."

"I hope not."

Mrs. Murphy leaned against the door catching her breath. "She loves us. We're all she's got, you know. I hate to think of Harry searching for us. It's been a terrible week."

"Yeah."

"If we're stuck here we might as well work."

"I'm game."

19

Pewter, hovering over the meat case, first heard Tucker howl. The sound was distant but she was sure it was Tucker. A huge roll of Lebanon baloney, her favorite, beckoned. Courtney lifted the scrumptious meat from the case. Sandwich duty occupied her morning. By 7:00 A.M. the farm crowd had wiped out the reserve she'd made up Sunday night.

"*Gimme some! Gimme some! Gimme some!*" Pewter hooked a corner of the roll with a claw.

"Stop that." Courtney smacked her paw.

"*I'm hungry!*" Pewter reached up again and Courtney cut her a hunk. Buying off Pewter was easier than disciplining her.

The cat seized the fragrant meat and hurried to the back door. Her hunger overwhelmed her curiosity but she figured she could eat, and listen at the same time. Another protracted howl convinced her the miserable dog was Tucker. She returned to Courtney, was severely tempted by the Lebanon baloney, summoned her willpower, and rubbed against Courtney's legs, then hustled to the back door. She needed to perform this identical routine three times before Courtney opened the back door for her. Pewter knew that humans learned by repetition, but even then you could never be sure they were going to do what you asked them. They were so easily distracted.

Once free from the store Pewter sat, waiting for another howl. Once she heard it she loped through the backyards, and came out into the alleyway. Another howl sent her directly to the back door of Maude Bly Modena's shop.

"Tucker!" Pewter yelled. "What are you doing in there?"

"Just get me out. I'll tell you everything later," Tucker pleaded.

Mrs. Murphy hollered behind the door: "Are there any humans around?"

"In cars. We need a walker."

"Pewter, if you run back to the store do you think you could get Courtney or Market to follow you?" Mrs. Murphy asked.

"Follow me? I can barely get them to open and close the door for me."

"What if you grabbed Mrs. Hogendobber on her way to the post office? She's around the corner." Tucker wanted out.

"She doesn't like cats. She wouldn't pay attention to me."

"She'll come down the alleyway. She walks it no matter what the weather. You could try," Mrs. Murphy said.

"All right. But while I'm waiting for that old windbag . . . What is it that Josiah calls her?"

"A ruthless monologist," Mrs. Murphy answered her, peeved that Pewter was insisting on a chat.

"Well, while I'm waiting why don't you tell me what you're doing in there?"

Mrs. Murphy and Tucker unfolded the adventure but only after swearing Pewter to secrecy. Under no circumstances was she to hint of any of this to Bob Berryman's dog, Ozzie.

"There she is!" Pewter called to them. "Let's try. Howl, Tucker."

Pewter thundered over to Mrs. Hogendobber. She circled her. She flopped on her back and rolled over. She meowed and pranced. Mrs. Hogendobber observed this with some amusement.

"Come on, Pruneface! Get the message," Pewter screeched. She moved toward Maude's shop and then returned to Mrs. Hogendobber.

Tucker emitted a piercing shriek. Mrs. Hogendobber halted her stately progress. Pewter ran around her legs and back toward Maude's shop, where Tucker let out another shriek. Mrs. Hogendobber started for the shop.

"I got her! I got her!" Pewter raced for the door. "Keep it up!"

Tucker barked. Mrs. Murphy meowed. Pewter ran in circles in front of the door.

Mrs. Hogendobber stood. She thought deeply. She put her hand on the doorknob, thought some more, and then opened the door.

"*Gangway!*" Tucker charged out of the door and hurried around the side of the house to relieve her bladder. Mrs. Murphy, with more bladder control, came out and rubbed Mrs. Hogendobber's legs in appreciation.

"*Thank you, Mrs. H.,*" Mrs. Murphy purred.

"What were you doing in there?" Mrs. Hogendobber said out loud.

Tucker ran around and sat next to Pewter. She gave the gray cat a kiss. "*I love you, Pewter.*"

"*Okay, okay.*" Pewter appreciated the emotion but wasn't overfond of sloppy kisses.

"*Come on. Mom's got to be at work by now.*" Mrs. Murphy pricked up her ears.

The three small animals chased one another down the alleyway as Mrs. Hogendobber followed, deeply curious as to why Mary Minor Haristeen's cat and dog were trapped inside Maude's shop.

Harry hadn't sorted the mail. She hadn't properly thanked Rob for the French postcard he'd smuggled to her. She'd burned the telephone wires calling everyone she could think of who might have seen her animals.

The sight of Mrs. Murphy and Tucker along with Pewter and Mrs. Hogendobber puffing up the steps astonished her. Tears filled her eyes as she flung open the door.

Mrs. Murphy leaped into her arms and Tucker jumped up on her. Harry sat on the floor to hug her family. She hugged Pewter too. This enthusiasm was not extended to Mrs. Hogendobber, but Harry did get up and shake her hand.

"Thank you, Mrs. Hogendobber. I've been worried sick. Where'd you find them?"

"In Maude Bly Modena's store."

"What?" Harry was incredulous.

"We found a secret compartment! And Bob Berryman stole letters!" Tucker's excitement was so great that she wiggled from stem to stern.

"Tucker bit the shit out of his ankle," Mrs. Murphy added.

"Inside the store?"

"Yes. The door was shut and they couldn't get out. I was walking down the alleyway—my morning constitutional on my way to see you—and I heard a ruckus."

"You would have waddled right on by if it weren't for me," Pewter corrected her.

"What on earth were my girls doing in Maude Bly Modena's shop?" Harry put her hands to her temples. "Mrs. Hogendobber, do you mind going back there with me?"

Mrs. Hogendobber would like nothing better. "Well, if you think it's proper. Perhaps we should call the sheriff first."

"He could arrest Mrs. Murphy and Tucker for breaking and entering." Harry realized the instant the joke was out of her mouth that Mrs. Hogendobber wouldn't get it. "Let me call Market over to mind the office."

Market happily agreed and said he'd even sort the mail. He, too, wanted to read other people's mail. It was an irresistible temptation.

The crepe myrtle bloomed along the alleyway. Bumblebees laden with pollen buzzed around the two women.

"I was right here when I heard Tucker."

"Ha!" Pewter sarcastically remarked.

Harry followed Mrs. Hogendobber, who recounted in minute detail her every step to the door.

"... and I turned the knob—it wasn't locked—and out they came."

And in they ran too. *"Come on!"*

"Me, too." Pewter followed.

"Girls! Girls!" Harry vainly called.

Mrs. Hogendobber, thrilled at the possibility of entering, said, "We'll have to get them."

Harry entered first.

Mrs. Hogendobber, hot on her heels, stopped for a second in front of the huge bags of plastic peanuts piled to the ceiling. "My word."

Harry, already in the front room, exclaimed, "Where are they?"

Mrs. Murphy stuck her head out from under the desk. *"Here!"*

Mrs. Hogendobber, now in the room, saw this. "There." She pointed.

Harry got down on her hands and knees and crawled under the desk. Pewter, grumbling, had to get out, as there wasn't room for all of them.

Mrs. Murphy sat in front of the secret compartment that she had opened the night before. A small button alongside the thin molding on the seam was the key. *"Right here. Look!"*

Harry gasped, "There's a secret compartment here!"

"Let me see." Mrs. Hogendobber, negotiating gravity, hunkered down on her hands and knees. Tucker moved so she could see.

"Right here." Harry flattened against the side of the desk the best she could and pointed.

"I declare!" Mrs. Hogendobber, excited, gasped. "What's in there?"

Harry reached in and handed over a large ledger and a handful of Xeroxed papers. "Here."

Mrs. Hogendobber backed up on all fours and sat in the middle of the floor.

Harry backed out and joined her. "There's another ledger in the desk." She got up and opened the middle drawer. It was still there.

"A second set of books! I wonder who she was filching from."

"The IRS, most likely." Harry sat down next to Mrs. Hogendobber, who was flipping through the books.

"I used to keep Mr. H.'s books, you know." She laid the two ledgers side by side, her sharp eyes moving vertically down the columns. The hidden ledger was on her left. "My word, what a lot of merchandise. She was a better saleswoman than any of us knew." Mrs. Hogendobber pointed to the right-hand book. "See here, Harry, the volume—and the prices."

"I can't believe she would get fifteen thousand dollars for seventy bags of plastic peanuts."

This gave Mrs. Hogendobber pause. "It does seem unlikely."

Harry took a page off the large pile of Xeroxed papers. They were the letters of Claudius Crozet to the Blue Ridge Railroad. Scanning them, she realized they involved the building of the tunnels.

"What's that?" Mrs. Hogendobber couldn't tear her eyes away from the accounting books.

"Claudius Crozet's letter to the Blue Ridge Railroad."

"What are you talking about?" Mrs. Hogendobber looked up from her books.

"I don't know."

Harry had to get back to work. "Mrs. Hogendobber, would you do something if I asked you? It isn't dishonest but it's . . . tricky."

"Ask."

"Xerox these letters and the accounting books. Then we'll turn it all over to Rick Shaw but we won't tell him we have copies. I want to read these letters and I think, with your training, you may find something in the accounting books that the sheriff would miss. If he knows we're studying the information he might take that as a comment on his abilities."

Without hesitation, Mrs. Hogendobber agreed. "I'll call Rick after I've completed the job. I'll tell him about the animals. About us coming back here. And that's all I'll tell him. Where can I Xerox without drawing attention to myself? This is a great deal of work."

"In the back room at the post office. I can buy some extra paper and reset the meter. No one will know if you don't come out of the back room. As long as I put in the ink and the paper, I'm not cheating Uncle Sam."

"Maude Bly Modena sure was."

20

Ned Tucker was informed by Barbara Apperton at Citizen's National Bank that the withdrawal from his account was correct and had been made with his credit card after hours. Ned fulminated. Barbara said she'd get a copy of the videotape, since these transactions were recorded. That way they'd both find out who used the credit card. Mrs. Apperton asked if the credit card was missing and Ned said no. He said he'd be down at the bank tomorrow.

The missing five hundred dollars wouldn't break the Tucker family but it was unwelcome news when Ned was paying the bills.

Troubled by this small mystery on top of the grotesque ones, Susan entered the post office only to witness Rick Shaw grilling Harry.

"You can't prove where you were Friday night or in the wee hours Saturday morning?" The sheriff stuck his thumbs in his Sam Browne belt.

"No." Harry patted Mrs. Murphy, who watched Rick with her golden eyes.

Susan came alongside the counter. Rick kept at it. "No one was with you on the nights of the two murders?"

"No. Not after eleven P.M. on the night of Maude's murder. I live alone now."

"This doesn't look good, with your animals in Maude Bly Modena's shop. Just what are you up to and what are you hiding?"

"Nothing." This wasn't exactly true, because under the counter, neatly placed in a large manila envelope, were the Claudius Crozet letters. Mrs. Hogendobber had smuggled the copies of the accounting books to her home.

"You're telling me your cat and dog entered the shop without your opening the door?" Rick's voice dripped disbelief.

"Yes."

"*Bob Berryman let us in,*" Mrs. Murphy said but no one listened to her.

"*Buzz off, Shaw,*" Tucker growled.

"You don't leave town without telling me, Miz Haristeen." Rick slapped the counter with his right palm.

Susan intruded. "Rick, you can't possibly believe that Harry's a murderer. The only people who can prove where they were in the middle of the night are the married ones faithful to their spouses."

"That leaves out much of Crozet," Harry wryly noted.

"And the ones who are together can lie for each other. Maybe this isn't the work of one person. Maybe it's a team." Susan hoisted herself up on the counter.

"That possibility hasn't escaped me."

Harry put her mouth next to Mrs. Murphy's ear. "What were you doing in Maude's shop, you devil?"

"*I told you.*" Mrs. Murphy touched Harry's nose.

"She's telling you something," Susan observed.

"That she wants some kitty crunchies, I bet." Harry smiled.

"Don't take this so lightly," Rick warned.

"I'm not." Harry's face darkened. "But I don't know what to do about this, any more than you do. We're not stupid, Rick. We know the murderer is someone close to home, someone we know and trust. No one's sleeping soundly anymore in Crozet."

"Neither am I." Rick's voice softened. He rather liked Harry. "Look, I'm not paid to be nice. I'm paid to get results."

"We know." Susan crossed her legs under her. "We want you to and we'll help you in any way that we can."

"Thanks." Rick patted Mrs. Murphy. "What were you doing in there, kitty cat?"

"I *told you*," Mrs. Murphy moaned.

After Rick left, Susan whispered, "How did they get in the shop?"

Harry sighed. "I wish I knew."

That night, after a supper of cottage cheese on a bed of lettuce sprinkled with sunflower seeds, Harry pulled out the postcards and her mother's huge magnifying glass. She shone a bright light over the card to Kelly and placed the card Rob lent her next to it. The inks were different colors. The true Paris postmark was a slightly darker shade. Also, the lettering of the cancellation stamp on Kelly's postcard was not precisely flush. This was also the case for the lettering on Maude's postcard. The "A" in Asheville was out of line the tiniest bit. She switched off the light.

The postcards were a signal. She remembered when Maude received hers. She didn't act like a woman under the threat of death. She was irritated that the sender hadn't signed his or her name.

The floorboards creaked as Harry paced over them. What did she know? She knew the killer was close at hand. She knew the killer had a sense of humor and was perhaps even sporting, since he or she had fired a warning shot, so to speak. She knew the mangling of the bodies was designed to throw people off the scent. Just why, she wasn't sure. The mess might have been to disguise the method of murder or it might have been to keep people from looking elsewhere, but why and for what? Or worse, it could have been a sick joke.

The other thing she knew was that Claudius Crozet was important to Maude. Tomorrow she was determined to call Marie, the secretary at the concrete plant, to find out if Kelly ever mentioned the famous engineer. She fixed a stiff cup of coffee—a spoon could stand up in the liquid—and sat down at the kitchen table to read the letters.

By one in the morning she was ravenous and wished that someone would figure out a way to fax a pizza. She ate more cottage cheese and kept reading. Crozet wrote in detail about the process of cutting the tunnels. The boring for the tunnels proceeded around the clock in three eight-hour shifts for eight solid years. The Brooksville tunnel proved extremely dangerous. The rock, seemingly sound, was soft as the men bit deeper into the mountain. Cave-ins and rockslides dumped on their heads like hard rain.

The physical difficulties occasionally paled beside the human ones. The tunnel rats were men of Ireland, but from two different parts of the Emerald Isle. The men of Cork disdained the Fardowners, the men of Northern Ireland. One bitter night, on February 2, 1850, a riot shook Augusta County. The militia was called out to separate the warring factions and the jail burst at the seams with bloodied Irishmen. By the next morning both sides agreed that they'd only desired a little fight and the authorities accepted that explanation. After breaking a few bones and sitting out the night in jail, the men got along just fine.

The Blue Ridge Railroad Company ran out of money with alarming frequency. The state of Virginia wasn't much help. The general contractor, John Kelly, paid the men out of his own pocket and accepted paper from the state—a brave man indeed.

When Claudius Crozet described the mail train rolling through the last completed tunnel on April 13, 1858, Harry was almost as excited as he must have been.

She finished the letters, eyes burning, and hauled herself into bed. She sensed that the tunnels meant something, but why? And which one? The Greenwood and Brooksville had been sealed since after 1944. She was going to have to go out there. She finally fell into a troubled slumber.

21

A full moon radiated silvery light over the back meadows, making the cornflowers glow a deep purple. Bats darted in and out of the towering conifers and in and out of the eaves of Harry's house.

Mrs. Murphy sat on the back porch. Tucker's snoring could be heard in the background. The cat was restless but she knew in the morning she'd blame it on Tucker, telling her that she'd kept her awake. Tucker accused Mrs. Murphy of making up stories about her snoring.

What was really keeping Mrs. Murphy awake was Harry. She wished her friend lacked curiosity. Curiosity rarely killed the cat but it certainly got humans in trouble. She feared Harry might trigger a response in the killer if she got too close. Mrs. Murphy had great pride where Harry was concerned, and if any human was smart enough to put the pieces of this ragged puzzle together it would be her Harry. But putting together a puzzle and protecting yourself were two different things. Because Harry couldn't conceive of killing another human being, she couldn't believe anyone would want to kill her.

Humans fascinated Mrs. Murphy. Their time was squandered in pursuing nonessential objects. Food, clothing, and shelter weren't enough for them, and they drove themselves and everyone around them crazy, including animals, for their toys. Mrs. Murphy thought cars, a motor toy, absurd. That's why horses were born. What's the big hurry, anyway? But if people wanted speed she could accept that—after all, it was a physical pleasure. What she couldn't accept was that these creatures worked and worked and then didn't enjoy what they worked for; they were too busy paying for things they couldn't afford. By the time they paid for the toy it was worn out and they wanted another one. Worse, they weren't satisfied with themselves. They were always on some self-improvement jag. This astonished Mrs. Murphy. Why couldn't people just be? But they couldn't just be—they had to be the best. Poor sick things. No wonder they died from diseases they brought on themselves.

One of the reasons she loved Harry was that Harry was more animal-like than other people. She loved the outdoors. She wasn't driven to own a lot of toys. She was happy with what she had. She wished that Harry didn't have to go to the post office every day but it was fun to see the other people, so if the woman had to work, this wasn't so bad. However, people disregarded Harry because she wasn't driven. Mrs. Murphy thought they were foolish. Harry was better than any of them.

Good as Harry was, she displayed the weaknesses of her breed. Mating was complicated for her. Divorce, a human invention, further complicated the simplicity of biology. Also, Harry missed communication from Mrs. Murphy. Although Harry wasn't afraid of the night, she was vulnerable in it. Perhaps because their eyes are bad, humans feel like prey in the darkness.

Night animals are associated with evil by humans. Bats especially scared them, which Mrs. Murphy thought silly. Humans didn't know enough about the chain of life to go about killing animals that offended them. They killed bats, coyotes, foxes—the night hunters. Their fears and their inability to comprehend how animals are connected, including themselves, would bring everyone to a sorry state. Mrs. Murphy, semidomesticated and enjoying her closeness to Harry, had no desire to see the nondomesticated animals killed. She understood why the wild animals hated people. Sometimes she hated them, too, except for Harry.

A shadowy movement caught her eye. Her ears moved forward. She inhaled deeply. What was he doing here?

A sleek, handsome Paddy moved toward the back porch.

"Hello, Paddy."

"Hello, my sweet." Paddy's deep purr was hypnotic. "How are you on this fine, soft night?"

"Thinking long thoughts and watching the clouds swirl around the moon. Were you hunting?"

"A little of this and a little of that. I'm out for the medicinal powers of the velvety night air. And what were your long thoughts?" His whiskers sparkled against his black face.

"That the so-called bad animals like coyotes, bats, and snakes are more useful to earth than human drug addicts."

"I don't like snakes."

"But they are useful."

"Yes. They can be useful far away from me." He licked his paw and then rubbed his face. "Why don't you come out and play?"

He was tempting, even though she knew how worthless he was. He was still the best-looking tom in Crozet. "I've got to watch over Harry."

"It's the middle of the night and she's safe."

"I hope so, Paddy. I'm worried about this killer."

"Oh, that. What's that got to do with Harry?"

"She's sticking her nose where it doesn't belong. Miss Amateur Detective."

"Does the killer know?"

"That's just it, isn't it? We don't know who it is, only that it's someone we know."

"Summer's a strange time to kill anyone," Paddy reflected. "I can understand it in the winter when the food supply is low—not that I approve of it. But in the summer there's enough for everyone."

"They don't kill over food."

"True enough." Humans bored Paddy. "See those fireflies dancing? That's what I want to do: dance in the moonlight, sing to the stars, jump straight up at the moon." He turned a somersault.

"I'm staying inside."

"Oh, Mrs. Murphy, you've become much too serious. I remember you when you would chase sunbeams. You even chased me."

"I did not. You chased me." Her fur ruffled.

"Ha, all the girls chased me. I thought it was wonderful to be chased by a bright tiger lass whose name, of all things, was Mrs. Murphy. Humans give us the silliest names."

"Paddy, you're full of catnip and moonshine."

"Not Muffy or Skippy or Snowball or Scooter or even Rambette, but Mrs. Murphy." He shook his head.

"I was named for Harry's maternal grandmother and well you know it."

"I thought they named their children after their grandparents, not their cats. Oh, come on out here. For old times' sake."

"Fool me once, shame on you. Fool me twice, shame on me," Mrs. Murphy said with firmness but without rancor.

He sighed. "I'm faithful in my fashion. I'm here tonight, aren't I?"

"And you can keep on going."

"You're a hard girl, M.M." He was the only animal that called her M.M.

"No, just a wise one. But you can do me a favor."

"What?" He grinned.

"If you hear or see or smell anything that seems suspicious, tell me."

"I will. Now stop worrying about it. Time will do justice all around." He flicked his luxurious tail to the vertical and trotted off.

22

The dark-red doors of Crozet Lutheran Church reflected the intense heat of the morning. Outside the church, sweltering, shuffled the camera crews from television stations in Washington, D.C., Richmond, and Charlottesville. What little peace remained in the town was shattered by the news teams, whose producers decided to bump up the story. The second murder was God's gift to producers in the summer news doldrums.

Inside the simple church, people huddled together, unsure of who was friend and who was foe, although externally everyone acted the same: friendly.

The casket, adorned with a beautiful spray of white lilies, rested before the altar railing. Josiah forgot nothing. Two chaste floral displays stood on either side of the gold altar cross. Maude's Crozet friends filled the church with flowers. Few knew her well but only one among the congregation wanted her dead. The others truly mourned Maude, as much for her as for themselves. She added something to the town and she would be missed.

The organ music, Bach, filled the church with somber majesty.

Sitting at the rear of the church and to the side was Rick Shaw. He was impressed that Josiah DeWitt and Ned Tucker canvassed the townspeople for this funeral. Ned refused to divulge who gave what but Rick shrewdly allowed Josiah the opportunity to tell all, which he did.

People of modest means, like Mary Minor Haristeen, gave as generously as they could. Mim Sanburne gave a bit more and begrudged every penny. Jim gave separately—a lot. The biggest surprise was Bob Berryman, who contributed $1,000. Apparently Bob's wife, a portly woman determined to wear miniskirts, was kept ignorant of this bequest until Josiah's judicious hints reached even her. Linda Berryman, glued to her husband's side, appeared more grim than sad.

After the mercifully short service, Reverend Jones, preceded by an acolyte, walked down the aisle to the front door. He stopped for a moment. Rick saw him wince. The good reverend did not want the camera crews to sully the sanctity of this moment. But the doors must open and news ratings meant more to producers than human decency. Reverend Jones nodded slightly and the acolyte opened the door.

Mim Sanburne discreetly fluffed her hair as she prepared to leave the church. Little Marilyn, less discreetly, checked her makeup and pointedly ignored Harry, who was immediately behind her. Josiah did not escort Mim, because he acted as next of kin to Maude and because Jim was there. Market Shiflett stood next to Harry, and Mim edged up even more lest someone (like a news reporter) think she would be accompanied by a—shudder—working man. Courtney Shiflett and Brookie and Danny Tucker quietly filed out the front door too. Susan and Ned stayed behind with Josiah to make certain nothing else needed to be done until the grave-site service.

A reporter rushed up to Mim. She stiffened and turned her back on him. He shoved his microphone under Little Marilyn's mouth. She started to open it when her mother clasped her wrist and yanked her away. Mrs. George Hogendobber waved her huge church fan in front of her face and made her escape.

Jim wheeled on the reporter. "I'm the mayor of this here town and I'll answer any questions you have, but right now leave these people alone."

As Jim was nearly a foot taller than the reporter, the squirt slunk off.

A woman reporter, straining to lower her voice to a more important register, buttonholed Harry, caught in the slow-moving mass of mourners.

"Were you a friend of the murdered woman?" the pert young thing asked.

Harry ignored her.

"Come on, girl." Market grabbed Harry's hand.

"Thanks, Market." Harry let him propel her toward his car.

Boom Boom Craycroft stayed away from Maude's funeral, which was appropriate. As she was still in deep mourning, no one expected her to make a public appearance anywhere but on the golf course, and everyone but Mrs. Hogendobber made allowances for that. As for Boom Boom, she would have taken apart the television crews, limb by limb.

The grave-site service progressed nicely until Reverend Jones tossed ashes on the casket. Bob Berryman began to sob. Linda was appalled. Bob moved away from the grave site and Linda didn't follow him. She sat like a stone in the tacky metal chair.

The moment the last syllable of the service was over, the "Amens" said, Josiah rushed to Bob's side. Harry and everyone else noticed him put his arm around Bob's shoulders, whispering earnestly in the shaken man's ear. Suddenly Bob pulled away from Josiah and slugged him square in the face. As the older man sank to his knees, Bob walked with deliberate control to his car. He turned to find his wife. She hurried to the car, opened the passenger door, and Bob drove off before she could even close it.

Ned reached Josiah first and found his face bloodied. Harry, Susan, and Mrs. Hogendobber got there next and Rick Shaw came more slowly. He was observing people's reactions to the outburst.

The cameras, zoom lenses intact, whirred away from a discreet distance. Jim Sanburne advanced on them, and the newspeople scurried like cockroaches. Susan pulled tissues from her bag but the gushing nosebleed poured through them.

Hayden McIntire took command. "Tilt your head back."

Josiah did as he was told. "What do you think? Broken?"

"I don't know. Come with me to the office and I'll do what I can. You're going to have two very black eyes tomorrow along with a fat nose."

Josiah wobbled to his feet with Hayden's assistance.

Mrs. Hogendobber, brimming with curiosity, blurted out what everyone else was thinking: "What did you say to him?"

"Well—I don't know." Josiah squinted. Everything hurt. "I told him this was a terrible thing, but for Maude's sake he should control himself. Those television vermin are across the road. What would people think?"

"That's all?" Harry asked, knowing perfectly well that what Josiah had just said would plant a fast-growing seed. Why would it look so bad? A nasty little emotional door had been opened and everyone would jam in front of it trying to peer inside.

Josiah nodded "yes" as Hayden led him off.

Rick silently watched this and then got in his squad car. He was going to tail Bob Berryman. He called to the dispatcher, gave a description of the car and the license plate number. He specified he didn't want Bob stopped unless he headed for the airport.

Rob Collier listened intently to the tale of Berryman's outburst. He lingered over his afternoon pickup.

". . . blood oozing onto his Turnbull and Asser shirt. I tell you, Rob, that must have hurt more than the blow."

Rob pulled his eyelashes, a nervous habit. "Something's not right."

"No shit, Sherlock."

Rob smiled good-naturedly. "Yeah, well, I'm not as dumb as you think. You're a woman and I'm a man. I know some things that you don't. Maybe a man cries because he killed someone and suddenly feels guilty."

Harry leaned over the counter, inadvertently touching Tucker, who was snoozing under it. The corgi awoke with a grunt.

"I don't know."

"See, what's going on here is, he's too full up to keep it to himself. Bob Berryman don't go 'round blubbering in public."

"Right."

Tucker yawned. Mrs. Murphy was sleeping with one eye open in a mail bin. Tucker could see the lump at the bottom of the canvas bin. She slunk over and very carefully, very gently bit the lump.

"Ah-h-h." Mrs. Murphy, startled, yelped. Tucker laughed and bit her again.

"Those two put on a real show, don't they?" Rob was diverted for a moment from his theory. "As I see it, Maude had something on Berryman. Bet your bottom dollar."

Harry drew in air between her teeth. "Well, something was going on."

"Maybe they were running drugs. Berryman travels nine states."

"I can't picture Maude as a drug dealer."

"Hey, sixty years ago booze was illegal. The son of one of the biggest bootleggers in the country became President. Business is business."

"Where does Kelly fit in?"

"Found out"—Rob shrugged—"or was in cahoots."

"Next you'll be telling me Mim Sanburne is a cocaine queen."

"Anything is possible."

"Let's don't talk about Mim, even though I brought her up. She's on my reserve shit list. She's mad at me. Oh, excuse me—ladies of Mim's quality don't get mad; they become agitated. She's agitated with me because I told Little Marilyn to invite her brother to the wedding."

Rob whistled. "Now there's an odd couple."

"Little Marilyn and Fitz-Gilbert Hamilton? He sure hasn't shown his face around here. Probably feels safe in Richmond."

"No, no—Stafford and Brenda Sanburne. She's about the prettiest thing I ever saw but . . . Well, I wish him happiness, but you can't go around breaking the rules and not expect to suffer for it."

"You're big on rules today." Harry thought, Love whomever you could. It was such a rare commodity in the world, you'd better take it where you could find it. No point arguing with Rob, who was a tender racist as opposed to the horrendous kind. Still, they did their damage, whether by trickle or by tidal wave.

Rob checked his watch. "Zip time."

He hopped into his mail truck as Mrs. Murphy hopped out of the mail bin. "Tucker, I was sleepy. Your snoring kept me awake last night."

"I don't snore."

"You do. Snort. Snort." Mrs. Murphy imitated a snore but she was far from it.

"What's with you two?" Harry walked over to the mail bin. "There's nothing in here." Mrs. Murphy rubbed against her leg. Harry gingerly stepped into the mail bin, pushed off with one leg, and then tucked that in the bin too. "Wheee!"

The door opened as she crashed into the wall.

"What are you doing, Miz Haristeen?" Rick Shaw stifled a laugh.

Harry stuck her head over the bin. "The cat has so much fun when she gets in here, I thought I'd try. Hell, anything to feel good these days."

Rick fished a cigarette out of his pocket, rolling it in his fingers. "I know what you mean."

"Thought you'd stopped."

"How'd you know?"

"Your eyes follow every lit cigarette."

"You're very observant, Harry." Rick appreciated that in a person. "Show me what you've got."

"I didn't think you'd answer my phone call today after the blowup at the funeral." She led him to the back room. "I'm impressed."

She shut the door behind them and brought out the two graveyard postcards. She handed him the magnifying glass and placed the legitimate French postcard on the table. He closed one eye and studied the cards, holding the unlit cigarette in his left hand.

"Uh-huh" was all he said.

"See the slight variation in the inks?"

"Yes."

"And the misalignment, very small, of the 'A' in 'Asheville.' "

"Yes." Rick twirled the magnifying glass. He handed the glass back to Harry. "Who else knows about this?"

"Susan Tucker. Rob knows I borrowed a postcard but he doesn't know why."

"Keep it to yourself. You and Susan."

"I will."

"Now, tell me what your cat and dog were doing in Maude's shop."

"I don't know."

"You were snooping in there, Harry. Don't lie to me."

"I wasn't. Somehow they got locked in there. I woke up in the morning. I couldn't find them. I drove around. I called around and just like I told you, Mrs. Hogendobber heard Tucker barking. She found them."

"I believe you. Thousands wouldn't." He dropped his bulk into a chair. "Gimme a Co-Cola, will you?" He lit up the cigarette as she brought him a soda from the little refrigerator. A long drag brought a smile to his lips. "It's a filthy habit but damn, it feels good. Next I'll try your mail bin." He inhaled. "I'm not really sorry I started up again. It's this or straight whiskey with a case like this, and with the whiskey I wouldn't be on the case long."

"What do you think—about the postcards, I mean."

"I think we've got someone so smart that he or she is laughing at us. I think we've got a fox that will lay a false trail."

Goose bumps dotted Harry's skin. "Scares me."

"Scares me too. If I only knew what the son of a bitch was after."

"Do you follow your hunches?"

"I do, but I do my homework first." Rick crossed his right leg over his left knee. "Okay, what's your hunch? You're itching to tell me."

"The old tunnels Claudius Crozet dug have something to do with this."

At the sound of the name Crozet, Rick sat up straight. "Why do you say that?"

"Because there was a letter from Crozet, a Xerox on Kelly's desk. Can you ride, Rick?"

"A little."

"Let's ride out to the closest tunnel, the Greenwood."

"In this heat, with the deer flies? No, ma'am. We're going in the squad car and we can walk up the rest of the way." He slapped her on the back. "I don't know why I'm doing this, but come on."

"You two stay here and be good now."

"No! No!" erupted the chorus of discontent.

Harry started to plead with Rick but he cut her off. "No way, Harry. They stay here."

Jungle vegetation couldn't have been much thicker than what Rick and Harry waded through.

"We should have taken horses," Harry grumbled.

"I haven't got two hours. This is quicker and you just be glad I'm including you."

"Including me? You wouldn't know about it if I hadn't told you. Hey, did you find Berryman?"

Rick slashed at pokeweed. "Yes. Was it that obvious after the funeral?"

"Where else would you go?"

"I found him at work. Selling a bronze stock trailer to the Beegles."

"Fireworks?"

"No, he was tired. Guess the excitement wore him out. He's got an alibi for the night Maude was killed. Home with his wife."

"She could lie for him."

"Do you honestly think, in your wildest dreams, Mary Minor Haristeen, that Linda Berryman would lie for Bob?"

"No." Harry stopped to catch her breath. The steamy heat sucked it right out of her.

Up ahead the outline of the tunnel loomed, covered and fantastic-looking with kudzu, honeysuckle, and a wealth of weeds unknown even to Harry. The old track, an offshoot of the newer line, ran up to the mouth of the tunnel.

"I've been keeping an eye out for broken grasses and tracks" —Rick wiped sweat off his forehead—"but with thick foliage like this, unless it's very recent, I don't have much hope. It's easier coming up the tracks but it takes twice as long."

As they reached the tunnel Harry cast her eyes upward. The chiseled remembrance of the men who built the tunnel, clear-cut and deep, was half covered by honeysuckle. The C. CROZET, CHIEF ENGINEER was visible. The rest was obscured except for A.D. 1852.

Harry pointed upward.

Kudzu grows about three feet a day, obscuring everything in its path.

"Treasure?" Harry said.

"The C and O searched the place top to bottom before they closed this off. And look at this rock. Nobody's getting through this stuff to hunt for treasure."

The mouth of the tunnel had been filled with debris, rock, and then sealed with concrete. The right side of the mouth was totally choked by vines.

Harry, crestfallen, reached out and touched the rock, warm from the sun. She withdrew her hand.

"There are three more tunnels to go."

"Brooksville is sealed off and Little Rock is still in use. I don't know if they shut off the Blue Ridge but it's so long and far away—"

"You're up on your tunnels." Harry smiled. She wasn't the only one sitting up at night reading.

"And so are you. Come on. There's nothing here."

As they trudged back Rick promised to send out a deputy to investigate the Brooksville, Little Rock, and Blue Ridge tunnels. They were outside his jurisdiction but he'd work that out with his counterparts in the other counties.

"What about calling the C and O?" Harry suggested.

"I did that. They got me the reports of closing the tunnels in 1944. Couldn't have been more helpful."

"And . . . ?"

"Just a dry recounting of shutting them up. There's no treasure, Harry. I don't know what the Crozet connection is. It's a dead end, kid."

He drove her back to the post office, where Tucker had chewed the corner of the door and Mrs. Murphy, with great violence, had thrown her Kitty Litter all over the floor.

23

Curving, sensuous, gilded pieces of Louis XV furniture dazzled Harry each time she entered Josiah's house. Gifted with a good eye and imagination, Josiah painted the walls stark white, which made the beautiful desks, bombé chests, and chairs stand out vividly. The floors, dark walnut, polished to perfection, reflected the glories of the furniture. The King Kong of pastel floral arrangements commanded the center of the coffee table. The flowers and the French pieces provided the only color in the room.

Josiah provided color of a different sort, valiantly sitting in a wing chair playing host to his callers, who had come as custom dictated. On a satinwood table next to the chair was a round cerise bowl that contained old marbles. Every now and then Josiah would reach into the bowl and run them through his fingers like worry beads. Another bowl contained old type bits; yet another contained doorknobs with mercury centers.

Susan rushed up to Harry to spill the rotten news about Danny's using his father's credit card to get money from the twenty-four-hour banking window. Ned had grounded him for the rest of the summer. Harry commiserated as Mrs. Hogendobber arrived with her famous potato salad. Mim, sleek in linen pants and a two-hundred-dollar T-shirt, glided over to assist Mrs. Hogendobber in carrying the heavy bowl. Hayden was just leaving as Fair came in. Little Marilyn served drinks out of a massive sterling-silver bowl.

Little Marilyn was spending a lot of time next to the liquor at these gatherings. Each time Harry looked her way, Little Marilyn found something fascinating to hold her attention. She wasn't going to acknowledge Harry with even a grimace, much less a smile.

"I've got to pay my respects to Josiah." Harry slipped her arm around Susan's waist. "The bank won't tell on Danny, so if you and Ned keep it quiet no one will know but me. I think a teenaged boy is allowed a few mistakes."

"A five-hundred-dollar one! And that's another thing. His father says he has to pay back every penny by Halloween."

"Halloween?"

"At first Ned said Labor Day but Danny cried and said he couldn't make enough from mowing lawns between the middle of July and Labor Day."

"This must be an up-to-date version of clipping a few bills from Mom's purse. Did you ever steal from your mother?"

"God, no." Susan's hand automatically covered her chest. "She would have beat me within an inch of my life. Still would, too."

Susan's mother was alive and extremely well in Montecito, California.

"My parents would not only have whopped me good," Harry said, "they would have told everyone they knew, to accent my humiliation, which would have made it ten times worse. Did I ever tell you about Mother not being able to get me up in the morning?"

"You mean when our classes started at six-thirty A.M.? I didn't want to get up either. Remember that? There were so many of us the schools couldn't handle it, so they staggered the times we'd arrive at school in the morning. If you missed your buddies at lunch hour, that was that."

"Poor Mom had to get up at five to try and get me up because I was on the 7:00 A.M. shift. I just wouldn't budge. Finally she threw water on me. She was not a woman to shy from a remedy once its potency was established."

Harry smiled. "I miss her. Odd, now I have no trouble getting up early. I even like it. It's too bad Mother didn't have more years to enjoy the fact that I've become an early bird." She collected herself. "I've got to say something cheery to Josiah."

Harry strolled over to Josiah, who was now being ministered to, literally, by Mrs. H., who was telling him about Lazarus. Josiah responded by saying that he, too, drew comfort from the thought of Lazarus waking from the dead but he, Josiah, was beat up, not dead. She needed to think of a better story. Then he reached for Harry.

"Dear Harry, you will forgive me for not rising."

"Josiah, this is the first time I've seen anyone's eyes match his shirt. Maroon."

"I prefer the descriptive burgundy." He leaned back in his chair.

"Now isn't that like you, making light of something terrible." Mrs. Hogendobber artlessly tried to pretend she liked Josiah and wished him well. Not that she disliked him, but she didn't feel he was exactly a man and she knew he wasn't a practicing Christian.

"It isn't so terrible. The man was distraught and lashed out. I don't know why Berryman's distraught, but if I were married to Our Lady of Cellulite perhaps I'd be distaught too."

Harry laughed. He was awful but he was on target.

"I had no idea that Linda Berryman evidenced an interest in film." Mrs. Hogendobber tentatively accepted a gin rickey—not that she was a drinker, mind you, but it had been an unusually difficult day and the sun was past the yardarm.

Fair, sitting across from Josiah, burst out laughing and then covered his mouth. Correcting Mrs. Hogendobber wasn't worth it.

"What's this I hear about the adorable Mrs. Murphy and the fierce Tee Tucker being caught red-handed, I mean red-pawed, in Maude's store—which I am buying, by the way?" Josiah asked Harry.

"I have no idea how they got in there."

"I found them, you know." Mrs. Hogendobber recounted, to the millisecond, the events leading to the discovery. She withheld the information about the desk but did give Harry a conspiratorial glance.

Josiah picked imaginary lint off his sleeve. "Don't you wish they could talk?"

"No." Harry smiled. "I don't want everyone to know my secrets."

"You have secrets?" Fair inclined his head toward Harry.

"Doesn't everyone?" Harry shot back.

The room quieted for a moment; then conversation hummed again.

"Not me," Mrs. Hogendobber said in a forthright voice, and then remembered that she had one now. She rather liked that.

"One teeny secret, Mrs. H., one momentary fall from grace, or at least a barstool," Josiah teased her. "I agree with Harry—we each have secrets."

"Well, someone's got a humdinger." Susan loathed the word humdinger, but it fit.

Harry exited the conversation on secrets as Mim joined it. She walked over to Little Marilyn, who couldn't weasel out of talking to her now.

"Marilyn."

"Harry."

"You're not talking to me and I don't much like it."

"Harry," Little Marilyn whispered, genuinely fearful, "not in front of my mother. I'm not mad at you. She is."

Harry also lowered her voice. "When are you going to cut the apron strings and be your own person? For chrissake, L.M., you're over thirty."

Little Marilyn flushed. She wasn't accustomed to honest conversation, since with Mim you glided around issues. Speaking directly about something was tactless. However, life in WASP nirvana was growing stale. "You have to understand"—she was now almost inaudible—"when I get married I can do what I want, when I want."

"How do you know you aren't exchanging one boss for another?"

"Not Fitz-Gilbert. He isn't remotely like Mother, which is why I like him." That admission popped out of Little Marilyn's mouth before she recognized what it meant.

"You can do what you want now."

"Why this sudden interest in me? You've never paid much attention to me before." A hint of belligerence crept into her voice. If she was going to rebel against Mama, why not practice on Harry?

"I love your brother. He's one of the most wonderful people I've ever known. He loves you and you'll hurt him if you keep him from your wedding. And I suppose if you'd stop hanging around with that vapid, phony chic set I could learn to like you. Why don't you motor out to the stables and get a little horse shit on your shoes? When we were kids you were a good rider. Go to New York for a weekend. Just . . . do something."

"Vapid? Phony? You're insulting my friends."

"Wrong. Those are friends your mother chose for you. You don't have any friends except for your brother." Tired, worried, and irritable underneath her public demeanor, Harry just blurted this out.

"And you're better off?" Little Marilyn began to enjoy this. "At least I'm getting the man I want. You're losing yours."

Harry blinked. This was a new Little Marilyn. She didn't like the old one. The new one was really a surprise.

"Harry?" Josiah's voice floated above the chatter. "Harry." He called a little louder. She turned. "It must be a glorious conversation. You haven't paid any attention to me and I've been calling."

Little Marilyn, defiantly, walked over to Josiah first. Harry brought up the rear.

"You two girls were jabbering like bluejays," Mim said with an edge. Then her husband, Jim, pushed open the front door with a booming greeting and Mim was truly on edge.

Harry eyed Little Marilyn's impeccable mother and thought that being in her company was like biting deeply into a lemon.

Fair saved the day, because Harry was teetering on the brink of letting everyone know exactly what she thought about them. He sensed that she was coiled, crabby. He knew he no longer loved his wife but after nearly a decade of being with someone, learning her habits, feeling responsible for her, it was a hard habit to break. So he rescued Harry from herself at that moment.

"What were you doing in Rick Shaw's squad car?" he asked.

A slow hush rolled over the room like a soft ground fog.

"We drove up to the Greenwood tunnel," Harry said, nonchalant.

"In this heat?" Josiah was incredulous.

"Maybe that was Rick's way of wearing her down for questioning," Susan said.

"I think the tunnels have something to do with the murders." Harry knew she should have shut her mouth.

"Ridiculous," Mim snapped. "They've been closed for over forty years."

Jim countered, "Right now no idea is ridiculous."

"What about the treasure stories?" Mrs. Hogendobber said. "After all, those stories must have some truth in them or they wouldn't have been circulated for over one hundred years. Maybe it's a treasure of a rare kind."

"Like my divine desk over there." Josiah swung his hand out like a casual auctioneer. "I've been meaning to tell you, Mim, that you need this desk. The satinwood glows with the light of the centuries."

"Now, now, Josiah." Mim smiled. "We're declaring a moratorium on selling until your eyes and your nose heal."

"If there were a treasure, the C and O would have found it." Fair fixed himself another drink. "People love stories about lost causes, ghosts, and buried treasure."

"Claudius Crozet was a genius. If he wanted to hide a treasure he could do it," Mrs. Hogendobber interjected. "It was Crozet who warned the state of Virginia that Joseph Carrington Cabell's canal company would never work. Cabell was a highly influential man in the decades before the War of Northern Aggression, and he deviled Crozet all his life. Cabell single-handedly held up the development of railroads, which Claudius Crozet believed heralded the future. And Crozet was right. The canal company expired, costing investors and the state millions upon millions of dollars."

"Mrs. Hogendobber, I'm quite impressed. I had no idea you were so knowledgeable about our ... namesake." Josiah sat up in his chair and then lapsed back again with a muffled moan.

"Here." Fair handed him a stiff Glenfiddich scotch.

"I—" Mrs. Hogendobber, unaccustomed to lying, couldn't think what to say next.

Harry jumped in. "I told you not to volunteer to head the 'Celebrate Crozet' committee."

"Me?" Mrs. Hogendobber mumbled.

"Mrs. H., you've got *too much* on your mind. Recent events plus the committee . . . I'll come over tomorrow and help you, okay?"

Mrs. Hogendobber got the hidden message. She nodded in the affirmative.

"Well, Harry, what did you find at the Greenwood tunnel? Lots of florins and louis and golden Russian samovars?" Josiah smiled.

"Lots of pokeweed and honeysuckle and kudzu."

"Some treasure." Little Marilyn minced on "treasure."

"Well"—Josiah breathed the scotch fumes—"I give you credit for going up there in this beastly heat. We've got to find out who this . . . person is, and nothing is too far-fetched." He raised his glass to Harry in a toast and then proceeded to regale the group with his plans for Maude's store.

Later that night, Harry, who forgot to eat a decent dinner, got the munchies. She cranked up her mother's old blender, putting in whole milk, vanilla ice cream, wheat germ, and almonds. The almonds clanked as the blades ground them. She drank the concoction right out of the blender glass.

Tucker screeched into the kitchen, jumping on her hind legs. *"That's it! That's it!"*

"Tucker, get down. You can lick the glass when I'm finished."

Mrs. Murphy, hearing the fuss, roused herself from the living room sofa. *"What's going on, Tucker?"*

"It's that smell." Tucker spun around in circles, her snow-white bib a blur. *"Close to the turtle smell, but much nicer, sweeter."*

Mrs. Murphy jumped on the counter and sniffed the bits of wheat germ and almonds. The ice cream smell was strong. She sniffed with intensity and then vaulted from the counter onto Harry's shoulder.

"Hey, now, that's enough! You didn't learn these bad manners at home." Harry put the milkshake on the counter and lifted Mrs.

Murphy off her shoulder. Gently, Mrs. Murphy was placed on the floor.

Tucker touched noses with the cat. *"What did I tell you?"*

"Close. The almonds don't smell exactly like a turtle, but then a turtle doesn't smell exactly like whatever we smelled at the concrete plant and up at the railroad track. I wonder what it is?"

Mrs. Murphy and Tucker sat next to each other and stared up at Harry as she drained the last drop.

"Oh, all right." Harry grabbed dog biscuits and kitty treats out of the cupboard. She gave one to each animal. They ignored them.

"Not only bad manners, but picky too." Harry waved the kitty treat under Mrs. Murphy's nose. "One little nibble for Mommy."

"If she starts the Mommy routine she'll coo and croon next. You'd better eat it," Tucker advised.

"I'm trying to keep the smell of almonds. . . . Oh, well, you're probably right." Mrs. Murphy daintily removed the treat from Harry's fingers.

Tucker, with less restraint, gobbled up her biscuit with its gravylike coating.

"Good kitty. Good doggie."

"I wish she'd stop talking to us as if we were children," Mrs. Murphy grumbled.

24

Saturday sparkled, quite unusual for sticky July. The mountains glistened bright blue; the sky was a creamy robin's-egg blue. Mim Sanburne swaggered down to the little dock on the lake, which also gleamed in the pure light. Her pontoon boat, Mim's Vim, sides scrubbed, deck scrubbed, gently rocked in the lap of the tiny waves. The bar overflowed with liquid delight. A huge wicker basket filled with special treats like cream-cheese-stuffed snow peas sat next to the pilot's wheel. Everything was splendid, including Mim's attire. She wore bright-white clamdiggers, red espadrilles, a horizontally striped red-and-white T-shirt, and her captain's cap. Her lipstick, a glaring red smear, reflected the light.

Jim and Rick Shaw were huddled up at the house. She'd heard her husband say they ought to bring in the FBI, but Rick kept repeating that the case didn't qualify for the FBI's attention.

Little Marilyn followed a servant carrying the lovely baskets filled with party favors. Upon seeing the baskets, Mim entertained a fleeting thought of Maude Bly Modena. She quickly pushed it out of her mind. Her theory was that Maude must have surprised Kelly's killer and that was why she had been killed. She'd seen on many TV programs that a killer often has to kill again to cover his tracks.

After arranging the little favors on her boat, Mim languidly strolled up the terraces and walked around her house to the front. Day lilies shouted in yellow and burnt orange. Oddly, her wisteria still bloomed and the lavender was at full tide. She couldn't wait for her friends Port and Elliewood and Miranda Hogendobber. Not that Miranda was their social equal but she had distinctly heard Harry say to her last night at Josiah's that she was to head the newly formed "Celebrate Crozet" committee, and Big Marilyn meant to be a part of such a committee. Anyway, the lower orders were violently flattered at being included in little gatherings of the elite. Mim was confident that Miranda would fall all over herself when Mim suggested that she, too, help head the committee. The trick of the day would be to keep Miranda off religion, to keep Port off the grandchildren, and to keep Elliewood off the murders. No murder talk today—she absolutely forbade it.

As Mim waited for the various ladies of quality and one of lesser quality to drive down the two-mile approach to the house, she allowed herself to recall her "White Party." Decorated in silver and white by Josiah, this was to have been Mim's *Town and Country* party. She'd arranged to have a reporter there. Josiah contacted the press. It would never do for her to seek publicity openly.

Jim kept the Learjet busy zooming to New York and California to pick up people. Just two hundred of her nearest and dearest friends.

Josiah, using the bulldozing talents of Stuart Tapscott, created a thirty-foot oval pond at the end of the formal gardens. The tables were laid out among the garden paths and the very special guests were seated around the pond. Josiah lined the bottom of the pond so that it was really a swimming pool. He painted the bottom cobalt blue, and lights shone under the water. However, apart from the lighting, the pond appeared to fit the lay of the land. Marvelous water lilies enhanced the surface, as did heavily sedated swans, floating serenely. As the evening wore on the drugs wore off, and the swans underwent a personality change from serene to pugnacious. They stalked from the pond, dripping, flapping and pecking vigorously at one another, to assert their right to the brandy and bonbons. They honked and attacked guests, some of whom, having consumed too much brandy, fled into the pond. Mim herself was accosted by one of the larger swans. She was saved at the last minute by Jim, who lifted her off the ground while abandoning the table to the greedy bird.

Photos of the debacle splashed across Town and Country. The copy, lighthearted, did not declare the night a disaster, but Mim was stung nonetheless.

Miranda Hogendobber, punctual to a fault, came up the driveway in her ancient but impeccable Ford Falcon. She was soon followed by Elliewood and Port. After fulsome greetings, Little Marilyn helped her mother load the ladies. She pushed off the pontoon boat and waved from the shore. Then Little Marilyn sat on the dock, toes in the water.

The first round of drinks loosened everyone. Miranda allowed alcohol to scorch her lips. A nifty cure for the stomach ailment that had plagued her last night. She refused the second round but did take a tiny nip on the third.

Mim broke out a fresh deck of cards, still smelling of ink. Port and Elliewood played against Miranda and Mim. Mim just couldn't do enough for Miranda, which amused Port and Elliewood, who knew Mim was angling for something. Occasionally Mim would wave to a sunbathing Little Marilyn on the dock. It was perfect, really perfect, because Mim was winning.

After the first round of cards, Mim insisted on cranking the boat up and motoring on the lake. Speed was her downfall. She frightened Port, who continually asked her to slow down, but Mim, three sheets to the wind, told Port, in so many words, to shut up and live dangerously.

Finally, she stopped the boat for lunch. At first no one noticed anything wrong. The effects of the drink and the profound gratitude of not having Mim at the wheel dulled their senses.

Then Port felt something rather wet. She glanced down. "Mim, my feet are wet."

Everyone looked down. Everyone's feet were wet.

"Well, put your feet on the table." Mim cheerily poured another round.

"I get the distinct sensation that we are lower in the water," Mrs. Hogendobber said, even-voiced.

"Miranda, we *are* lower in the water," Port echoed, her face now white despite the sunburn.

Mim took off her soaking shoes and settled back for another swig. The group stared at her.

"Can you bail? I mean, Mim darling, do you have a pump?" Elliewood asked. Not a cursing woman, Elliewood had to exercise willpower to say "darling." She wanted to say "jerk," "asshole," anything to get Mim's attention.

By now the water was mid-calf. Port, unable to control herself any longer, emitted a heartrending shriek. "We're sinking! Help, my God, we're sinking."

She so startled the other women that Miranda put her hands to her ears and Elliewood fell out of her chair. She did not, however, spill her drink.

"I'll drown. I don't want to die," Port wailed.

"Shut up! Shut up this minute. You're embarrassing me." Mim spat the words. "Little Marilyn is there on the dock. I'll get her attention. There's not one thing to worry about."

Mim waved at her daughter. Little Marilyn didn't budge.

Elliewood and Miranda waved too.

"Little Marilyn," her mother called.

Little Marilyn sat still as a post.

"Little Marilyn! Little Marilyn!" the other three called.

"I can't swim! I'm going to drown," blubbered Port.

"Will you please be quiet," Mim demanded. "You can hold on to the boat."

"The goddamned boat is sinking, you bitch!" Port shouted.

Mim, outraged, pushed Port off her chair. Port sloshed in the water but bounced back up. She hauled off and caught Mim in the neighborhood of the left bosom.

Elliewood grabbed Mim, and Miranda grabbed Port.

"That's quite enough," Miranda ordered. "It won't settle anything."

"Who are you to tell me what to do?" Port got snotty.

"Bag it, Port." Mim, although in deep water, was not going to have her chances ruined. She returned her attentions to Little Marilyn.

She screamed. She hollered. She boldly took off her red-and-white T-shirt and waved it over her head, her lift-and-separate bra dazzling in the sun for all to see.

Little Marilyn, who was staring at them the entire time, finally rose to her feet and walked—not ran, but walked—up to the house.

"She's leaving us to die," Port sobbed.

"Can you swim?" Miranda matter-of-factly asked Elliewood. "I can't."

"I can't," howled Port.

"I can," replied Elliewood.

"Me too," said Mim.

"You'll leave me here. I just know you will. Mim, you're a cold-hearted, self-centered snake. You always were and you always will be. I curse you with my dying breath." Clearly, Port had once harbored secret dreams of being an actress.

"Shut the fuck up!" Mim shouted.

The use of the "f" word stunned the girls more than the fact that they were sinking.

Mim continued. "If help does not come in time, and I'm sure it will, we will nonetheless get you to shore, but you've got to lie on your back and shut up. I emphasize *shut up.*"

Port put her head in her hands and cried.

Miranda, with calm resolution, prepared to meet her Maker.

Within minutes Jim, Rick Shaw, and Little Marilyn appeared on the shore. Little Marilyn pointed to the distressed band. Mim forgot she had taken her shirt off. Miranda did not. She covered Mim.

Jim and Rick ran in opposite directions. Jim hauled a canoe out of the dock house and Rick hopped in his squad car. He roared to the neighbor's on the other side of the lake. They really didn't want him to use their small motorboat. The sight of Mim's sinking was pleasing to their eyes but they gave in. The women were rescued as the water crept above their waistlines.

Later, Jim and Rick overturned the boat. One of the pontoons had been slashed and then covered with some manner of water-soluble pitch. Mim, fully recovered from her plight, stood next to the boat. Jim wished she hadn't seen this.

"Someone tried to kill me." Mim blinked.

"Well, it could have been ripped on the bottom," Jim lied.

"Don't tell me what I know. I never came near the bottom. Someone tried to kill me!" Mim was more angry than scared.

"Perhaps they only meant to give you a hard time." Rick hunkered down again to inspect the tear.

Mim, now in full hue and cry, whipped out her cellular phone to call the girls.

"Don't do that, Mrs. Sanburne." Rick pushed down the phone's aerial.

"Why not?"

"It might be prudent to keep this to ourselves for a while. If we withhold information, the guilty party might make a mistake, ask a leading question—you understand?"

"Quite." Mim pursed her lips.

"Now, Mim honey, don't you worry. I'll hire day and night bodyguards for you." Jim put his arm around his wife's shoulders.

"That's too obvious," Mim replied.

After further discussion Jim convinced her, saying he'd get female bodyguards and they'd pass them off as exchange students.

Later, when grilled by her mother concerning her inaction on the dock, Little Marilyn declared the sight of Mim sinking was so traumatic that she was temporarily paralyzed by the prospect of losing her mother.

25

Mondays made Harry feel as if she were shoveling a ton of paper with a toothpick. Susan's junk mail piled up like the Matterhorn. Harry couldn't fit it in her mailbox. Josiah received *Country Life* magazine from England and a letter from an antiques dealer in France. Fair's box was jammed with advertisements from drug companies: *End Heartworms Now!* Mrs. Hogendobber would be happy to receive her Christian mail-order catalogue. Jesus mugs were a hot item, or you could buy a T-shirt printed with the Sermon on the Mount.

Harry envied Christ. He was born before the credit card. Owning a credit card in the age of the mail-order catalogue was a dicey business. Bankruptcy, a phone call away, could be yours in less than two minutes.

Cranky, she upended the last duffel bag, and letters, postcards, and bills poured out like white confetti. Mrs. Murphy crouched, wiggled her behind, then pounced into the delicious pile.

"No claws. Citizens will know you're fooling with their mail and that's a federal offense." Harry scratched the base of her tail.

Tucker watched from her bed under the counter while Mrs. Murphy darted to the end of the room, rose up on her hind legs, pulled a 180, and charged back into the pile.

"Gangbusters!"

Tucker twitched her ears. *"You love paper. I don't know why. Bores me."*

"The crinkle sounds wonderful." Mrs. Murphy rolled in the letters. *"And the texture of the different papers tickles my pads."*

"If you say so." Tucker sounded unconvinced.

By now Mrs. Murphy was skidding on the mail, much like kids skidding on ice without skates.

"That's enough now. You're going to tear something." Harry reached for the cat but she eluded her. Harry noticed a postcard on top of the latest pile Mrs. Murphy had assaulted. A pretty etching of a beetle was printed on the postcard. Harry picked it up and turned it over.

Written in computer script and addressed to her, it read: "Don't bug me."

Harry dropped the postcard as if it were on fire. Her heart raced.

"What's the matter with Harry?" Tucker called to Mrs. Murphy, still sliding on the letters.

The cat stopped. *"She's white as a sheet."*

Harry sorted the mail slowly, as if in a trance, but her mind was moving so quickly she was nearly paralyzed by the speed. The killer had to be someone at Josiah's house, telling her to mind her own business. Her amateur sleuthing had struck a nerve. What the killer didn't know was that Harry knew the postcards were his or her signal. Nor did the killer realize that both Harry and Mrs. Hogendobber knew more about Maude than they were letting on. Harry sat down, put her head between her hands, and breathed deeply. If she put her head between her knees she'd pass out. Her hands would have to do. Her thoughts going back to Mrs. Hogendobber, Harry realized she would have to impress upon her the absolute necessity of not telling anyone about the second ledger. Even if Mrs. Hogendobber had a guardian angel, there was no point in testing him.

It flitted through her mind that Fair could have sent the bug postcard. This was his idea of sick humor. Really sick. The card might not have come from the killer. She clung to this hope for an instant. Fair had his faults but he wasn't this weird. Like a dying light bulb, her hope fizzled out. She knew.

Harry dialed Rick Shaw and gave him her latest report. He said he'd be right over. Then she finished sorting the mail, the one bright spot being another postcard from Lindsay Astrove, still in Europe.

Mrs. Hogendobber appeared on the doorstep. Tucker ran to the door and wagged her tail. Ever since Mrs. H. had released them from Maude's shop, Tucker harbored warm feelings for her.

Harry opened the door, reached for Mrs. Hogendobber, and yanked her into the post office. She shut the door behind her.

"Harry, I am capable of self-propulsion. You must have heard about my near-death experience on Mim's boat. I thank the Lord for my deliverance."

"No, I haven't heard a peep. I do want to hear about it but not right this instant. I want to remind you, to beseech you, not to tell anyone about those accounting books. You'll be in danger if you do."

"I know that," Mrs. Hogendobber replied. "And I know more than that, too. I've studied those books to the last penny, the last decimal point. That woman ordered enough packing to move everyone in Crozet. It makes no sense, and the money she was getting! Our Maude would never have been on food stamps."

"How much money?"

"She'd been here for five years—a rough average of one hundred and fifty thousand dollars per year on the left side of the ledger, if you know what I mean."

"That's a lot of plastic peanuts." Fear ebbed from Harry as her curiosity took over.

"I haven't a clue." Mrs. Hogendobber threw up her hands.

"I do—sort of." Harry peered out of the front window to make sure no one was coming in. "We have as our first victim a rich man who owned a concrete plant and heavy, heavy hauling trucks. The second victim was a woman who operated a packing shop. They were shipping something."

"Dope. Maude could fix up anything. She could pack a diamond or a boa constrictor. Remember the time she helped Donna Eicher ship ant farms?"

"That!" Harry recalled three years back, when Donna Eicher started her ant farms. Watching the insects create empires between two Plexiglas plates held an appeal for some people. It lost its appeal for Donna when her inventory escaped and devoured the contents of her pantry.

"If Maude could ship ants, she sure could ship cocaine."

"They've got dogs now that smell packages. I read it in the newspaper." Harry thought out loud. "She'd have to get it past them."

"*We can smell anything. My nose detects a symphony of fragrance,*" Tucker yapped.

"Oh, Tucker, can it. You've got a good nose. Let's not get carried away with it." Mrs. Murphy wanted to hear what the women were saying.

"Piffle." Mrs. Hogendobber waved her hand. "She'd wrap the drugs with some odor to throw them off—Vicks VapoRub would do the job. A hundred fifty thousand a year, well, where else would one make profits like that?" Her back was to the door, which had just opened.

Harry winked at Mrs. Hogendobber, who stopped talking. Harry smiled. "Hi, Courtney. How's your summer going?"

"Fine, Mrs. Haristeen. Good morning, Mrs. Hogendobber." Courtney was down at the mouth but polite.

"How bad is it?" Harry asked.

"Danny Tucker is under house arrest for the rest of the summer. He even has a curfew! I can't believe Mr. and Mrs. Tucker are that cruel."

"Did he tell you why?" Harry inquired.

"No."

"Mr. and Mrs. Tucker aren't that cruel, so whatever he did, it was a doozy," Harry said.

"Doozy is such a funny word." Courtney wrinkled the mail by twisting it in her hands. She wasn't paying attention to it.

"Comes from Dusenberg," Mrs. Hogendobber boomed. "The Dusenberg was a beautiful, expensive car in the 1920's but to own one you also needed a mechanic. It broke down constantly. So a doozy is something spectacular and bad."

"Oh." Courtney was interested. "Did you own one?"

"That was a little before my time, but I saw a Dusenberg once and my father, who loved cars, told me about them."

Courtney thought the 1920's were as distant as the eleventh century. Age was something she didn't understand, and she wasn't sure if she'd just insulted Mrs. Hogendobber. She did know that her question would have insulted Mrs. Sanburne. Courtney left under this cloud of confusion.

"She's a dear child." Mrs. Hogendobber swung her purse to and fro. "No one ever forgets anything in this town. I know I never do."

"Yes?" Harry waited for the connective sentence.

"Oh, I don't know," Mrs. Hogendobber said. "Just crossed my mind. Now listen, Harry, I was due at the Ruth Circle five minutes ago but I'll be in constant touch and I want you to do the same."

"Agreed."

Mrs. Hogendobber rushed out for her women's church group meeting and Harry waited for the troops to march through, eagerly opening their mailboxes for a love letter and groaning when they found a bill instead. She waited for Rick Shaw too. She didn't know if he was a good sheriff or not. Too soon to tell, but she felt safer for having him around.

26

Fair Haristeen was washing his hands after performing surgery on an unborn ten-month-old fetus. Given the foal's bloodlines, he was worth a hundred thousand before he dropped. Fetal surgery was a new technique and Fair, a gifted surgeon, was in demand by Thoroughbred breeders in Virginia. His skill and the deference paid to him didn't go to his head. Fair still made the rounds to humble barns. He loved his work and when he allowed himself time to think about himself he knew it was his work that kept him alive.

Opening the door from the operating room, he found Boom Boom Craycroft sitting in his office. She smiled.

"Horse trouble?"

"No. Just . . . trouble. I came to apologize for the way I treated you the day Kelly was killed. I took it out on you in my own bitchy way—you must be used to that by now."

Fair, unprepared for an apology, cleared his throat. "S'okay."

"It's not okay and I'm not okay and the whole town is crazy." Her voice cracked. "I've done some serious thinking. It's about time, you'll say. No, you wouldn't say anything. You're too much the gentleman, except for once in a blue moon when you lose your temper. But I have thought about myself and Kelly. He never grew up, you see. He was always the smart kid who puts one over on people, and I never grew up either. We didn't have to. Rich people don't."

"Some rich people do."

"Name three." Boom Boom's black eyes flashed.

"Stafford Sanburne, in our generation."

She smiled. "One. Well, I guess you're right. Maybe you have to suffer to grow up and usually we can pay someone to suffer for us. That didn't work this time. I can't run away from this one." She tilted her head back, exposing her graceful neck. "I also came to apologize for not understanding how important your work is to you. I don't think I will ever see how reaching into a horse's intestinal tract is wonderful, but—it's wonderful to you. Anyway, I'm sorry. I'm apologized out. That's what I came to say, and I'll go."

"Don't go." Fair felt like a beggar and he hated that feeling. "Give me a chance to say something. You weren't a spoiled rich brat each and every day and I wasn't a saint myself. We were kids when we married our spouses. Harry's a decent person. Kelly was a decent person. But what did we know in our early twenties? I thought love was sex and laughs. One big party. Hell, Boom Boom, I had no more idea of what I needed in a woman than ... uh, nuclear fusion."

"Fission."

"Fission's when they pop apart. Fusion's when they come together," Fair corrected her.

"I corrected you. That's a rude habit."

"Boom Boom, I can accept that you're thinking about your life but do you have to be so overpoweringly polite?"

"No."

"Anyway, I made mistakes, too, and I made them on Harry. I wonder if everyone learns by hurting other people."

"Isn't it odd? I feel that I know Kelly better now than when he was alive. I guess in some ways you feel you know Harry better now that you have some distance. You know, this is the first time we've had a heart-to-heart talk. God, is it like this for everyone? Does it take a crisis to get to the truth?"

"I don't know."

"Do we have to savage our marriages, give up the sex, before becoming friends? Why can't people be friends and lovers? I mean, are they mutually exclusive?"

"I don't know. What I know"—Fair lowered his eyes—"is that when we're together I feel something I've never felt before."

"Do you still love Harry?" Boom Boom held her breath.

"Not romantically. Right now I'm so mad at her I can't imagine being friends with her but people tell me that passes."

"She loves you."

"No, she doesn't. In her heart of hearts she knows. I hate lying to her. I know all the reasons why but when she finds out she'll hate me most for the lying."

Boom Boom sat quietly for a moment. Being female, there were many things she could say to Fair about his feelings for Harry but she'd taken enough of a risk by coming here to apologize. She wasn't going to take any more, not until she felt stronger, anyway. "I'm running the business, you know." She changed the subject.

"No, I didn't know. It will be good for you and good for the business."

"Isn't it a joke, Fair? I'm thirty-three years old and I've never had to report to work or be responsible to anyone or anything. I'm . . . I'm excited. I'm sorry it took this horror to wake me up. I wish I could have done something, made something out of myself while Kelly was alive but . . . I'm going to do it now."

"I'm happy for you."

She paused for a moment, and tears came to her eyes. "Fair"—she could barely speak—"I need you."

27

A swift afternoon thunderstorm darkened and drenched Crozet. It was a summer of storms. Harry couldn't see out to the railroad tracks during the downpour. Tucker cowered in her bed and Mrs. Murphy, herself not fond of thunder, stuck to Harry like a furry burr.

She heard a sizzle and a pop. The power had shut down, a not uncommon occurrence.

The sky was blackish green. It gave Harry the creeps. She felt under the counter for her ready supply of candles, found them, and lit a few. Then she stood by the front window and watched the deluge driven by stiff winds. Mrs. Murphy jumped onto her shoulder, so Harry reached up and brought the cat into her arms. She cuddled her like a baby, rocking her, and thought about Rick Shaw's response to the postcard—which was "Lay low."

Easier said than done. The death of two citizens must be accounted for somehow. And she felt that she had the end of a ragged thread. If she could follow that thread back, step by step, she would find the answer. She also knew she might find more than she bargained for—an answer in this case didn't mean satisfying her curiosity. Secrets are often ugly. She was peeling away the layers of the town. It might mean her own life. Rick forcefully impressed this upon her. She had been of help to him and he was grateful but she wasn't a professional so she should butt out. She wondered, too, if underneath his concern there might not be a hint of face-saving. The Sheriff's Department seemed to be running in circles. Better the citizens didn't know. She wondered, if Rick did solve the murders, whether he would get a gold star behind his name or at least a promotion. Maybe he didn't want to share the limelight.

Well, whatever, he was doing his job, and part of that job was protecting the citizens of Albemarle County and that meant her too.

A figure appeared in the swirling rain, oilskin flapping in the wind. It headed toward the post office. The hair on Harry's neck stood up. Mrs. Murphy sensed it, jumped down, and arched her back.

The door flew open and a bedraggled Bob Berryman swept in, leaves in his wake. He leaned against the door with his body close to it.

"Goddamn!" he roared. "Even nature's turned against us." He seemed unhinged.

Paralyzed by fear, Harry edged back by the counter. Bob followed her, dripping as he went. In this weather, if Harry screamed at the top of her lungs no one would hear her.

Tucker scurried out from under the counter. *"She's scared of Bob Berryman?"*

"Yes." Mrs. Murphy never took her eyes from Bob's glowering face.

"What can I do for you?" Harry squeaked.

Bob reached across the counter, pointing. "Gimme one of those registered slips. Harry, are you sick? You look . . . funny."

"Tucker, can you get out the door if I open it?" Mrs. Murphy asked. *"He stole those letters. If he's the one and he makes a move for Harry, we can attack."*

"Yeah." Tucker hurried to the door that separated the work area from the reception area.

Mrs. Murphy stretched her full length and began playing with the doorknob. This one was the right height for her. If she opened the door Harry would be on to one of her best tricks but Mrs. Murphy didn't think she had a choice. She strained and held the knob between her two paws. With a quick motion she forced the knob to the left and the door popped open.

"Smart cat," Berryman commented.

"So that's how she does it," Harry said weakly.

Tucker sauntered out, nonchalant, and sat three paces from Bob's juicy ankle. Mrs. Murphy leaped back up to the counter to watch and wait.

"The slip, Harry." Berryman's voice filled the room.

Harry pulled out a registered mail slip and filled it out as candlelight flickered and a sheet of rain lashed at the front window. She tore up the first copy and started another.

"I'll get it right," she mumbled.

Berryman reached across and held her hand. She froze. Tucker moved forward and Mrs. Murphy crept to the edge of the counter. Berryman observed the cat and looked down at the dog. Tucker's fangs were bared.

"Call off your dog."

"Let go of my hand first." Harry steadied herself.

He released her hand. Tucker sat down but continued to stare at Berryman.

"Don't be afraid of me. I didn't kill Maude. That's what you're thinking, isn't it?"

"Uh—"

"I didn't. I know it looks bad but I couldn't take any more at her funeral. Josiah's words of *wisdom*," he said bitterly, "were the straw that broke the camel's back. What does he know about men and women?!"

Harry, confused, said, "I expect he knows a great deal."

"You must be kidding. He uses Mim Sanburne to party in Palm Beach and Saratoga and New York and God knows where else."

"I didn't mean that. He's observant, and because he isn't married or involved he has more time than other people. I guess he—"

"You like him. All women like him. I can't for the life of me figure out why. Maude adored him. Said he made her laugh so hard her sides ached. He yapped about clothes and makeup and decorating. They always had their heads together. I used to tell her he was nothing but a high-class salesman but she told me to stop acting like

Joe Six-Pack—she wasn't going to give him up. She said he gave her what I couldn't and I gave her what he couldn't." Bob's lips compressed. "I hate that silly faggot."

"Don't call him a faggot," Harry admonished. "I don't care who he sleeps with or who he doesn't. You're mad at him because he was close to Maude. He made you jealous."

"So the cat's out of the bag." He sighed. "I don't care anymore. You want to know why I hit him? Really? He came over and told me to pull myself together. 'Think of your wife,' he said. I was afraid that Maude had told him about us, and then I knew she had. Damn him! Coming over and oozing concern. He didn't want Linda to go into a huff and ruin his orchestrated funeral. He didn't care about Maude."

"Of course he did. He paid for much of it."

"We all paid for the funeral. He wants to look good so he can take over her store. He and Maude talked business as much as they talked mascara. He knows what a moneymaker it is. I—well, I don't care about the business. Okay, it's out in the open. I loved Maude. She's dead and I'd give anything to have her back." He paused. "I'm leaving Linda. She can have the house, the car, everything. I'm keeping my business. I'm alone but at least I'm not living a lie." This admission calmed him. "I didn't kill Maude. I wouldn't have harmed a hair on her head."

"I'm so sorry, Bob."

"So am I." He handed over the envelope to be sent to the IRS. "Rain slacked off." Realizing what he'd said, he was embarrassed. He hesitated a minute before leaving.

Harry understood. "I'll keep my mouth shut."

"You can tell anyone you like. I apologize for fulminating. I'm not sorry for what I told you. I'm sorry for how I told you. You don't need to put up with that. I'm so up and down. I—I don't know myself. I mean, I go up and down." This was the only way he could describe his mood swings.

"Under the circumstances, I think that's natural."

"I don't know. I feel crazy sometimes."

"It will even out. Be easier on yourself."

He smiled a tight smile, said, "Yeah," and then left.

Harry, exhausted from the encounter, sat with a thud. Tucker walked back to her.

"So the letters were love letters," Mrs. Murphy thought out loud.

"Probably, but we don't know," Tucker replied. "Anyway, he could have killed her in a lovers' quarrel. Humans do that. I overheard on the TV that four hundred and thirty-five Americans are killed each day. I think that's what the newscaster said. They'll kill over anything."

"I know, but I don't think he killed her. I think he told Harry the truth."

"What are you meowing about, kitty cat? Now I'm on to your tricks. You've been opening doors all along, haven't you? You little sneak." Harry stroked Tucker's ears while Mrs. Murphy rubbed against her legs. Vitality seeped back into her limbs, which felt so heavy with fear when Bob first came into the post office. She hoped the rest of the day would pick up. But unfortunately, Harry's day went from bad to worse.

Mrs. Hogendobber drove up in her Falcon. She opened an umbrella against the rain. Mrs. H. saw no reason to trade in a useful automobile, and the interest rates on car loans were usury as far as she was concerned. Although once a month she drove over to Brady-Bushey Ford to allow Art Bushey the opportunity to sell her a new car, Art knew she had no intention of buying anything. She swooned over him, and being gallant, he took her to lunch each time she careened onto the lot.

"Harry! I made a mistake, a tiny mistake, but I thought you ought to know. I should have told you before now but I didn't think about it. I just ... didn't. After you left the party or whatever you want to call it at Josiah's, I stayed on. Mim and I were commenting on the state of today's morals. Then Mim mentioned that you had encouraged Little Marilyn to contact Stafford in New York. I spoke about forgiveness and she haughtily told me she didn't need a sermon, she attended Saint Paul's for that, and I said that forgiveness extended through the other six days of the week as well."

"I'm sorry you got on the bad side of her." Harry leaned on the counter.

"No, no, that's not it. You see, then Josiah mentioned that the government, the federal government, has never forgiven the draft evaders, not really, and Ned, who arrived after you left—quite drawn-looking, too, I must say—well, Ned laughed and said the IRS never forgives anyone. The power to tax is the power to destroy, and I said maybe it was just as well that Maude was dead because they'd catch up with her sooner or later."

"Oh, no!" Harry exclaimed.

"Conversation ran to other topics and I didn't think about it until now."

"Why now?"

"I don't know exactly. The rain made me remember all that water in Mim's boat. What if—what if Mim wasn't the killer's target? After all, Mim can swim."

"I see." Harry rubbed her temples. This felt worse than a head-ache.

The entire town knew about Mim's slashed pontoon because the workers Jim used to lift the boat onto his truck saw the damage. By now everyone was jumping to conclusions, so the gossip all over town was that Mim was the intended victim.

Mrs. Hogendobber breathed in sharply. "What do I do now?"

"If anyone brings up your slip—you know, asks a leading ques-tion about Maude and the IRS—pick up the phone and call me. Better yet, call Rick Shaw."

"Oh, dear."

"Mrs. H., you must trust me. The killer gives a signal before he strikes—I can't tell you what it is. He gives warning, which makes me wonder if the slashed pontoon was really aimed at you."

"Do you think he'll kill me? Is that what you're saying?" Her voice was quite calm.

"I hope not."

"If I tell Rick Shaw he'll know what we've done."

"I think we'd better tell him. What's he going to do? Arrest us?

Listen to me. You have absolutely got to remember who was there after I left."

"Myself, Mim, Little Marilyn, Jim, old Dr. Johnson, and Ned. That reminds me, what is going on with Ned and Susan? Oh, Susan was there, of course."

"Just remember the names and I'll tell you about Ned."

This encouraged her. "U-m-m, Fair and Josiah—well, that's obvious."

"No, nothing is obvious. Are you certain there wasn't anyone else? What about Market? What about any of the kids?"

"No, Market wasn't there, nor Courtney."

"This isn't good."

Mrs. Hogendobber put her back to the wall for support. She wiped her brow. "I'm not used to not trusting people. I feel horrible."

Harry's voice softened. "None of us is used to that. You can't be expected to change a behavior overnight—and maybe it's better that you don't. Except until we catch this killer, well, we're going to have to be on our toes. Why don't you have Larry's wife stay with you tonight, or better yet, go over there."

"Do you think it's that bad?"

"No," Harry lied. "But why take chances?"

"You believe that Maude and Kelly were shipping out dope, don't you? I do. They had to be in business together. So who's the kingpin?"

"Some sweet Crozet person we play tennis with or go to church with. A woman or a man we've known for years."

"Why?" Mrs. Hogendobber might preach about evil, but when confronted with it she was at a loss. She expected the Devil with green horns or a human being with a snarling face. It had never once occurred to her in her long and relatively happy life that evil is ordinary.

Harry shrugged in answer to Mrs. Hogendobber's question. "Love or money."

After Mrs. Hogendobber drove off, Harry returned to work with renewed vigor. Since she felt helpless about Mrs. Hogendobber, she could feel purposeful in cleaning the office. She could get one thing to work right in her life.

Then Fair walked into the post office.

"I tried to be a good husband—you know that, don't you?" Fair cleared his throat.

"Yes." Harry held her breath.

"We never discussed what we expected from each other. Perhaps we should have."

"What's wrong? Come out and say it. Just come out with it, for chrissake." Harry reached out to touch him and stopped herself.

Fair stammered, "Nothing's wrong. We made our mistakes. I just wanted to say that."

He left. He wanted to tell her about Boom Boom. The truth. He tried. He couldn't.

Harry wondered, Was he mixed up in these murders? He was acting so strange. It couldn't be. No way.

28

Mrs. Hogendobber's fears were justified. Rick Shaw seethed when Harry and Mrs. Hogendobber confessed about Xeroxing the second ledger.

By the time Harry got home she decided if this wasn't the worst day in her life, it certainly qualified as so bad she didn't want it repeated.

She called Susan, telling her about Fair's peculiar behavior. Susan declared that Fair was in the grief stage of the divorce. Harry asked her to come to the post office in the morning for a long coffee break. After she hung up she decided she'd tell Susan about the bug postcard she had received. She needed Susan's response. Anyway, if she couldn't trust her best friend, life wasn't worth living.

29

Tucker chewed a big knucklebone behind the meat counter. Market Shiflett, in a generous mood, gave her a fresh one. Mrs. Murphy and Pewter received smaller beef bones. They happily gnawed away while catching up on recent events. Ozzie, Bob Berryman's Australian shepherd, had been down at the mouth. Pewter claimed he hardly wagged his tail and barked. Mim Sanburne's snotty Afghan hound had lost his testicles yesterday. The animal news, usually rich in the summer, lagged behind the human news this year.

Tucker recounted Rick Shaw's livid explosion. Poor Mrs. Hogendobber thought she was going to jail.

Courtney paid scant attention to these three animals cracking bones and talking among themselves. Her large hoop earrings clattered.

"When did Courtney start dressing like a gypsy?" Mrs. Murphy, conservative about attire, wanted to know.

"She's trying to attract Danny Tucker's attention. He'll be mowing Maude Bly Modena's lawn today. He'll hear her before he sees her." Pewter had eaten so much she lay down on one side and rested her head on her outstretched arm.

"Guess you heard what he did?"

"Mrs. Murphy told me yesterday while you were out doing potty, as Harry calls it." Pewter laughed. "I don't mind Harry's expressions so much except when she tells you to go potty her voice rises half an octave. Say, not only is

Courtney sticking big hoops in her ears but last night when Market was out she made herself a martini. She wants to be sophisticated and she thought drinking a martini would do it. Ha! Tastes like lighter fluid.''

"She's young." Mrs. Murphy tore off a slender thread of red meat.

"Tell me about it. Human beings take forty years to grow up and half of them don't do it then. We're ready for the world at six months."

"We're not really grown up though, Pewter." Mrs. Murphy licked her chops. "I'd say we're fully adult at one year. I wonder, why does it take them so long?"

"Retarded," came Pewter's swift reply. "I mean, will you look at Courtney Shiflett. If she were a child of mine those earrings would be out of those ears so fast she wouldn't know what hit her."

"At least she works. Think of all those humans who don't even earn a living until their middle twenties. She works after school and she works in the summer. She's a good kid." Mrs. Murphy thought most humans lazy, the young ones especially.

"If you like her so much, you live with her. If I hear her George Michael tape one more time, I'm going to shred it with these very claws." She flashed her impressive talons. "Furthermore, the girl will make herself deaf—and me, too —if she doesn't turn down that boom box. Sometimes I think I'll walk out the door and never come back—live on field mice."

"You're too fat to catch mice," Mrs. Murphy taunted her.

"I'll have you know that I caught one last week. I gave it to Market and he went 'O-o-o.' He could have thanked me."

"They don't like mice." Tucker slurped at her bone.

"Try giving them a bird." Mrs. Murphy rolled her eyes. "The worst. Harry hollers and then buries the bird. She likes the moles and mice I bring her. I break their necks clean. No blood, no fuss. A neat job, if I do say so myself."

Pewter burped. "Excuse me. A neat job ... Mrs. Murphy, the human murders were messy," she thought out loud.

"Why?" Tucker sat up but put her paw on her bone just in case. Pewter was known to steal food. "It's not efficient to kill a person that way. Throw one in a cement mixer and tie another one to the railroad track. Originally, it was a neat job. After they were dead the killer ground them into hamburger."

Pewter lifted her head. "*The killer's not a vegetarian.*" Then she dropped her head back and laughed.

Mrs. Murphy pushed Pewter with her paw. "*Very funny.*"

"*I thought so.*"

Tucker said, "*The police aren't revealing how Kelly and Maude died—if they know. The mess has to be to cover up something inside the bodies or to divert us from what the people were doing before they died.*"

"*That's right, Tucker.*" Mrs. Murphy got excited. "*What were they doing in the middle of the night? Kelly was at the concrete plant. Working? Maybe. And Maude willingly went out to the railroad tracks west of town. Humans sleep at night. If they were awake it had to be important, or*"—she paused—"*it had to be something they were used to doing.*"

30

"Mrs. Murphy and Tucker are at the back door." Susan interrupted Harry, who was sorting the mail and telling all simultaneously.

"Will you let them in?"

Susan opened the back door and the two friends raced through, meowing and barking. "They're glad to see you."

"And in a good mood too. Market handed out bones today."

"*We think we've got part of the puzzle,*" Mrs. Murphy announced.

"*They were in cahoots, Kelly and Maude, with something—*" Tucker shouted.

"*In the nighttime when no one could see,*" Mrs. Murphy interrupted.

"All right, girls, calm down." Harry smiled and petted them.

Mrs. Murphy, discouraged, hopped into the mail bin. "*I give up! She's so dense.*"

Tucker replied, "*Find another way to tell her.*"

Mrs. Murphy stuck her head over the bin. "*Let's go outside.*" She jumped out.

Tucker and the cat dashed to the back door. Tucker barked and whined a little.

"Don't tell me you have to go to the bathroom. You just came in," Harry chided.

Tucker barked some more. "*What are we going to do when we get out?*"

"*I don't know, yet.*"

Harry, exasperated, opened the door and Tucker nearly knocked her over.

"Corgis are a lot faster than you think," Susan observed.

After replaying yesterday's conversation with Fair one more time, both Susan and Harry were depressed. Harry shook out the last mailbag, three-quarters full. Susan made a beeline for the postcards. They both held their breath. A series of Italian postcards scared them but there were no graveyards on the front, and when turned over they revealed a number in the right-hand corner and the signature of their traveling friend, Lindsay Astrove. They exhaled simultaneously.

"I'll read you Lindsay's cards while you finish stuffing the mailboxes." Susan sat on a stool, crossed her legs, put the postcards in order, and began.

" 'Being abroad is not what it's cracked up to be. I took a train across the Alps and when it pulled into Venice my heart stopped. It was beautiful. From there, everything went downhill.

" 'The Venetians are about as rude as anyone could imagine. They live to take the tourists for all they can. No one smiles, not even at each other. However, I was determined to transcend these mortal coils, so to speak, and drink in the beauty of the place. Blistered and exhausted, I tramped from place to place, seeing the Lord in painting after painting. I saw Jesus on the cross, off the cross, in a robe, in a loincloth, with nails, without nails, bleeding, not bleeding, hair up, hair down. You name it. I saw it. Along with the paintings were various other art forms of the Lord and his closest friends and family.

" 'Naturally, there were many, many, many pieces of the Virgin Mother. (A slight contradiction in terms.) In all of Venice, however, I was not able to find a snapshot of Joseph and the donkey. I could only conclude that they are ashamed of his stupidity for believing Mary's story about her and God and the conception thing and they only bring him out for Christmas.

" 'I did arrive at one possible conclusion. Since all of this artwork looks exactly alike, maybe one man is to blame. I find it plausible that one man did all of it and used many names. Or maybe all the little Italian boys born between 1300 and 1799, if their last name ended in "i" or "o," were given a paint-by-number kit. I am sure there is a logical explanation for all this.

" 'One closing thought and I will move on to my visit to Rome. I am grateful that Jesus was Italian and not Spanish. All of that art would have been Day-Glo on velvet instead of oil on canvas.

" 'On to Rome—the Infernal City.

" 'Rome combines the worst of New York and Los Angeles. The one thing the Romans do well is blow their horns. The noisiest city in the world. The Romans rival the Venetians for rudeness. The food in both cities is not nearly as good as the worst Italian restaurant in San Francisco.

" 'As you can probably guess, I got to go to the Vatican Museums. I also got to leave the Vatican Museums because I proclaimed in an audible voice that it is just disgusting to see the wealth the church is hoarding. On the interest alone, they could cure cancer, AIDS, hunger, and homelessness in less than a year. All of a sudden the people who did not speak English were fluent in the language. I was ushered out. I didn't even get to see the Pope in his satin dresses.

" 'The rest of Rome was no big deal either. The Colosseum was in shambles, the Spanish steps were littered with addicts and drunks, and the Trevi fountain was like any cruise bar.

" 'The designer shops were a delight. A designer outfit is one that does not fit, does not match, and does not cost less than your permanent residence. Did not shop in that city.

" 'I left Rome wondering why the Visigoths bothered to conquer it. However, Monaco was fabulous. The people, the food, the attitude, the absence of Renaissance culture!

" 'I'll see you all in September when I will have soaked up about as much of the Old World as I can possibly stand. I'm beginning to think that Mim, Little Marilyn, Josiah, and company are gilded sheep to rave on about Europe, furniture, and a face-lift in Switzerland. Oh, well, as you know, I think Mim impersonates the human condition. And don't show this to Mrs. Hogendobber! Do show Susan.

" 'Love, Lindsay' "

Susan and Harry laughed until tears rolled down their cheeks. Once they finally got hold of themselves they realized they hadn't laughed, true laughter, since Kelly's murder. Stress was exacting its toll.

"How many postcards did that take?"

Susan shuffled them like playing cards. "Twenty-one."

"Who are they addressed to?"

"You. You're the only one she could write this to."

Harry smiled and took the postcards. "I'll be glad when Lindsay comes home. Maybe this will be over by September."

"I hope so."

"*Shred it up, like this.*" Mrs. Murphy ripped into the sparrow corpse, and feathers flew everywhere. A squeamish expression passed over Tucker's pretty face. "*Oh, come on, Welsh corgis are supposed to be tough as nails. Tear that mole I caught into three pieces.*"

"*She's going to hate this.*"

"*So she hates it. Our message might sink in subliminally.*"

"*She's smart for a person. She knows there's a connection between Kelly and Maude.*"

"*Tucker, stop shilly-shallying. I want her to know we know. Maybe she'll start to listen to us for a change.*"

Tucker, with singular lack of enthusiam, tore the still-warm mole into three pieces. If that wasn't bad enough, Mrs. Murphy made her carry the hunks to the back door of the post office.

The cat reared up on her hind legs and beat on the door. A soft rattle echoed in the post office.

Harry opened the door. Neither animal budged. Instead they sat next to their kill, carefully placed together by Mrs. Murphy.

"How revolting," Harry exclaimed.

"*I told you she'd hate it,*" Tucker snapped to the tiger cat.

"*That's not the point.*"

"What?" Susan called out.

"The cat and dog brought back the remains of a mole and what must have been a bird only a short time ago." Harry peered for a closer look. "Ugh. The mole's in three pieces."

Susan stuck her head out the back door. "Like Maude."

"That's horrible. How could you say that?"

"Well—it's not hard to think of those things." Susan petted Tucker on the head. "Anyway, they're doing what comes naturally and they brought these pathetic corpses back to you as a present. You should be properly grateful."

"I'll be properly grateful after I clean them up."

Whether or not the bird and mole corpses inspired Harry, the animals couldn't say, but she did drive her blue truck to Kelly's concrete plant, leaving them outside while she went in for a chat.

After delicately dancing around the subject in Kelly's office, now taken over by his wife, Harry felt the time was right. She quietly leaned toward Boom Boom and asked, "Did Kelly ever do business with Maude?"

A wave of relief swept over the sultry woman's features. "Oh—sure. She packed up his Christmas business mailing for him. Is that what you mean?"

"No." Harry noticed the photos of Kelly with the county commissioners, the president of the University of Virginia, the state representatives. "What about business on a larger scale?"

"There's no record of it." Just to make certain, Boom Boom jangled Marie on the intercom and Marie confirmed the negative.

"What about a more intimate connection?" Harry whispered, and waited for the reaction.

Extramarital sex, shocking to many, barely dented Boom Boom's psyche. She expected it, even from her husband. "No. Maude wasn't Kelly's type, although she seems to have been Bob Berryman's."

"All over town?" Harry asked, knowing it was.

"Linda's given to fainting spells. Next come the faith healers, I guess. Hard to believe either Linda or Maude loved him, but then you really never know, do you?" Her long eyelashes, which reached into next week, fluttered for an instant.

"No."

Boom Boom's face flushed. "Kelly wasn't a saint and our marriage was far from perfect. If he strayed off the reservation, so to speak, he'd never have done it close to home. What do you think? You obviously believe something was going on between my husband and Maude."

"I don't know. My hunch is they were in business together. Illegal."

Boom Boom stiffened slightly. "He made tons of money legally."

"Kelly loved to screw the system. An enormous untaxable profit would have been a siren call to his rebellious self—if they were shipping drugs, I mean."

Realistic about Kelly, Boom Boom hesitated. It was not as if the thought hadn't occurred to her once or twice since his murder. "I don't know, but I sure hope you keep these thoughts to yourself. He's dead. Don't go about ruining his name."

"I won't, but I have to get to the bottom of this. Do you think Kelly's murder and Maude's murder are connected?"

"Well, at first I didn't think, period. The shock left me empty, and into the emptiness rushed anger. I just want to kill this son of a bitch. Barehanded." She put her hands together in a choking motion. "As the days have gone by—seems like years, in a funny way—I go over it and over it. I don't know why but yes, I believe they are connected."

"Shipping something—that's what I come up with no matter how I examine this."

"Contrary to what the public has been told by government types, drugs are easy to ship. It's possible. God knows they're also easy to hide. They don't take up that much space. You could cram two million dollars' worth of cocaine into these desk drawers."

"Whatever they did, they fell afoul of a partner or partners." Harry said this, realizing as the words were out of her mouth that Boom Boom could be one of those partners. She'd be committed to profit, but Harry couldn't imagine Boom Boom at her hardest doing business with Kelly's killer.

"If you find out, Mary Minor Haristeen, tell me twenty minutes before you tell Rick Shaw. I'll pay you ten thousand dollars for that information."

Harry choked. Ten thousand dollars. God, how she needed it.

A silence wrapped around them, an air of static antagonism. Boom Boom broke it: "Think it over."

Harry swallowed. "I will." She paused. "Why do I feel like you're holding out on me?"

Boom Boom's face became suddenly still. "I'm telling you everything I know about Kelly. If he had a secret, then he kept it from me too."

"What about Fair?" Harry's lips were white.

"I don't know what you mean." Boom Boom's eyes darted around the room. "Did you come here looking for clues about Kelly or clues about Fair? I mean, you threw him out, Harry. What do you care what he does?"

"I'll always care what he does. I just can't live with him." Harry's face flushed. "He just wasn't . . . there."

"What do you mean?"

"He wasn't there emotionally." She sighed. "It's one thing to lose your marriage, but it's just as bad to lose your friends. Everyone's taking sides."

"What did you expect?" No sympathy from Boom Boom.

That put the match to the tinderbox. "More of you!" Harry clenched her teeth. "He and Kelly were never the same after Fair made that pass at you, but we stayed friends."

"That was last year. Everyone was drunk! Look, Harry, people don't want to look at themselves. Let me give you some advice about Crozet."

Harry interrupted. "I've lived here all my life. What do you know that I don't?"

"That divorce frightens people. From the outside your marriage seemed fine. People want to accept appearances. Now you've gone and upset the apple cart. You might be looking inside yourself but no one in these parts will give you credit for it. This is Albemarle County. No change. Keep everything the same. You stay the same.

To change is viewed as an admission of guilt. Hell, people would rather live in their familiar misery than take a chance to change it."

Harry had never weathered blunt truth from Boom Boom before. She opened her mouth but nothing came out. Finally she found her voice. "I can see you've been doing a lot of thinking."

"Yes. I have."

The discussion had magnified tension instead of dispelling it.

As Harry drove home she noticed the late afternoon shadows seemed longer. A sense of menace began to haunt her.

She kept to her routine, as did everyone else. At first the routine cushioned the shock of the murders, as well as her separation, but now she felt off balance, the routine a charade. The macabre killings, the reality of them, began to sink in.

She touched down on the accelerator but she couldn't outrun the shadows of the setting sun.

31

" 'Wish you were here.' " Harry's hands shook as she read the post-card addressed to Mrs. George Hogendobber. The front of the postcard was a beautiful glossy photograph of Pushkin's grave. Another carefully faked postmark covered the upper right-hand corner.

Harry called Rick Shaw but he wasn't in the office. "Well, get him!" she yelled at the receptionist. Next she depressed the button and dialed Mrs. Hogendobber.

"Hello."

Harry never thought she would be thrilled to hear that hearty voice. "Mrs. Hogendobber, are you all right?"

"You call me first thing in the morning to see if I'm all right? I'll be over there in fifteen minutes."

"Let me walk over for you." Harry fought for a deep breath.

"What? Mary Minor Haristeen, I've been walking to the post office since before you were born."

"Please do as I say, Mrs. H. Go out on your front porch so that everyone can see you. I'll be there in one minute flat. Just do it, please." She hung up the phone and flew out the door, Tucker and Mrs. Murphy at her heels.

Mrs. Hogendobber was rocking in her swing, a perplexed Mrs. Hogendobber, an irritated Mrs. Hogendobber, but an alive Mrs. Hogendobber.

Harry burst into tears at the sight of her. "Thank God!"

"What in the world is wrong with you, girl? You need an Alka-Seltzer."

"You must get out of here. Get out of Crozet. What about your sister in Greenville, South Carolina?"

"It's just as hot there as it is here."

"What about your nephew in Atlanta?"

"Atlanta is worse than Greenville. I'm not going anywhere. Are you suffering from heat stroke? Maybe you're overworked. Why don't we go inside and pray together? You'll soon feel the hand of the Lord on your shoulder."

"I sincerely hope so but you're coming with me to the post office and you aren't leaving until Rick Shaw gets there."

Tucker licked Mrs. Hogendobber's ankles. Mrs. Hogendobber shooed her away, but Tucker returned. Finally, Mrs. Hogendobber let her lick. She was sweaty already on this blistering morning. What were wet ankles?

"Are you going to tell me what's going on here?"

"Yes. Each murder victim received an unsigned postcard. The handwriting was in computer script. It looks like real handwriting but it isn't. Anyway, on the face of each postcard was a photograph of a famous graveyard. The message read, 'Wish you were here.' You received one this morning."

Mrs. Hogendobber's hand fluttered to her ponderous bosom. "Me?"

Harry nodded. "You."

"What did I do? I've never even seen a marijuana cigarette, much less sold dope."

"Oh, Mrs. H. I don't know if this has anything to do with drugs or not but the killer knows you've seen the second set of books. At Josiah's gathering."

Mrs. Hogendobber's eyes narrowed. She might lack a sense of humor but she didn't lack a quick mind. "Ah, so it isn't just the IRS Maude was cheating. That ledger is an account of her turnover with whomever her partner was." She placed her hands on either side of the hanging swing. "Someone at Josiah's party. It's preposterous!"

"Yes—but it's real. You're in danger."

With great composure Mrs. Hogendobber rose and accompanied Harry back to the post office. She recovered sufficiently to say, "I always knew that you read the postcards, Harry."

When Rick Shaw arrived with Officer Cooper, he herded everyone into the back room.

"Harry, you act normal. If you hear anyone, go on out and talk to them." He studied the postcard.

"What about prints?" Officer Cooper asked.

"I'll send them to the lab. But the killer's smart. No prints. Not on the postcards. Not on the bodies. No nothing. This guy—or gal—must be invisible. We're checking with the computer companies in town to see if there's anything distinguishable in the script. Unfortunately, computers aren't like typewriters, which can be traced. A letter from a typewriter is almost like a fingerprint. Electronic printing is, well, homogenized. We're trying, but we're not hopeful on that front."

Officer Cooper watched Mrs. Murphy try to squeeze into a Kleenex box on the shelf.

"He's sporting, too. He gives us a warning even if the victims don't know it's a warning," Harry said.

"I hate the kind that put on finishing touches." Rick grimaced. "Give me a good old domestic murder any day." He swiveled his chair, facing Mrs. Hogendobber. "You're getting out of Dodge, ma'am."

"I'm prepared to accept what God has in store for me." Her chin jutted out. "I was prepared to drown on Mim's lake. This isn't any different."

"The Lord moves in mysterious ways, but I don't," Rick countered. "You can visit a relative and we'll make certain you arrive there safe and sound. We'll alert the authorities there to keep a close watch over your welfare and we won't inform anyone of your whereabouts. If you won't leave town, then we'll put you in jail. We'll treat you well, but, my dear Mrs. Hogendobber, you are not going to be the third victim of this cold, calculating murderer. Am I understood?"

"Yes." Mrs. Hogendobber's reply was not meek.

"Fine. You and Officer Cooper go home and pack. You can decide what you want to do, and tell no one but me."

"Not even Harry?"

"Not even Harry."

Mrs. Hogendobber reached over and squeezed Harry's hand. "Don't you worry about me. You'll be in my prayers."

"Thank you." Harry was touched. "You'll be in mine."

After Mrs. Hogendobber and Officer Cooper left through the back door, Harry crumpled a mailbag.

"He'll know that I know and that you know," the sheriff said. "He won't know if anyone else knows. Does anyone else know?"

"Susan Tucker."

Rick's eyebrows clashed together. "Oh, dammit to hell, Harry. Can't you keep your mouth shut about anything?!"

"She's my best friend. Besides, if anything happens to me I want someone to know at least as much as I did."

"How do you know Susan isn't the killer?"

"Never. Never. Never. She's my best friend."

"Your best friend. Harry, women who have been married to men for twenty years find out they've got another wife in another city. Or children grow up and find out that their sweet daddy was a Nazi war criminal who escaped to the United States. People are not what they seem and this killer appears normal, well-adjusted, and hey, one of the gang. He or she *is* one of the gang. Susan is under suspicion as much as anyone else. And what about Fair? He's got medical knowledge. Doctors make clever killers."

"Susan and Fair just wouldn't, that's all."

Rick exhaled through his nostrils. "I admire your faith in your friends. If it isn't justified you've got a good chance of meeting your Maker." He picked up a pencil and tapped it against his cheek. "Do you think Susan told Ned?"

"No."

"Wives usually talk to their husbands and vice versa."

"She gave me her word and I've known her far longer than Ned has. She won't tell."

"So it's only you and Susan and Mrs. Hogendobber who know the postcard signal?"

"Yes."

He kept tapping. "We're a small force but I'll assign Officer Cooper to guard you. She'll stay here in the post office and she'll go home with you too. For a couple of days, at least."

"Is that necessary?"

"Very necessary. Within twelve hours, max, the killer will know that Mrs. Hogendobber left town and he'll figure out the rest. She won't show up for her Ruth Circle at church. They'll ask questions. I'll have her make some calls from the station. She can say that her sister's taken ill and she's hurrying to Greenville. Whatever location she gives out won't be true, of course. But Mrs. Hogendobber's cover won't fool the killer, any more than Mim's exchange students are fooling anyone. Her departure is too abrupt and Mrs. Hogendobber talks for days if she's going into Charlottesville. For an emergency trip out of state, she'd take an ad out in the *Daily Progress*. See, that's what's tough about this one—he or she knows everyone's habits, foibles, routines. If he can't get to Mrs. H., I'm not sure what he'll do next. He might turn on you or he might get nervous and make a mistake. A tiny one but something we can use."

"I hope it's the latter and not the former."

"Me, too, but I'm not taking any chances."

Mrs. Murphy and Tucker drank in every word. If Harry was in danger, there was no time to lose.

32

Officer Cooper's presence at the post office electrified everyone. Mim, Little Marilyn, and the bodyguard stopped at the sight of her.

Little Marilyn hovered at her mother's elbow, as did the daytime female bodyguard, who could have used a shave.

"Uh, Harry, I've been meaning to talk to you about the Cancer Ball this year." Little Marilyn bit her lip as Mim watched.

Harry had served on the committee every year for the last six years. "Yes."

"Given that you're divorcing, well, it just won't do for you to be on the committee." Little Marilyn at least had the guts to tell her face-to-face.

"What?" Harry couldn't believe this—it was too silly and too painful.

Mim backed up her daughter. "We can't have you on the program. Think what it would do to dear, sweet Mignon Haristeen."

Mignon Haristeen, Fair's mother, was also in the Social Register and therefore important to Mim.

"She's living in Hobe Sound, for Christ's sake," Harry exploded. "I don't think she much cares what we do in Crozet."

"Really, have you no sense of propriety?" Mim sounded like a schoolmarm.

"Who the hell are you two to bump me off the Cancer Ball?" Harry seethed. "Mim, you're in a poisonous marriage. You sold out cheap. I don't care if Jim has umpteen million dollars. You can't stand him. What's umpteen million dollars compared to your emotional health, your soul?"

Mim roared back: "I came to the marriage with my own money."

In saying that, she said it all. Her life was about money. Love had nothing to do with it.

She slammed the door, leaving Little Marilyn and the bodyguard running to catch up.

Bad enough that Harry had lost her temper, she had criticized Mim in front of Officer Cooper.

Mim, entombed as she was in the white sepulcher of her impeccable lineage, was jarred by a person of low degree, Harry. Oh, she'd made allowances for Harry. After all, Fair had little money but the Haristeens had bloodlines. They'd once had money but lost it in the War Between the States. Never bounced back financially, but then that was the story of the South. It took vulgarians like Jim to make money again.

Mim about ripped the door off her Volvo. She was calling Mignon Haristeen the second she got home.

Courtney breezed in as Mim blew out. "Hey, what's the matter with her?"

"Change of life," Harry said.

Officer Cooper laughed. Courtney didn't get it. She banged open the postal box.

"Courtney, be careful. You'll twist the hinges if you keep that up."

"I'm sorry, Mrs. Haristeen. Officer Cooper, what are you doing here?"

"Guarding your post box from fraud and bent hinges."

Mrs. Murphy stuck her paw in the opened box from the inside. She could reach most of the boxes if the mail cart was underneath, which it was. Courtney touched her paw. Mrs. Murphy had performed this trick for Mrs. Hogendobber, who screamed when she saw the hairy little paw. Here she was, brave about her nasty postcard but scared of a cat's paw. Well, she wasn't used to animals. Mrs. Murphy thought about that as Courtney played with her.

Danny Tucker opened the door and carefully closed it, a change from his usual slam bang. Ever since the credit-card episode, he had walked on eggshells.

"Hello, Harry, Officer Cooper." He glanced at Courtney. "Hello, Courtney."

"Hello, Danny." Courtney shut the box, thereby depriving Mrs. Murphy of a great deal of satisfaction.

Danny leaned over the counter. "Mom says you should come over for supper tonight," he told Harry. "Dad's staying over in Richmond."

"Thank you. Officer Cooper will accompany me."

"You in trouble?" Danny half hoped Harry was, so he wouldn't be the only person with a black cloud hanging over his head.

"No."

"Terminal speeding tickets," Officer Cooper said laconically.

"You?" Danny exclaimed. "That old truck can't do but fifty full-out."

"The condition of my truck is much to be lamented but the condition of my bank account is even sorrier. Hence the truck. And I do not have a speeding ticket. Not even one."

"Why don't you drop a new engine in it or a rebuilt engine? My buddy Alex Baumgartner—he can do anything with an engine. Cheap, too."

"I'll give it my bright regard." Harry smiled. "And tell your mom we'll be over about six-thirty. Is that all right with you, Coop?"

"Great." Officer Cynthia Cooper lived alone. A home-cooked meal would be a little bit of heaven.

Danny's eyes twinkled. He wanted to appear suave but he still resembled the fourteen-year-old he in fact was. "Courtney, you come too."

"I thought you were grounded." Why seem eager?

"I am but you can visit me. It's only for supper, and Mom thinks you're a good influence." He laughed.

"You can ride in the squad car with us," Officer Cooper offered.

"Let me ask Daddy." She rushed out and was back within seconds. "He said it's okay."

Josiah came in. "I heard you were being watched, and I was nearly run over by Mim, Little Marilyn, and that bodyguard. Hello, kids." He noticed Courtney and Danny.

"Hello, Mr. DeWitt." They left the post office to talk outside.

Josiah's lower lip protruded; he pretended to be serious. "I vouch for the character of this woman. Pure as the driven snow. Clean as mountain water. Honest as Abe Lincoln. If only we could corrupt her."

"Try harder." Harry smiled.

He got his mail and yelled around the corner: "Is there anything I can do to relieve you of Officer Cooper's presence? Not that we don't think you're wonderful, Officer Cooper, but you'll ruin the poor girl's sex life."

"What sex life?" Harry said.

"My point exactly." Josiah returned to the counter. His tone was more serious. "Are you all right?"

"I'm fine."

"I'll take your word for it then." He hesitated, lowered his eyes, then raised them. "Any word from Stafford?"

"Not that I know of, and Mim let me know I wasn't winning any personality contest, but then she isn't winning one with me either, the stuck-up bitch."

Josiah's eyes opened wider. He'd rarely seen Harry angry. "She exhausted every adjective in describing to me her feelings about 'the Stafford episode,' as she calls it. Mim and I have an understanding of sorts. She doesn't meddle in my personal life and I don't meddle in hers, but she's quite wrong about this. Of course, just why Little Marilyn selected Fitz-Gilbert remains a mystery. Any quieter and the man would be in a coma."

"When's he going to show his face?" Harry inquired.

"Mama plans a small 'do' at Farmington Country Club but she keeps moving the date. She's more rattled than she lets on about . . . things."

"Aren't we all?" Harry pushed around the rubber-stamp holder.

He smoothed his salt-and-pepper hair. "Yes—but I prefer not to think about it. I can't do anything about it anyway."

Mrs. Murphy, ear cocked to catch mouse sounds, prowled in the barn. It had been a long day at the post office. When they arrived home Mrs. Murphy hurried toward the barn, accompanied by Tucker. High in the hayloft she caught sight of a black tail hanging over the side of a bale. She climbed up the ladder to the loft. "Paddy?"

He opened one golden eye. "You gorgeous thing. I've been waiting for you. It's a good thing you woke me up or I would have slept right through until tonight." He stretched. "I remembered our brief conversation under a full moon and a canopy of stars. . . ."

She twitched her tail. His flowery speech made her impatient. He continued.

"And spurned though I was, your words were engraved on my heart. I saw something odd. I didn't think about it at the time and I wish I had, because I would have investigated, but my blood was up and you know how that is."

"What?" Mrs. Murphy's ears pitched forward; her whiskers swept forward. Every muscle was on alert.

"I was hunting out near the old Greenwood tunnel. A rabbit shot out of the tunnel and I chased him clear down to the Purcell McCue estate. That damned golden retriever of theirs lumbered out, mouth running, and I lost my rabbit."

"Go up a tree?"

"Me? That toothless old hound. No, I dashed right in front of his nose and walked on home. Then I remembered what you said and I came here."

"The tunnel's sealed."

"But I saw the rabbit come out of it."

"Do you remember exactly where?"

"He moved pretty fast but I think it was near the bottom. It's covered with foliage. Hard to see."

"How do you know he wasn't hiding in the foliage and you flushed him out?"

"I don't, but I swear I saw him pop out of a hole at the very bottom. Can't be sure but, well—I thought you'd like to know."

"Thanks, Paddy. I don't know how I can make it up to you."

"I do."

"Not that way." Mrs. Murphy cuffed his ears. "Come on, let's tell Tucker."

The two cats joined Tucker. Conversation grew excited.

"We've got to get up there!" Tucker shouted above the voices. "That's the only way we'll ever know."

"I know we've got to get up there but it's a good day's journey, and we can't leave Harry now that she's in danger." Mrs. Murphy spat, she was so vehement.

"How are you going to convince her to go up there in the first place?" The human race didn't rank high in Paddy's book.

"Harry catches on if you keep after her." Tucker defended her friend.

"If we can just think of something—"

"More dead birds and moles?"

"No." Mrs. Murphy jumped on the water trough. "The Xeroxed papers. Let's try that when we get inside."

"Oh." Tucker's liquid brown eyes clouded. "That will fry her."

"Better mad than dead," Paddy said matter-of-factly.

"I'd better learn to quack, since I'm going to waddle for the next three days." Officer Cynthia Cooper rubbed her stomach as she entered Harry's house.

"Mim spends a fortune on her cook, and Susan Tucker's much better—for free, too." Harry dumped her satchel on the kitchen table, since they had come in through the back door. The last time Harry used the front door was for her father's funeral party. "Let me show you the guest bedroom."

"No, I'll sleep in your room and you sleep in the guest bedroom. If anyone sneaks around looking for you, he or she will come to your bedroom first."

"You don't really believe the killer is going to sneak around up here in the middle of the night just because he or she knows I've figured out the postcard signal?" Harry wanted to think she was safe.

"It seems unlikely, but then everything about this crime is unlikely."

"*Follow me!*" Mrs. Murphy shouted over her shoulder. She galloped into Harry's bedroom, knocked over a lamp, and threw the Xeroxed papers on the hooked rug.

"*Yahoo!*" Tucker pretended to chase Mrs. Murphy. "*Should I chew the papers?*"

"*No, nitwit. Circle the bed,*" Mrs. Murphy ordered the dog. "*When she gets here to spank us, hide under the bed with me.*"

Harry, followed by Officer Cooper, charged into the room. "All right, you two!"

Mrs. Murphy hopped on the bed, performed a perfect somersault, and then as Harry reached for her she scooted off and flattened herself under the bed. Tucker was already there.

The muslin material underneath the mattress hung invitingly. From time to time Mrs. Murphy would lie on her back and pull herself, paw over paw, from one end of the bed to the other. Shreds of material gave testimony to her lateral rappeling technique. She reached up and sank in her claws.

"Don't," Tucker warned. "*She's furious enough as it is.*"

"That's enough, you two! I mean it. I really mean it this time. Damn, the lamp is broken."

"Was it valuable?" Officer Cooper knelt down to pick up the pieces. She could see a doggie, ears down, staring at her. "That dog is laughing at me, I swear it."

"A real comedienne." Harry hunkered down too. "Mrs. Murphy, what have you done to my bed?"

"*If you'd clean under here more often you'd have noticed by now,*" Mrs. Murphy answered.

"The lamp not only wasn't valuable, it was the ugliest lamp in three counties. I never got around to buying a good one. Actually, I barely have time to brush my teeth and eat."

"H-m-m," said Cooper.

"Oh, jeeze," Mrs. Murphy moaned. "*Here comes the lament of Father Time, gray hair and slowed reflexes. I wish she'd get over it! Dammit, Harry, the papers!*"

"Don't yowl at me, pussycat. I can sit on this bed and wait a long time for you to come out," Harry threatened while still on her knees. "Might as well clean up this mess." She began picking up the papers.

Officer Cooper read one as she helped. "Where'd you find these?"

"You know perfectly well, or doesn't Rick Shaw tell you anything?"

"Oh, this and the ledger is what you filched from Maude's desk? That got his knickers in a twist." She giggled.

"Yeah." Harry put the papers on the bed. "Mrs. Hogendobber and I only copied them. It's not as if we obstructed justice."

"Our sheriff wants to know everything. He's a good sheriff." She began reading again.

"Which one is that?" Harry's knees cracked when she unbent to sit on the bed.

"November 4, 1851. Addressed to the President and Directors, Board of Public Works, from the Engineer's Office of the Blue Ridge Railroad."

"Too bad he couldn't start with 'Dear Honey'—think of the stationery it would have saved him," Harry remarked. "I think that letter is about the temporary bridge built at Waynesboro so the men could haul materials over the mountains."

"Yeah, that's the one. Wow. I can't believe this. The original price of labor when the tunnel was contracted was seventy-five cents per day, and it shot up to eighty-seven and a half cents for some workers and even one dollar for others. Men risked their lives for eighty-seven and a half cents!"

"A different world." Harry handed Officer Cooper another sheet, the overhead light casting a dim shadow on the policewoman's blond hair. "This one's interesting." She started to read.

"November 8, 1853. He wrote a lot in November, didn't he?" She read on. " '. . . we were suddenly taken by surprise by the eruption of a large vein of water, for which we were obliged to take hands from their work, and set them to pumping, until we could obtain machinery for the same purpose, working by horsepower. This circumstance has been repeated several times during the year, successive veins of water having been encountered, until the body of water we have now to keep down amounts to no less than one and a half hogshead per minute, ninety hogshead per hour.' " She whistled. "They could have drowned in there."

"Digging tunnels is dangerous work and this is before dynamite, remember. He created a siphon to evacuate the water and it was the longest siphon on record. Here's another one."

Mrs. Murphy grumbled under the bed. "I don't feel like sleeping under the bed. Are they ever going to get it or not?"

"*Beats me.*" Tucker yawned.

"H-m-m." Cooper squinted at the page. "December 9, 1855. Lot of technical stuff about the grades and curves and timbering the excavation." She selected a more dramatic passage. " ' . . . some time in February, 1854, an immense slide from the mountain completely blocked up the western entrance, and, coming down as fast as removed, from a height of about one hundred feet, effectually prevented the construction of the arch at this end, until late in the fall of the same year.' " She turned to Harry. "How old was Claudius Crozet at this time?"

"He was born December 31, 1789, so he would have been just shy of his sixty-sixth birthday."

"Enduring this kind of physical labor? He must have been tough as nails."

"He was. He was a genius really. Politics cost him his job as First Engineer of the state, and twelve engineers couldn't do the work of one Crozet, so Richmond had to eat humble pie and ask him back in 1831. This was long before he built the tunnels. Know what else he did?"

"Not a clue."

"Brought the first blackboard to West Point. He taught there starting in 1816. Can you imagine teaching without a blackboard? America must have been primitive. The level of education was so low at West Point that he had to teach his class math before he could teach them engineering. It's a wonder we didn't lose the Mexican War."

"Guess he raised the standard of education. Lee was an engineer, you know."

"I know. Every good Southern kid knows that—that and Stonewall Jackson's Valley Campaign. And that 'you all' is plural, never singular, and that corn bread— How'd I get on this?"

"You're wound up. All that sugar in Susan's sauce on the veal."

"Maybe so. This is my favorite." Harry plucked a letter from the disorganized pile. "Crozet was being criticized in the newspapers both for the length of time the tunnels were taking and for their location, so he wrote to a friend: 'Strange things are now going on, of which you may have seen some notice. Most scurrilous and unfair attacks directed against me have appeared in some papers, especially the "Valley Star." Though few will notice such things, except with disgust, yet it is proper I should be informed of them, otherwise the seeds of slander may grow around me, without my having a chance to cut them off in time.' He then asks his friend to send him clippings he might come across. He gave as his address 'Brooksville, Albemarle.' " She kicked off her shoes and put down the letter. "The more things change, the more they stay the same. Try to do something new, something progressive, and you're crucified. I don't blame him for being touchy."

"Do you think there's treasure in one of the tunnels?"

"Oh—I'd like to think there is." Harry curled her toes.

"*Car! Car! Car!*" Tucker warned and ran from under the bed to the front door.

"Cut the lights," Officer Cooper commanded. "Get on the floor!"

Harry hit the floor so hard she knocked the wind out of herself and found herself nose to nose with Mrs. Murphy, who had started to wiggle out from under the bed.

Officer Cooper, pistol in hand, crept toward the front door. She waited. Whoever was in the car wasn't getting out, although the headlights had been turned off. The living room light gave evidence that someone was home and Tucker was hollering her head off.

"*Shut up.*" Mrs. Murphy bumped the dog. "*We know there's a car outside. Cover the back door. I'll take the front.*"

Tucker did as she was told. Officer Cooper flattened herself beside the front door.

The car door slammed. Footsteps clicked up to the front door. For a long agonizing moment nothing happened. Then a soft knock.

A harder knock, followed with "Harry, you in there?"

"Yes," Harry called out from the bedroom. "It's Boom Boom Craycroft," Harry told Officer Cooper.

"Stay on the floor!" Cooper yelled.

"Harry, what's wrong?" Boom Boom heard Cynthia Cooper's voice and didn't recognize it.

"Stay where you are. Put your hands behind your head." Officer Cooper flicked on the front porch light to behold a bewildered Boom Boom, hands clasped behind her head.

"I'm not armed," Boom Boom said. "But there's a thirty-eight in the glove compartment. It's registered."

Mrs. Murphy slunk behind Officer Cooper's heels. If anything went wrong she would climb up a leg—in Boom Boom's case a bare one—and dig as deeply as she could.

Officer Cooper slowly opened the door. "Stay right where you are." She frisked Boom Boom.

Harry, on all fours, peeked around the bedroom door. Sheepishly she stood up.

Boom Boom caught a glimpse of her. "Harry, are you all right?"

"I'm fine. What are you doing here?"

"Can I come inside?" Boom Boom's eyes implored Officer Cooper.

"Keep your hands behind your head and the answer is yes."

As Boom Boom entered the house, Cooper shut the door behind her, gun still cocked. Boom Boom had plenty she wanted to say to Harry but the presence of Officer Cooper inhibited her.

"Harry, I've ransacked Kelly's office. Ever since you dropped by I've just gone wild and—I found something."

35

Crumpled sheets of yellow legal paper, the penciled-in mileage numbers smeared, shone under the kitchen light. Harry, Boom Boom, Officer Cooper, Mrs. Murphy, and Tucker gathered around the old porcelain-topped table. Still leery, Coop kept her pistol in her hand.

"I checked the mileages of the trucks against the depreciation in Marie's ledger. They don't jibe," Boom Boom pointed out. "Nor is there any accounting for this bill." She produced a faded invoice for a huge amount of epoxy and paint resin. The bill was from North Carolina.

"Maybe the added mileage on the trucks reflects hauling the materials back here?" Harry said.

"It's three hours to Greensboro and three hours back. We're looking at thousands of miles." Boom Boom's misty-mocha fingernail pinned down the long number as though it were a butterfly. "Another thing. I asked around the plant if anyone had done extra hauling over the last four years. No one had. This isn't to say that someone might not be lying but my hunch is, whatever was being carried, Kelly drove it."

Officer Cooper flipped through the four years of mileage figures. "There's no way to tell if these were short hops or long ones. You only have the monthly figures."

"Right. But I subtracted them from Marie's figures, or rather I subtracted Marie's figures from these, and it averages out to one thousand miles per month for the big panel truck. The other trucks have less mileage on them."

"Jesus, that's a lot of resin." Harry pushed back her chair. "Anyone want a drink?"

"No, thanks," they both said.

"He wasn't transporting resin and epoxy. I found one bill for that. I mean, there could be others but that's all I found, so I think he was taking something else in the panel truck as well as occasionally using a smaller truck."

"Boom Boom, one thousand miles a month is a one-way trip to Miami, drug capital of the U.S.," Coop observed. "I take that back. Any city over five hundred thousand people is a drug capital these days."

"If Kelly was moving drugs he'd certainly be smart enough to disguise it as something else." Harry had always liked Kelly. "And he often drove the trucks. He liked being outside; he liked physical work. I suppose he and Maude linked up four years ago. She must have helped him package the stuff—if it was drugs."

"Don't get fixated on cocaine, or even heroin," Officer Cooper advised. "There's a big market in speed and steroids. He'd avoid the South Americans that way. Those boys play rough."

"He brought in drugs before, though, didn't he?" Harry asked.

Boom Boom closed her mouth.

"He's dead. There isn't anything I can do about crimes of the past," Coop said.

Boom Boom sighed. "He gave it up. He gave up using the stuff. He used to say that the drug lords and high government officials were in collusion over the drug trade. The congressmen and senators on the take, as well as the people under them, didn't want their nontaxable income removed. 'It's a damned sin,' he'd say. 'The American people are losing billions of dollars in taxes from drugs, taxes that could help people. Why is alcohol a state-supported drug to the exclusion of other drugs? You can't stop the trade. You can't legislate human behavior.' He was impassioned about it."

"Tobacco," Officer Cooper added laconically.

"What?" Boom Boom asked.

"It's a legal drug. Most addictive drug we've got. Ask Rick Shaw." The vision of Rick sneaking another cigarette made Coop laugh.

"Here in Virginia we know all about tobacco." Harry examined the yellow pages. "Where'd you find these?"

"Behind the frame of the poster he had on the wall. You know, the one where the duck is sitting in the lawn chair sipping a drink and there are bullet holes over his head. It was the last place I looked, and the corner of the backing was bent."

"I'm going to confiscate these." Cooper reached for the papers in Harry's hand.

"I don't want any of this in the paper. When you finally find out who the killer is you'll find out what they were really doing. The publicity has been grueling enough. No more!"

"I can't control the press, Boom Boom," Cooper truthfully replied.

"That's up to Rick, not Officer Cooper," Harry reminded Boom Boom.

"Do what you can, please," Boom Boom begged.

"I'll try."

Boom Boom left. Harry and the policewoman watched her pull out of the driveway.

Mrs. Murphy, who had politely listened to the coversation, emitted a loud shout. *"Go up to the tunnels. That's why I threw the papers on the floor. It's worth another look."*

"What lungs." Cooper grinned.

"You ate leftovers from Susan's tonight." Harry used her Mother voice.

"Listen to me!" Mrs. Murphy bellowed.

Tucker sniffed at Mrs. Murphy's tail, hanging over the table. *"Save your breath."*

"Damn."

"All right." Harry got up and opened the big jar of Best Fishes. She placed four of the delicious tidbits under the cat's bright whiskers. Mrs. Murphy, in a fit, knocked the treats off the counter and stalked out of the room.

"So emotional," Officer Cooper said as Tucker scarfed down the treats.

"Like people," Harry said.

36

At seven forty-five the next morning, the phone rang in the Crozet post office.

"Hello," Harry answered.

"Did you catch the killer yet?" Mrs. Hogendobber's voice boomed.

"How are you?" Harry was surprised at how happy Mrs. Hogendobber's call made her.

"Bored. Bored. Bored. Being under threat of death isn't as much torture as being out of the swim. Did you catch him?"

"No."

"Any clues?"

"Yes."

"Tell me. I'm far away. I can't blab."

"Get thee behind me, Satan."

"Mary Minor Haristeen, how dare you quote the New Testament to me like that? Why, I'm appalled at the suggestion that I would tempt you. I'm not tempting you. I'm simply trying to help. Sometimes a person considering the same evidence will see something new. Many cases have been solved that way."

"If you're far away, Rick Shaw can't make your life miserable. He can sure muck up mine."

This idea dawned on Mrs. Hogendobber and set. "He'd be thrilled for an answer. Now, I've known you since the day you were born. Prettiest little baby I ever saw. Even prettier than Boom Boom Craycroft—"

"Don't stretch the truth," Harry interrupted.

"You were—upon my soul, you were. You know I won't breathe a word of this and I do have good ideas."

"Mrs. Hogendobber, I can't speak as freely as I would wish."

"Oh, I see." Mrs. Hogendobber's voice registered her thrill with the development. "Someone we know?"

"Yes, but not of the inner circle."

"Reverend Jones."

"Now why would you mention his name?"

"He's a lovely man but he's not of my denomination. I don't consider him of the inner circle."

"Hardly any of us attend your church. I'm an Episcopalian."

Mrs. Hogendobber, a self-confessed expert on Protestant churches, corrected Harry. "You are entirely too close to the Catholic church and so is Reverend Jones. The real Reformation came when churches such as mine, The Holy Light, freed The Word to the people. However, you don't even attend Saint Paul's, so you ought to stop claiming that you are an Episcopalian. You are a lapsed Episcopalian."

"Is that like fallen arches?"

"Harry, such subjects are not humorous and it grieves me that you don't see the light. That's why we're called The Holy Light."

"Yes, ma'am."

"Who's there? Will they be offended if you tell?"

"I don't think so. It's Officer Cooper."

"Really?" The husky voice shot upward.

"Really. Now I've got to get back to work. You take care of yourself."

"I want to come home." Mrs. Hogendobber sounded like a miserable child.

"We want you to come home." Harry thought to herself: Some of us do. Harry missed her.

"I'll call tomorrow. I can't give you my number. 'Bye."

" 'Bye." Harry hung up the phone. "She's a pip."

"There's another one at the door."

Harry smiled and kept silent as she unlocked the door for Mim

Sanburne, who was unusually early. She paused but did not say hello.

"Good morning, Mim." Harry decided a lesson in manners might be amusing.

Big Marilyn's expertly frosted hair caught the light. "Are you under house arrest?"

"We're rehashing the Stamp Act and how it led up to the Revolution," Officer Cooper retorted.

"Deference is greatly to be sought after in public servants. Our sheriff prides himself on his staff. But then—" Mim didn't finish what would have been a threat, for Josiah jauntily opened the door. Nor did she tell Harry that she had indeed called Mignon Haristeen, who told her to mind her own goddamned business and reinstate Harry on the Cancer Ball committee. Yes, Mignon deplored the divorce but Harry had worked hard for the charity and the charity should come first. That made Mim back down.

"Stop what you're doing and come on over to the shop," Josiah said. "I've worked a miracle."

"I'll come over when Larry gives me my lunch break."

"That's no fun. We should go now—the more the merrier." He swept his arm to include Mim and Officer Cooper.

"Thrilled," Mim said without conviction.

Susan pulled up at the same time as Rick Shaw.

Josiah watched them through the window. "I envy you, Harry. You're at the hub of Crozet—Grand Central."

"Hi," Susan called out.

Rick Shaw came in on her heels. "I need a buddy today when I ride," she said. "You're it, Harry."

"Okay—but I think we'll melt."

Rick ushered himself behind the counter and collected Boom Boom's papers from Officer Cooper. He made no attempt to hide this collection, but he didn't draw attention to it either. "Has she been a good girl?" He nodded in Harry's direction.

"Good as gold."

"Officer Cooper, how long are you going to shadow Harry? Will I

ever be able to have an intimate dinner with her?" Josiah empha-
sized the "intimate."

"Only if you do the cooking," came Cooper's swift reply.

"Where's Mrs. Murphy?" Susan inquired.

"Pouting in the mail bin," Harry said.

"Sheriff Shaw, would you like to see the shop before I open it?
You wouldn't know it was the same shop," Josiah persisted.

It wasn't. Harry dropped by after lunch. Well, after what started
out as lunch and ended up being an appetite killer. She zipped into
Crozet Pizza, only to behold Boom Boom and Fair in earnest conversation at a table. She was beginning to like Boom Boom more
and Fair less but she couldn't bear them together. She left without
even a slice of that famous pizza.

Maude's shop, transformed into a high-quality antiques show-
room, conveyed that sleek, urbane yet country mix that was Josiah's
forte. The packing materials were arranged in the back room and
even they looked inviting. Officer Cooper rummaged around. She
loved antiques.

"You're glum, sweetie. What's up?" Josiah sidled over to Harry.

"Oh, Fair and Boom Boom were at Crozet Pizza. It's silly for it to
hurt, but it does."

He curled his arm around her shoulders. "Harry, anyone who
ever died of love deserved it. There are other fish in the sea and
besides, you've wasted far too much time, far too much, on
Pharamond Haristeen."

"I guess."

Officer Cooper rested herself in a cushy wing chair to better
appreciate the discussion.

"It's a new day tomorrow, brighter and better." He turned to
Cooper. "You and I are going to be friends. You have exquisite taste,
I can see, but tell me, is my favorite postmistress really in danger?"

"I can't answer that."

Josiah pulled Harry even closer to him. "I wasn't born yesterday.
Mrs. Hogendobber certainly was packed off in great haste. If she's
on vacation, so to speak, and you've got a police dogsbody—pardon

me—that means the authorities are worried about her and you. Well, so am I."

Officer Cooper crossed her legs. "I know you've spoken to Rick but for my satisfaction, who do you think is the killer?"

"I don't know, which is so frustrating ... unless it was Mrs. Hogendobber and you've locked her up to keep the townies from lynching her. Mrs. H., a killer—unlikely, although she can kill a conversation faster than Limburger cheese."

"Any idea about motive?" Harry asked.

"Some sort of grudge, I should think."

"Why do you say that?" Officer Cooper shifted her position.

"He's humiliated the bodies, if you think about it. I think that bespeaks some kind of powerful emotion. Anger. Jealousy perhaps. Or he was spurned."

"You're such a romantic. I think it's over money, pure and simple." Harry folded her arms across her chest. "And the mutilation of the bodies is to keep us away from the real issue."

"Which is?" Josiah's eyebrows raised.

"Damned if I know." Harry threw up her hands.

"No. Damned if you do, because he would kill you—according to your analysis. According to my analysis you're perfectly safe."

"Let's hope you're right." Officer Cooper smiled up at Josiah.

37

Lolling under the crepe myrtle behind Maude's shop, Mrs. Murphy, Tucker, and Pewter waited for Harry to be released from her obligatory socializing.

Pewter batted at a red ant scooting through the grass. "*Black ants are okay but these little red ones bite like blazes.*"

"*Better than fleas.*" Mrs. Murphy lay on her back, her four legs in the air, tail straight out.

"*Last year was the worst, the absolute worst.*" Tucker pricked her ears, then relaxed them. "*Every week I was drenched with a bath, doused with flea killer, the worst.*"

"*For me it was flea mousse. Harry doesn't like bathing me, for which I am grateful. But Pewter, this mousse smells like rancid raspberries and it's sticky. Rolling in dirt, grass, even rubbing against the bark of a tree does no good. This year I've been moussed once.*"

"*Market embraces the concept of the flea collar. The first week the fumes were so intense my eyes watered. After that I figured out how to wriggle out of them. He's so slow it took four lost flea collars before he gave up.*"

"*Do you like humans?*" Tucker addressed Pewter.

"*Not especially. A few I like. Most I don't*" was her forthright reply.

"*Why?*" Mrs. Murphy twisted her head so she could better observe Pewter. She stayed on her back.

"*You can't trust them. Hell's bells, they can't even trust each other. Take a cat, for instance. If you wander into another cat's territory, you know it right* away. Unless there's an important reason to be there, you leave. The lines are clear. Nothing is clear with humans, not even mating. A human being will mate with another human being for social approval. They rarely sleep with the person who's right for them. But humans are much more like sheep than cats. They're easily led and they don't look where they're going until it's too late."

"They aren't all like sheep," Tucker responded.

"No, but I agree with Pewter—most of them are. Something terrible happened to the human race way back in time. They separated from nature. We live with a human who has some connection to the seasons, to other animals, but she's a country person. They're few and far between. And the further humans move from nature, the crazier they get. In the end it's what will destroy them."

"I don't give a damn if they die, every last one. I just don't want to go with them, if it's the bomb you're talking about." Pewter slashed her tail through the grass.

"The bomb's the least of it." Mrs. Murphy shook herself and sat up. "They'll kill the fish in the rivers and then the fish in the oceans. They'll wipe out more and more species of mammals. They won't have good water to drink after they kill the fish. They won't even have good air to breathe. If you don't have an adequate oxygen supply, how can you think clearly? Worse, they have no sense of when and how much to breed. Even a squirrel can read a bad acorn harvest and hold back breeding. A human can't read harvests. They keep reproducing. Do you know there are over five billion humans on the earth right now as I speak? They can't feed what they've got and they're breeding more."

"Plus they're breeding sick ones because they won't cull." Tucker's eyes were troubled. "Sick in body and sick in mind. If I have a weak puppy, I'll kill it. It's my obligation to the rest of the litter. They won't do that."

"Do it! My God, they scream murder, and when they have to raise taxes to pay for the criminal acts of the sick in mind, or pay for the increased care of the physically weak, they pitch a fit and fall in it. They just won't realize they're another animal and the laws of nature apply to them too." Pewter's pupils expanded.

"They think it's cruel. You know, Pewter, you are right. They are crazy. They won't kill a diseased newborn but they'll flock by the millions to kill one another in a war. Didn't World War II kill off about forty-five million of them? And *World War I* axed maybe ten million? It almost makes me laugh." Mrs. Murphy watched Harry and Officer Cooper leave Maude's shop by the back door. "I don't much care if they die by the millions, truth be told, but I don't want Harry to die."

Pewter trilled, a sound above a purr. "Yeah, Harry's a brick. We should make her an honorary cat."

"Or an honorary dog," Tucker rejoined. "She says that cats and dogs are the lares and penates of a household, the protective household gods. Harry's big on mythology but I fancy the comparison."

Harry and Officer Cooper walked over to the crepe myrtle.

"A kitty tea party." Harry scratched Pewter at the base of her tail. Tucker licked her hand. "Excuse me, a kitty and doggie tea party. Well, come on, troops. Back to work."

38

Bob Berryman prided himself on his physical prowess. Stronger in his early fifties than when he played football for Crozet High, he'd grown even more vain about his athletic abilities. Time's theft of speed made Berryman play smarter. He played softball and golf regularly. He was accustomed to dominating men and accepting deference from women. Maude Bly Modena didn't defer to him. If he thought about it, that was why he had fallen in love with her.

He thought about little else. He replayed every moment of their time together. He searched those recollections, fragments of conversation and laughter for clues. Far more painfully, he returned to the railroad tracks today. What was out here halfway between Crozet and Greenwood?

Immediately before her death, Maude had jogged this way. She took the railroad path once a week. She liked to vary her routes. Said it kept her fresh. She didn't run the railroad path more frequently than other jogging routes, though. He backtracked those also, with Ozzie at his heels.

Kelly and Maude had never seemed close to him. He drew a blank there. He reviewed every person in Crozet. Was she friendly to them? What did she truly think of them?

A searing wind whipped his thinning hair, a Serengeti wind, desert-like in its dryness. The creosote from the railroad tracks stank. Berryman shaded his eyes with his hand and scanned east toward town, then west toward the Greenwood tunnel.

She used to joke about Crozet's treasure, and given Maude's thoroughness, she'd read about Claudius Crozet. The engineer fascinated her. If she could only find the treasure she could retire. Retail was hard, she said, but then they shared that thought, since Berryman moved more stock trailers than anyone on the East Coast.

It wasn't until ten o'clock that evening, in the silence of his newly rented room, that Berryman realized the tunnel had something to do with Maude. Impulsively, driven by wild curiosity as well as grief, he hurried to his truck, flashlight in hand, Ozzie at his side, and drove out there.

The trek up to the tunnel, treacherous in the darkness on the overgrown tracks, had him panting. Ozzie, senses far sharper than his master's, smelled another human scent. He saw the dull glow at the lower edge of the tunnel where dappled light escaped through the foliage. Someone was inside the tunnel. He barked a warning to his master. Better he'd stayed silent. The light was immediately extinguished.

Berryman leaned against the sealed tunnel mouth to catch his breath. Ozzie heard the human slide through the heavy brush. He dashed after him. One shot put an end to Ozzie. The shepherd screamed and dropped.

Berryman, thinking of his dog before himself, ran to where Ozzie disappeared. He crashed through the brush and beheld the killer.

"You!"

Within one second he, too, was dead.

39

Rick Shaw, Dr. Hayden McIntire, and Clai Cordle and Diana Farrell of the Rescue Squad stared at Bob Berryman's body. He was seated upright behind the driver's wheel of his truck. Ozzie, also shot, lay beside him. Bob had been shot through the heart and once again through the head for good measure. In his breast pocket was a postcard of General Lee's tomb at Lexington, Virginia. It read, "Wish you were here." There was no postmark. His truck was parked at the intersection of Whitehall Road and Railroad Avenue, a stone's throw away from the post office, the train depot, and Market Shiflett's store. A farmer on his way to the acres he rented on the north side of town found the body at about quarter to five in the morning.

"Any idea?" Rick asked Hayden.

"Six hours. The coroner will be more exact but no more than six, perhaps a little less." Hayden thought his heart would break every time he looked at Ozzie. He and Bob had been inseparable in life and were now inseparable in death.

Rick nodded and reached into his squad car. Picking up the mobile phone, he commanded the switchboard to get him Officer Cooper.

A sleepy Cynthia Cooper soon greeted him.

"Coop. There's been another one. Bob Berryman. But this time the killer was in a hurry. He abandoned his usual *modus operandi*. No cyanide. He didn't have time to slice and dice the body either. He just left two bullet holes and a postcard. Stick to Harry. I'll talk to you later. Over and out."

40

Mrs. Murphy and Tucker learned the news from the town crier, Pewter. The fat gray cat, asleep in the store window, heard the truck in the near distance early that morning. Pewter was accustomed to hearing cars and trucks before dawn. After all, the drunks have to come home sometime; so do the lovers, and the farmers have to be up before dawn. Ozzie's death hit the animals like a bombshell. Was he killed protecting Berryman? Was he killed so he couldn't lead Rick Shaw to the murderer? Or was the murderer losing his marbles and going after animals too?

"If only I'd known, I would have jumped on the ice cream case and seen who did this," Pewter moaned.

"There was no way for you to know," Tucker comforted her.

"Poor Ozzie." Mrs. Murphy sighed. The hyper dog had tried her patience but she didn't wish him dead.

Bedlam overtook the post office. Harry had time to adjust to this latest horror because Officer Cooper prepared her, but nobody was prepared for the onslaught of reporters. Even the New York Times sent down a reporter. Fortunately, Crozet had no hotels, so this swarm of media locusts had to nest in Charlottesville, rent cars, and drive west.

Rob Collier fought his way through a traffic jam to deliver his mail.

"Goddamn!" He chucked the bags on the floor, quickly shutting the door behind him as one reporter in a seersucker jacket tried to come through.

"Maybe we'd better bolt the windows," Harry remarked.

Mrs. Murphy, Tucker, and Pewter scratched at the back door. Officer Cooper let them in. "I think your children have relieved themselves. Pewter's in tow."

"*I refuse to stay in the market another minute!*" Pewter bitched loudly. "*You can't move in there.*"

Mrs. Murphy noted, "*You stayed long enough to push you mug in front of the TV cameras.*"

"*I did not! They chose to highlight me.*"

"Girls, girls, calm yourselves." Harry poured crunchies in a bowl for everyone and returned to the front.

Rob stared out the window. "I heard on the radio that the killer leaves a mark, a momento. That's how Rick knows it's the same fellow. Bob Berryman . . . well, ladies, at least he exited this life with speed."

Officer Cooper joined him at the window. "Strange country, isn't it?"

"We're more excited by bad news than by good news. Think these reporters would be here if you'd saved a child from drowning?"

"Locals, maybe. That's about it." He turned to Harry. "See you this afternoon. Might be late."

"Take care, Rob."

"Yeah. You too." He pushed open the front door and shut it quickly behind him, then sprinted for the truck.

The phone rang.

"Harry," the familiar voice rang out, "I just saw the *Today* show. Bob Berryman!"

"Mrs. Hogendobber, the world's gone mad," Harry said. "Don't come home. Whatever you do, stay put."

"The times. The morals. People have abandoned God, Harry—He hasn't abandoned us. It's time for a New Order."

"I always suspect that under a New Order, women will be kept in their old place."

"Feminism! You can think of feminism at a time like this?" Mrs. Hogendobber was both aghast and furious at being out of the center of events.

"I'm not talking about feminism but who runs your church. The women?" Harry would prefer to talk about anything but this latest murder. She was more frightened than she let on.

"No—but we contribute a great deal, Harry, a great deal."

"That's not the same thing as running the show or sharing in the power." Susan rapped on the window. Harry cradled the receiver between shoulder and ear and made a T for time sign with her hands. "Mrs. Hogendobber. I apologize. I'm so upset. The reporters have parachuted in. I'm taking it out on you. Forget everything I've said."

"Actually, I won't. You've given me something to think about," she uncharacteristically replied. Travel seemed to make Mrs. H. more liberal. "Now you watch out, hear?"

"I hear."

"I'll call tomorrow. Bye-bye."

Harry hung up the phone. Officer Cooper let Susan in.

"Jesus, Mary, and Joseph. If the killer has any heart maybe he'll fire on these reporters. What are we going to do? I had to walk over here. It's gridlock out there."

"You know"—Harry shoved a mail sack in Susan's direction; to hell with rules—"I think the killer is loving this."

Officer Cooper grabbed a mail bin. "I think so too."

"Well, I've got an idea." Harry motioned for Susan and Coop to get close. She whispered: "Let's give him a little zinger of our own. Let's put graveyard postcards in everyone's mailbox."

"You're kidding." Susan's hands involuntarily flew up to her chest as though to protect herself.

"No, I am not. No one knows about the postcards but me and you, and Rick and Coop. They know there's some telling sign, but they don't know what it is. Think Rick told anyone else?"

"Not yet," Coop answered.

"We won't scare anyone but the killer," Harry said. "He won't know who sent the postcard. But he'll know we're playing with him."

"You'd better damn well hope he doesn't figure out who we are." Susan folded her arms across her chest.

"If he does, I guess we'll fight it out," Harry replied.

"Harry, forget fighting. He'll blindside you." Coop's voice was low.

"Okay, okay, I shouldn't sound so cocky. He's killed three times. What's another one? But I think we can rattle his chain. Dammit, it's worth a try. Susan, will you buy the postcards? I know there are postcards of Jefferson's grave. Maybe you can find others."

"I'll do it, but I'm scared," Susan admitted.

41

Rick went through the roof. A third murder on his hands, the press tearing at him like horseflies, and Mary Minor Haristeen hit him with a crackbrained idea about postcards.

He screeched into Larry Johnson's driveway and slammed his squad car door so hard it was a wonder it didn't fall off. The retired doctor, tending his beloved pale yellow roses, calmly continued spraying. By the time Rick joined him he was somewhat calmed down.

"Larry."

"Sheriff. Bugs will take over the world, I swear it." The hand pump squished as the robust old man annihilated Japanese beetles. "What can I do for you? Tranquilizers?"

"God knows I need them." Rick exhaled. "Larry, I should have come to you before now. I hope I haven't offended you. It was natural to interview Hayden because he's practicing now, but you've known everybody and everything far longer than Hayden. I'm hoping you can help me."

"Hayden's a good man." Squish. Squish. "Ever hear that line about a new doctor means a bigger cemetery?"

"No, I can't say that I have."

"In Hayden's case it isn't true. He's catching on to our ways. Not like he's some Yankee. He was raised up in Maryland. Young man, bright future."

"Yes. We must be getting old, Larry, when thirty-eight seems young. Remember when it seemed ancient?"

Larry nodded and vigorously sprayed. "*Banzai*, you damned winged irritants! Go meet the Emperor." He had been a career Army physician in World War II and Korea before returning home to practice. His father, Lynton Johnson, practiced in Crozet before him.

"I'm going to ask you to break confidentiality. You don't have to, of course, but you're no longer practicing medicine, so perhaps it's not so bad."

"I'm listening."

"Did you ever see signs of anything unusual? Prescribe medications that might alter personality?"

"One time, I prescribed diet pills, back in the 1960's, to Miranda Hogendobber. My God, she talked nonstop for weeks. That was a mistake. Still only lost two pounds in two years. Mim suffers a nervous condition—"

"What kind of nervous condition?"

"This and that and who shot the cat. That woman had a list of complaints when she was still in the womb. Once through the vaginal portals, she was ready to proclaim them. What put her over the top was Stafford marrying that colored girl."

"Black, Larry."

"When I was a child that was a trash word. It's awful hard to change eighty years of training, you know, but all right, I stand corrected. That pretty thing was the best, the best thing that coulda happened to Stafford. She made a man out of him. Mim teetered perilously close to a nervous breakdown. I gave her Valium, of course."

"Could she be unstable enough to commit murder?" It occurred to Rick that Mim could have slashed her pontoon boat herself, so as to appear a target.

"Anyone could be if circumstances were right—or maybe I should say wrong—but no, I think not. Mim has settled down since then. Oh, she can be as mean as a snake shedding its skin but she's no longer dependent on Valium. Now the rest of us need it."

"Did you treat Kelly Craycroft?"

"I checked Kelly into the drug rehabilitation center."

"Well?"

"Kelly Craycroft was a fascinating son of a bitch. He recognized no law but his own, yet the man made sense. He had an addictive personality. Runs in the family."

"What about hereditary insanity? What family does that run in?"

" 'Bout ninety percent of the First Families of Virginia, I should say." A wicked grin crossed his face. The spraying slowed down.

"Gimme that. I'd like to knock off a couple." Rick attacked the beetles, their iridescent wings becoming wet with poison. A buzz, then a sputter, and then the bugs fell onto the ground, hard-backed shells making a light clinking noise. "What about Harry? Ever sick? Unstable?"

"Pulled out her back playing lacrosse in college. When it flared up I used to give her Motrin. I think Hayden still does. Harry's a bright girl who never found her profession. She seems happy enough. You don't think she's the killer, do you?"

"No." Rick rubbed his nose. The spray smelled disagreeable. "What do you think, Larry?"

"I don't think the person is insane."

"Fair Haristeen doesn't have an alibi for the nights of any of the killings . . . and he has a motive as regards Kelly. Since he lives alone now, he says there's no one to vouch for him."

Larry rubbed his brow. "I was afraid of that."

"What about cyanide? How hard is it to produce?" Rick pressed.

"Extremely hard, but a man with a medical background would have no trouble at all."

"Or a vet?"

"Or a vet. But any intelligent person who took a course in college chemistry can figure it out. Cyanide is a simple compound, cyanogen with a metal radical or an organic radical. Potassium cyanide shuts off your lights before you have time to blink. Painters, furniture strippers, even garage mechanics have access to chemicals that, properly distilled, could yield deadly results. You can do it in your kitchen sink." Larry watched the rain of dying beetles with satisfaction. "You know what this is all about, don't you?"

"No." Rick's voice rose high with curiosity.

"It's something right under our noses. Something we're used to seeing or passing every day, as well as someone we're used to seeing or passing. It's so much a part of our lives we no longer notice it. We've got to look at our community with new eyes. Not just the people, Rick, but the physical setup. Bob Berryman did. That's why he's dead."

42

Rick arrested Pharamond Haristeen III. He had no alibi. He was physically strong, highly intelligent, and possessed of expert medical knowledge. He bore a grudge against Kelly and vice versa. What he had against Maude Bly Modena, Rick wasn't sure, but if he did arrest him it would be an action soothing to the press and the public. It could also ruin Fair's life if he wasn't the killer. He weighed that fact but arrested him anyway. He had to play safe. He also said yes to Harry's plan. What did he have to lose, unless it was Harry? He issued her a revolver and no one except Cynthia Cooper knew Harry was now armed.

Mrs. Murphy sprawled on the butcher block in Harry's kitchen. Rhythmically, her tail flicked up and down. Tucker sat by Harry at the kitchen table. Harry, Susan, and Officer Cooper hunched over their postcards, writing again and again, "Wish you were here."

The phone rang. It was Danny for his mother. Susan grabbed the phone. "What is it this time?" She listened as he groaned that Dad had clicked off the TV in order to make him clean his room. Susan knew as she soaked up the litany of woes that having a teenaged child was aging her rapidly. Having a middle-aged husband sped up the process too. "Do as your father says." This was followed by a renewed outburst. "Danny, if I have to come home and negotiate between you and your father you are going to be grounded until Christmas!" Another howl. "I'll ground him, too, then. Go clean your room and don't bother me. I wouldn't be here if it wasn't important. Goodbye." Bang, she slammed the receiver down.

"Happy families," Harry said.

"Having a teenaged son isn't difficult. It's the combination of father and son that's difficult. Sometimes I think that Ned resents Danny growing stronger. He's already two inches taller than Ned."

"An old story." Cooper reached for another postcard. Dolley Madison's tombstone graced the front. "How many more of these to go?"

"About one hundred twenty-five. There are four hundred and two post boxes and we're on the home stretch."

"Why so few?" Susan asked.

"You want more?" Cooper was incredulous.

"No, I don't want more, but there are three thousand residents of Crozet, by my count."

"Rest of them didn't buy post boxes. Most of my people are right in town itself." Harry's index and middle fingers began to hurt.

As the three women continued to scribble Mrs. Murphy opened a cupboard and crawled in.

Tucker hated that she couldn't climb around like the cat. *"Don't go in there. I can't see you if you do."*

Mrs. Murphy stuck her head out. *"I like to smell the spices. There's an aromatic tea in here that reminds me of catnip."*

"Nothing up there that smells like a beef bone, I guess?"

"Bouillon cubes. They're in a package. I'll get them out." She examined the package. *"I'm sorry we couldn't sniff Bob Berryman. Wonder if that smell was on him?"*

"I doubt it. Bullet did him in. I've checked out everyone that comes into the post office just in case that smell would be on them—you know, like something in their work. Rob smells like gas and sweat. Market smells delicious. Mim drenches herself in that noxious perfume. Fair reeks of horses and medicine. Little Marilyn's hairspray makes my eyes water. Josiah smells like furniture wax plus his after-shave. Kelly smelled like concrete dust. Their smells are like their voices, individual."

"What does Harry smell like to you?"

"Us. Our scent covers her but she doesn't know it. I make sure to rub up against her and sit in her lap and so do you. Keeps other animals from getting ideas."

Harry glanced up and beheld Mrs. Murphy chewing the bouillon package. "Stop that." The cat jumped out of the cupboard before Harry reached her.

"Bet you get a bouillon cube." Mrs. Murphy winked.

"Well, this is useless," Harry fumed. She opened the package and gave Tucker one of the cubes Mrs. Murphy chewed. Brazenly, the tiger kitty sat on the counter. "Oh, here, dammit, you worked hard enough for it, but your manners are going to hell." Mrs. Murphy delicately took the cube from Harry's fingers.

"Last one!" Officer Cooper rejoiced.

"Now we'll see if the other shoe drops." Harry's eyes narrowed.

What dropped was Harry's jaw when she turned on the TV and saw Fair being led to jail. Damn Rick Shaw. He'd told nobody. Just let it come out on the eleven o'clock news.

She put on her shoes and dragged Cooper to the jail. Too late. Fair had been released. An alibi had been established, an alibi as upsetting to Harry as it was to Fair.

43

Ned puffed his pipe. At Harry's request, Officer Cooper waited in the living room with Susan. The murders were ghastly but this was painful.

Upon learning that Boom Boom freed Fair by confessing that he was with her on the night of Kelly's murder, as well as on the night of Maude's murder, Harry called Susan.

Logically, she knew it was absurd to be shaken. Her husband had been unfaithful. Millions of husbands are unfaithful. She knew, too, in her heart that this affair must have flourished before the separation. She would be divorcing him, affair or no affair, but when she learned the details at the jail she burst out crying. She couldn't help herself.

She called Ned. He told her to come right over.

". . . irreconcilable differences. You can change that, of course, and now sue on grounds of adultery. You see, Harry, Virginia divorce law is, well, let's just say this isn't California. If you sue on grounds of adultery and the court finds in your favor, you won't have to divide up the monies you've acquired during the marriage."

"In other words, this is his punishment for fooling around." Harry's eyes got moist again.

"The law doesn't state punishment—"

"But that's what it is, isn't it? Suing on the grounds of adultery is an instrument of revenge." She sank back in the chair. Her head ached. Her heart ached.

Ned's words were measured. "In the hands of some lawyers and people, you might say it's an instrument of revenge."

After a long, deep pause Harry spoke with resolution and clarity. "Ned, it's bad enough that divorce in this town becomes public spectacle. This . . . this adultery suit, well, that would turn spectacle into nightmare for me and a real three-ring circus for the Mim Sanburnes of the world. You know"—she glanced at the ceiling—"I can't even say that he's wrong. She has something I don't."

The friend in Ned overcame the lawyer. "She can't hold a candle to you, Harry. You're the best."

That made Harry cry again. "Thank you." When she'd regained her composure she continued. "What do I have to gain by hurting him because I'm hurt? I can't see anything in this but more money if I win, and my divorce isn't about money—it really is about irreconcilable differences. I'll stick with that. Sometimes, Ned, even with the best of intentions and the best people"—she smiled—"things just don't work out."

"You've got class, honey." Ned came over, sat on the edge of the chair, and patted her back.

"Maybe." She half laughed. "On the odd occasion, I'm capable of acting like a reasonable adult. I want to put this behind me. I want to go on with my life."

44

Like clockwork, Mrs. Hogendobber called for her gossip bulletin at seven forty-five the next morning. Pewter visited from next door. The post boxes, filled, awaited their owners, and when the door opened at 8:00 A.M., Harry and Officer Cooper acted normal. Well, they thought they were normal but Officer Cooper positioned herself so she could see the boxes. Harry burned off energy in giving Mrs. Murphy, Pewter, and even Tucker rides in the mail bin.

Danny Tucker arrived first, scooped out the mail, and didn't go through it. "Sorry I didn't get to see you last night. Mom said you had business with Dad."

"Yeah. We got things straightened out."

Just then Ned Tucker bounded up the steps. "Hello, everyone." He gave Harry a big smile, then noticed the mail in his son's hands. "I'll take that." He rapidly flipped through it, blinked when he saw the postcard, read it, and said aloud, "That's Susan's handwriting. What's she up to now?"

Harry hadn't thought of that. They should have assigned names. She wondered who else would recognize their handwriting.

"Dad, I've been really good and there's a party tonight—"

"The answer is no."

"Ah, come on. I could be dead by Halloween."

"That's not funny, Dan." Ned opened the door. "Harry, I will relieve you of our presence." Ned unceremoniously ushered his protesting son outside.

"Are you a regular letter writer?" Harry asked Coop.

"No. What about you?"

"Not much. We bombed that one."

"Let's hope he doesn't say anything except to Susan. Wonder what she'll tell him."

Market was next. He sorted out his mail and tossed the junk mail, including the postcard, into the trash. "Damn crap."

"Doesn't sound like you, Market." Harry forced her voice to be light.

"Business is booming but I'd rather make less and have peace of mind. If one more reporter or sadistic tourist tramps into my store, I think I'll paste them away. One newspaper creep leered at my daughter and had the gall to invite her to dinner. She's fourteen years old!"

"Remember Lolita," Harry said.

"I don't know anyone named Lolita and if I did I'd tell her to change her name." He stalked out.

"I'm not going home until he's in a better mood," Pewter remarked to her companions.

"So far, Harry's idea has been a bust." Mrs. Murphy licked her paw.

Fair sheepishly came in. "Ladies."

"Fair," they replied in tandem.

"Uh, Harry—"

"Later, Fair. I haven't got the strength to hear it now." Harry cut him off.

He went to his post box and yanked out the mail.

"What the hell is this?" He walked over to Harry and handed her the postcard.

"A pretty picture of Jefferson's marker."

" 'Wish you were here,' " Fair read aloud. "Maybe Tom thinks I should join him. Well, plenty of others do now; I guess I've made a mess of it." He skidded the card down the counter. "If T.J. returned to Albemarle County today, he'd die to get away from it."

"Why do you say that?" Officer Cooper asked.

"People come to worship at the shrine. I mean, the man stood for progressive thought, politically, architecturally. We haven't progressed since he died."

"You sound like Maude Bly Modena," Harry observed.

"Do I? I guess I do."

"Guess you'll be dating Boom Boom out in the open now."

Fair glared at Harry. "That was a low blow." He stormed out.

"Jesus, it isn't even ten in the morning. Wonder who else we can offend?" Officer Cooper laughed.

"It's the tension, and all those reporters keep rubbing the wound raw. And . . . I don't know. The air feels heavy, like before a storm."

Reverend Jones, Clai Cordle, Diana Farrell, and Donna Eicher picked up their mail. Nothing much came of that. Donna also got Linda Berryman's mail for her.

Once the post office was empty again, Harry remarked, "We were probably tasteless to put a card in Linda Berryman's box."

"In this case, the end justifies the means and the meanness."

Hayden McIntire dropped by. He, too, left without examining his mail.

Boom Boom Craycroft, however, caught the meaning immediately as she put her mail into three piles: personal, business, junk. "This is attractive." She handed the postcard to Harry. "Is this what you wish for me now?"

"I got one too," fibbed Harry.

"Sick humor." Boom Boom's lips curled. "These murders flush out every weirdo we've got. Sometimes I think all of Crozet is weird. What are we doing festering here like a pimple on the butt of the Blue Ridge Mountains? Poor Claudius Crozet. He deserved better." She paused and then said to Harry: "Well, I guess you deserve better, too, but I can't bring myself to apologize. I don't feel guilty."

As she walked out an astonished Harry noticed Mrs. Murphy heading for the stamp pads. Quickly she sped toward them and snapped them shut. Mrs. Murphy trotted right by them as though they were of no concern to her, and wasn't Harry silly? This upheaval over Boom Boom and Fair had upset the cat too. She hated seeing Harry suffer.

The name Crozet fired a nerve in Harry's brain. "Cooper, if I found the buried treasure would I have to pay income tax on it?"

"We even pay death duties in this country. Of course you'd have to pay."

"*She may be getting it at last.*" Mrs. Murphy pranced.

"*Getting what?*" Pewter hated being left out of things, so Tucker filled her in.

"The profits in Maude's ledger. Maybe they involved selling the treasure in bits and pieces."

"You're soft as a grape." Cooper smiled. "But it's as good an explanation as any other. This doesn't address the small, trifling fact that the tunnels are sealed shut. Rock, debris, concrete. Poor Claudius. I'd be more worried about him returning than Thomas Jefferson. Imagine coming back and seeing your life's work, a world-class engineering feat, sealed up and forgotten."

"Let's go up there after work."

"Yeah—okay."

Just then Mim, Little Marilyn, and bodyguard entered the building. Josiah, like a well-groomed terrier, was at their heels.

Mother and daughter, strained with each other, cast a pall over the room. Josiah discreetly sorted his mail at the counter while the two women spoke in low tones.

The low tone erupted as Mim yanked the mail from Little Marilyn's hands. "I'll do it."

"I can sort the mail as easily as you can."

"You're too slow." Mim frantically flipped through the mail. The postcard barely dented her consciousness. She was looking for something else.

"Mother, give me my mail!"

Josiah read his postcard, Dolley Madison's tomb. He smiled at Harry. "Is this one of your jokes?"

"I'll give you your mail in a moment." The cords stood out on Mim's neck.

Little Marilyn, face empurpled, backhanded her mother's hands, and the mail flew everywhere. Mrs. Murphy leaped on the counter to watch, as did Pewter. Tucker, behind the counter, begged to go into the front and Harry opened the door for her. She sat by the stamp machine and watched.

"I know what you're looking for, Mother, and you won't find it."

Mim pretended to be in control and bent down to pick up wedding invitation replies. Josiah, leaving his mail on the counter, joined her. "Why don't you get some fresh air, Mim? I'll do this."

"I don't need fresh air. I need a new daughter."

"Fine. Then you won't have *any* children," Little Marilyn screamed at her. "You're looking for a letter from Stafford. You won't find one, Mother, because I didn't write him." Little Marilyn paused for breath and dramatic effect. "I called him."

"You what?" Mim leaped up so quickly the blood rushed from her head.

"Mim, darling—" Josiah attempted to calm her. She pushed him off.

"You heard me. I called him. He's my brother and I love him and if he's not coming to my wedding, then you aren't coming either. I'm the one getting married. Not you."

"Don't you dare speak to me like that."

"I'll speak to you any way I like. I've done everything you've ever asked of me. I attended the right schools. I played the appropriately feminine sports—you know, Mother, the ones where you don't sweat. Excuse me—glow. I made the right friends. I don't even like them! They're boring. But they're socially correct. I'm marrying the right man. We'll have two blond children and they'll go to the right schools, play the right sports *ad nauseam*. I am getting off the merry-go-round. Now. If you want to stay on, fine. You won't know you aren't going anywhere until you're dead." Little Marilyn shook with fury, which was slowly subsiding into relief and even happiness. She was doing it at long last. She was fighting back.

Harry, hardly breathing, wanted to cheer. Officer Cooper's eyes about popped out of her head. So this was the way the upper class behaved? The public display would eventually upset Mim more than the raw emotions.

"Darling, let's discuss this elsewhere. Please." Josiah gently cupped Mim's elbow. She allowed him to guide her this time.

"Little Marilyn, we'll talk about this later."

"No. There's nothing to talk about. I am marrying Fitz-Gilbert Hamilton. Excitement is not his middle name, but he's a good man and I honestly hope we make it, Mother. I would like to be happy, even if only for one day in my life. You are invited to my wedding. My brother's wife will be my matron of honor."

"Oh, my *Gawd!*" Mim fainted.

45

It wasn't until the diminishing hours of sunlight, the spreading of coppery-rich long shadows, about seven in the evening, that Harry understood what really happened in the post office.

Josiah and Officer Cooper revived Mim. Little Marilyn left. Whatever sorrow she might feel over her mother's acute distress was well hidden. Mim had caused her enough distress over the years. If she fainted in the post office and cracked her head, so be it.

When Mim came to, with the bodyguard shoving amyl nitrite under her nostrils, she said, "I don't fit here anymore. My life's like an old dress."

For a brief moment Harry pitied her.

Josiah tended to Mim, walking her to his shop.

People poured in and out of the post office for the rest of the day. Harry and Officer Cooper barely had time to go to the bathroom, much less think.

The thinking came later, in the oppressive heat redolent with the green odor of vegetation, as the two women, armed, climbed the grade on the old track up to the Greenwood tunnel. Mrs. Murphy and Tucker refused to stay in the parked car far below. They, too, panted.

"People hauled timbers up here. Even with mules, this was a bitch."

"The old tracks run to the tunnel. Crozet built serving roads and tracks before—" Harry stopped. A yellow swallowtail butterfly twirled before her and winged off.

"Is this one of your jokes? Coop . . . Coop! Josiah said that to me after reading his card."

"So what? Ned recognized Susan's handwriting. 'Wish you were here' fizzled."

"Don't you see? The killer knows that apart from the sheriff, I'm the one who recognized the postcard signal. I'm the one who ran to Mrs. Hogendobber even before your people got to her. I see the mail first. He slipped. It's him! Jesus Christ, Josiah DeWitt. I like him. How can you like a murderer?"

Officer Cooper's face, taut, registered the information. "Well, if there is someone in that tunnel, we're sitting ducks."

"Like Kelly Craycroft's poster." Harry's mind raced. "I don't know how long it will take him to realize what he's done."

"Not long. Our people are everywhere. He may not be able to leave his shop early. When he does he'll come for you."

"He doesn't know where I am."

"Then he'll come up here in the night if there really is anything here, or he'll slip away. I don't know what he'll do but he's not fearful."

The closed mouth of the tunnel, wreathed in kudzu, loomed before them.

"Let's go." Harry pressed on.

Cooper, mental radar scanning, cautiously stepped up to the mouth. Harry, paces behind, checked out the top of the tunnel. It would be rough going, coming up behind the tunnel. In fact, it would take hours, but it could be done.

The tunnel mouth was indeed sealed shut. Only dynamite would open it.

"Look for Paddy's rabbit hole." Mrs. Murphy and Tucker fanned out.

Nose to the ground, Tucker smelled the faintest remains of Bob and Ozzie. "Ozzie and Berryman were here."

Mrs. Murphy nodded. "Paddy's got to be right. If Berryman came up here, there is a treasure!" She raced ahead of the corgi while Harry and Coop tiptoed along the mouth of the tunnel.

Hidden behind the foliage, there was a small hole at the base of

the tunnel. A rabbit could easily go in and out of it. So could Mrs. Murphy.

"*Don't go in there,*" Tucker warned. "*We'll do it together.*"

"*Okay. I'll go first. My eyes are better.*" Mrs. Murphy slipped through the hole. "*Holy shit!*"

"*Are you all right?*" Tucker, half in and half out of the hole, was digging for all she was worth.

"*Yes.*" Mrs. Murphy ran back to her buddy. "*Can you see yet?*"

"*Barely.*" Tucker blinked and blinked but she felt in a sea of India ink.

Slowly her eyes adjusted and she saw the treasure. It wasn't Claudius Crozet's treasure, but it was a king's ransom in paintings, Louis XV furniture, carpets painstakingly rolled in heavy protective covers. Mrs. Murphy soared onto a Louis XV desk. A golden casket rested atop it. She lifted up the lid with one paw. Old, expensive jewelry glistened inside. Near the mouth of the tunnel rested an old railroad handcart. A huge bombé cabinet was on it.

"*Get Harry.*"

Tucker dashed to the rabbit hole and barked.

"Where's the dog?" Officer Cooper glanced around. "Sounds like she's inside the tunnel. That's impossible."

Harry pulled away brush, kudzu, and vine to reach the farthest right-hand corner of the tunnel. Tucker barked at her feet. "There's a rabbit hole. Tucker, come out of there."

Officer Cooper got down on her hands and knees. A black, wet nose twitched. "Come on, pooch."

"*You come in here,*" Tucker replied.

"*They won't fit.*" Mrs. Murphy joined her. "*Let's go out. There has to be another way in.*"

Tucker grunted her way out and Mrs. Murphy danced out. Tucker jumped up at Harry. Mrs. Murphy circled her human friend. Harry understood. She crouched down, then lay flat on her belly as Cooper stepped out of the way. "There's something in there. I need a flashlight."

Cooper lay down. She cupped her hands around her eyes as

Harry moved so she could get a better look. "Antiques. I can't see how much but I see a big chest of drawers."

Harry leaped up and ran her hands along the tunnel mouth. Cooper joined her. Harry knocked on the right-hand side of the sealed mouth. It sounded hollow.

"Epoxy and resin. Makes sense now, doesn't it?" Harry said. "That furniture was not squeezed through the rabbit hole unless Josiah has Alice in Wonderland potions. Must be a trigger or a latch somewhere. I bet Kelly loved making this. I wonder how long it took him?"

"Working nights, I don't know, a couple of months. A month. I've got it." Coop found a thick vine covering a latch. The vine, kudzu, was affixed to the false front. The natural foliage grew around it.

With a click the door opened, large enough to get a railroad lorry through. The two women entered the tunnel. Mrs. Murphy and Tucker scurried inside.

"There's a fortune in here," Harry whispered.

Tucker's ears went up. Mrs. Murphy froze.

"*Don't bark, Tucker. He knows the humans are here but he doesn't know we are. Whine. Give Harry a warning.*"

Tucker whined, softly. Harry leaned over to pat her. "*Mommy, please pay attention,*" the dog cried.

"*Hide, Tuck, hide.*" Mrs. Murphy jumped from a desk to the top of a wardrobe near the doorway. Tucker hid behind the lorry.

Harry felt their fear. "Cooper, Cooper," she whispered and grabbed Cynthia's arm. "Something's wrong."

Cooper pulled her pistol. Harry did too.

A light footfall played on their ears. Inside the tunnel, sounds were magnified and distorted in the 536 feet of rock. Harry crept to the right side of the opening. She stood on the other side of the lorry. Cooper remained in the deep shadows to the left.

A familiar, charming voice reached them. Josiah was too smart to appear in the opening. "I underestimated you, Harry. Never underestimate a woman. Officer Cooper, I know you're armed. I suggest you toss out your weapon. No reason to defile Claudius Crozet's handiwork with bloodshed—especially mine." Cooper kept silent.

"If you don't toss out your weapon I'm going to throw in this gasoline-soaked rag and just the tiniest Molotov cocktail I happen to have with me for the evening's enjoyment. I also have a gun, as I guess you know. It's Kelly's. When ballistics files its report on Bob Berryman, it will frustrate that stellar public servant Rick Shaw, and tell him Bob was killed with a dead man's gun. It's nasty dying in a fire and if you run out I'll be forced to shoot you. If you throw out your weapon, Officer Cooper, perhaps we can make a deal. Something more lucrative than your vast public salaries—both of you."

"What was the deal you made with Kelly? Or Maude?" Harry's voice, sharp and hard, reverberated through the tunnel.

"Kelly enjoyed excellent terms, but after four years at twenty percent he got a little greedy. As you can see, there's enough stockpiled in the tunnel that I could dispense with his services for the future. When my inventory runs low I shall find another feckless fellow eager for profit."

"You used his paving enterprise."

"Of course."

"And his trucks."

"Harry, don't try my patience with the obvious. Officer Cooper, throw out your gun."

"First, I want to know why you killed Maude. It's obvious what she did, too."

"Maudie was a dear woman but her ovaries ruled her head, I fear. You see, she really was in love with Bob Berryman. When business reasons compelled me to remove Kelly Craycroft from our board of directors, she didn't want to be an accessory to murder."

"Was she?"

"No. But she became frightened. What if I were caught and what if our profitable venture were disclosed? Berryman, stringing her along, kept telling her he would leave Linda, and Maude loved that cretin. A shaky partner is worse than no partner at all. She could have given us away, or worse, she could have spilled the beans to Bob Berryman—pillow talk—who with his amusing sense of honor would have traipsed directly to the authorities. You see, poor Maude had to go. Now, darlings, I've indulged you long enough. Throw out the gun."

"Did you try to drown Mrs. Hogendobber?" Harry wanted to keep him talking. She had no plan, but it gave her time to think.

"No. Throw out your gun."

Harry dropped her voice to the gossip register, a tone she prayed would be irresistible to Josiah. "Well, if you didn't slash those pontoons, who did?"

He laughed. "I think it was Little Marilyn. A real passive-aggressive, our Little Marilyn. She didn't go for help until she realized that two of the ladies on Mim's yacht couldn't swim. She just wanted to ruin her mother's party. I can't prove it, but that's what I think." He laughed again. "I would have given anything to have seen that boat sink. Mim's face must have been fuchsia." He paused. "Okay, enough chat. Really, there's no point in anyone's being hurt. Just cooperate."

"Well, how did you get your victims to eat cyanide?"

"You are prolonging this." Josiah sighed. "I simply poured cyanide on a handkerchief, pretending it was cologne, and quickly put it over their mouths! Presto! An instant dead person. Now get with the program, girls."

Harry intoned. "You didn't have to mutilate them."

"An artist's touch." He sniggered.

"One more teeny-weeny question." Harry gulped for air. Her voice was steely calm in the suffocating atmosphere. "I know you brought the goods up here in a lorry, but where did you get them in the first place?"

Josiah hooted. "That's the best part, Harry. Mim Sanburne! I've been her 'walker' for years. The finest homes. New York, Newport, Palm Beach, Richmond, Charleston, Savannah, wherever there is an elegant party, a must gathering. I'd appraise the merchandise and then one or two years later, voilà—I'd return for an engagement of a different sort. No engraved invitations. That was the easy part. You bribe a servant—the rich are notoriously cheap, you know. Pay someone enough to live on for a year and a one-way ticket to Rio. How simple to get in when the master and mistress were gone. The hard part was lifting the lorry off the track and rolling it inside the tunnel each time we were finished—that and trying to stay awake the next day. We never had to work that hard, though. Perhaps three houses a year. Distribution is easy once the fuss dies down. A small load to Wilmington or Charlotte. A side trip to Memphis. Wouldn't snooty Mim just die? She looks down her long nose at thee and me, yet she's consorting with a criminal—an elegant criminal."

"Big profits, huh?"

"Ah, yes, sweet are the workings of capitalism—a lesson you've never learned, my girl. Now, time's up." His voice, hypnotic, promised all would be well. This was just a glorious lark.

Harry edged closer to the mouth and in pantomime to Coop said that she would throw out her gun. Cooper nodded. Mrs. Murphy fluffed her tail, ready to strike.

"You won't toss in that Molotov cocktail. The fire would ruin your inventory. The smoke and commotion would bring all of Crozet up here to the tunnel. Now that would spoil everything. If we're going into business, we'd better trust one another right now. You throw down your gun first and Officer Cooper will throw out hers."

"Don't take me for a fool, Harry. I'm not throwing down my gun first," he snapped.

"You're the creative one, Josiah. Think of something," Harry taunted him. "You can starve us out but Rick Shaw will notice you're missing. That won't do. We'd better reach an agreement now."

"You drive a hard bargain."

"Never underestimate the power of a woman," Harry mocked. "I'd hate for one of us to kill the other, because you couldn't remove the body until the middle of the night, and in this flaming heat the corpse will start to stink in two to three hours. That's disagreeable."

"Quite so," came Josiah's clipped response. "What would you do if you killed me?"

"What you did to Maude. Then I'd wait a year, and Coop and I would sell off your stash. Oh, we don't have your contacts, Josiah, but I'm sure we'd make some kind of profit." She lied through her teeth.

"Don't be an ass! With me you can make a fortune. By yourself, you'll get caught."

"I got this far, didn't I?"

A long silence followed. The unlit Molotov cocktail was placed at the opening. Josiah's hand quickly withdrew.

"Proof positive of what a saint I am. There's the Molotov cocktail."

"Josiah"—Harry hoped to keep him talking—"how did you fake the postmarks?"

"My latent artistic impulses surged to the fore." He smiled. "I've got waxes, inks, stains, bits of ormolu, you name it, to repair the furniture. I mixed up a color and then tapped the postmark letters with old typeface. The inscription came compliments of my computer. I thought the postcards a flourish. I rather relished the picture of poor Rick Shaw's face as he tried to make sense of it—once he realized the postcards were a signature. You realized quite quickly. I was terribly impressed."

"But not scared?"

"Me? Never."

"Your gun." Harry's voice made the demand sound like a social request.

"What about Coop? Is she really in there? I want to hear her voice. How do I know you haven't killed her?" Josiah made a demand of his own. What he wanted was to hear where she was.

"Here." Cooper nodded to Harry. She then swiftly moved to stand right beneath Mrs. Murphy. Tucker put her front paws on the lorry.

Harry, on Coop's signal, said, "On the count of three, you throw down your gun. She'll throw down hers. One ... two ... three." She tossed out her gun as Josiah threw his in the opening.

He had a second gun. He didn't waste time. He bolted into the tunnel, firing randomly. Mrs. Murphy jumped, claws at the ready, onto his head. Then slid to his back. Tucker, on her hind legs, pushed the lorry, which, despite its slow pace, knocked him off balance when it bumped into him. Tucker then bit his gun hand as he stumbled to the tunnel floor, his knee hitting a steel rail. Josiah lifted his gun hand, the dog still hanging on his wrist, and aimed straight for Harry, who dropped and rolled. Mrs. Murphy hung on his back, digging into him full force. Cooper, with deliberate precision and trained self-control, fired once. Josiah grunted as the bullet sank into his torso with a thud. He fired wildly. Cooper fired one more shot. Between the eyes. He twitched and was dead.

"Tucker!" Harry rushed to the dog, bruised but wagging her tail.

Cooper scooped up Mrs. Murphy as she walked over to Harry. She kissed the kitty, whose fur still stood straight up. "Bless you, Mrs. Murphy." She reached down and felt for Josiah's pulse. She dropped his arm as if it were rotten meat. "Harry, if these two hadn't thrown him off balance he would have hit one of us. His gun was on rapid fire. The tunnel isn't that wide. He was no dummy, except for his little slip in the post office."

Harry sat on the moist earth, Tucker licking the tears from her face. Mrs. Murphy stood on her hind legs, her front paws wrapped around Harry's neck. Harry rubbed her cheek against Mrs. Murphy's soft fur.

"It's a funny thing, Cooper. I didn't think about myself. I thought about these two. If he had hurt Mrs. Murphy or Tucker, I would have killed him with my bare hands if I could have. My mind was perfectly composed and crystal-clear."

"You've got guts, Harry. I was armed. You threw out your gun to sucker him in."

"He wouldn't have come in otherwise. I don't know—maybe he would have. God, it seems like a dream. What a cunning son of a bitch. He had two guns."

Cooper frisked the body. "And a stiletto."

46

Mrs. Hogendobber rapturously returned on the day following Harry's shoot-out with Josiah. The media had a field day with the heroic postmistress, her valiant cat and gallant dog, as well as stalwart Officer Cooper, so cool under fire. Harry found the hoopla almost as bad as being trapped in the tunnel.

Rick Shaw, fully briefed on the engagement with Josiah DeWitt, never mentioned in his prepared statement that Josiah's entry into wealthy homes was on Mim Sanburne's arm. Naturally, all of Crozet knew it, as well as Mim's rich friends, but at least that detail wasn't splashed across America. Jim secretly relished that his wife's snobbery had been her undoing, and he was thrilled to be rid of Josiah.

Pewter envied her friends terribly and ate twice as much to make up for being denied stardom.

Fair and Boom Boom dated. No promises were made yet. They struggled to find some equilibrium amid the torrid gossip concerning them. Harry went from being the tough wife who threw out her husband to the innocent victim—in public, but not Harry's, opinion.

Susan got Harry to take up golf for relaxation. Harry wasn't certain that it relaxed her, but it began to obsess her.

Little Marilyn and Mim made up, sort of. Mim had brains enough to know that she would never dominate her daughter again.

On schedule, Rob brought the mail and picked it up. Harry kept reading postcards. Lindsay Astrove returned from Europe, sorry to have missed the drama. Jim Sanburne and the town council of Crozet decided to make money from the scandal. They offered tours of the tunnel. Tourists rode up in handcarts. A nice booklet on the life of Claudius Crozet was printed and sold for $12.50.

Life returned to normal, whatever that is.

Crozet was an imperfect corner of the world with rare moments of perfection. Harry, Mrs. Murphy, and Tucker witnessed one of them on a crisp September day.

Harry looked out the post office window and saw Stafford Sanburne, with his beautiful wife, step off the train. He was greeted by Mim and Little Marilyn. He had a big smile on his face. So did Harry.

Afterword

I hope you enjoyed my first crime novel. Tell my publishers if you did. Maybe they'll give me an advance for another one.

Uh-oh, I hear footsteps in the hall.

"Sneaky Pie, what is this in my typewriter?"